TORTUGA

A Confection of Blood and Gold

TORTUGA

*   *   *

A Confection of Blood and Gold

Thomas Erikson

CVP
CASCADE VIEW PUBLISHING

ISBN: 0615957641
ISBN 13: 9780615957647
Library of Congress Control Number: 2017913106
Cascade View Publishing, Bothell WA

For my sons Wade and Maxwell, and
most of all for my wife Joan,
for the unending encouragement, support,
and patience --- with all my love.

You do not come to Euphemia only to buy and sell, but also because at night, by the fires . . . at each word that one man says --- such as "wolf," "sister," "hidden treasures," "battle," "scabies," "lovers" --- the others tell, each one, his tale of wolves, sisters, treasures, scabies, lovers, battles. And you know that in the long journey ahead of you, when you start summoning up your memories one by one, your wolf will have become another wolf, your sister a different sister, your battle other battles.

ITALO CALVINO
Invisible Cities

CONTENTS

Part I

CAYONA

1 A WAYLAYING

A fat moon hung low and yellow over the path behind these thatch-roofed, clamorous taverns. Its glow cast dead black shadows between the kegs and firewood stacked against the adobe walls, shadows black as the narrow alley they watched.

Behind a tall-wheeled wagon, rank with its load of stiff cowhides, the three boys crouched, still and hidden. They peered under the wagon's bed like mousers at a rat hole, staring into the alley's mouth. The palm trees above them shuffled and clicked in the rising breeze, a sound barely heard against the ragged hullabaloo from the taverns.

A sharp belch erupted out of the alley.

"Care," said Jack, slowly rising up on his toes. He brushed his fingers against the knife in his belt and leaned forward beneath the wagon bed. Louis and Will beside him did the same.

A much longer and indulgent belch announced a grizzled pirate who shuffled drunkenly out of the alley. The man stopped and swayed stupidly, squinted at the moon with one good eye and rubbed the patch over the other with the curve of his hook. Using his one good hand he absently fished out his prick, ready to add to the reeking puddles at his feet.

"That's 'im," Louis whispered.

Jack cuffed his head and put a finger to his lips.

"Ahoy," a high voice called from far back in the alley. The pirate looked back over his shoulder as the piss began dribbling from his roger. "Ahoy, Bristolman."

"That's 'im," said Jack. He scampered left, jumping over the wagon tongue. Will and Louis went right and instantly the three had the fumbling sea-artist at bay. The man's single pale eye grew wide at the three knives glinting before his belly and his mouth dropped open, unleashing a third, short, astonished belch.

Flying out of the alley came little Jesús in mid leap, marlin spike raised high to slash down on the back of the pirate's skull just as Louis lowered his head and butted into the man's bulging gut.

A salmagundi laced with wine and bile spewed from the cutthroat's mouth and over Louis' back. Louis squealed in disgust, jumping away and falling on his butt. Groaning, the pirate fell to his knees, then face first to the dirt. He retched again, sputtering in his own parbreak.

Louis, cursing the saints, wriggled out of his stinking, sopping shirt and tossed it against the tavern wall.

"That's an extra share for Louis," Jack said with a laugh, ducking away from a backhand swing.

"Certain as damnation," Louis said. He bent over and fished in the moaning man's greasy, gray ringlets and tore the gold ring from his ear.

"No," said Jesús dancing nervously over to the pirate. "It's in his ear. In his ear."

Always their lookout, the tiny mestizo boy spied up and down the path at the leather-curtained doorways of the tavern kitchens. Then he jumped knees first onto the pirate's back.

"A pearl the size of a pistol ball. It's stopped in his ear with wax." Jesús laughed high and gleefully, jerking their victim's hair to turn his head. "In his ear for safekeeping. Ha!"

The old pirate lurched up on his elbows, tumbling Jesús into the dirt. Jack kicked, putting his big toe right in the eye-patch. The man shouted berserkly, spinning over and swinging his hook wide. The barb etched a burning scratch across Jack's foot as he leapt backward.

"God's eyes," Jack yelped, stumbling into a woodpile and poking his ribs on an ax handle.

The pirate bellowed curses, now up on all fours. From behind Louis kicked him a hard kick in the cods and his shouting ended with a profound grunt. He fell again into his own muck. Now Will took aim at the sprawled form and quick-kicked him in the crotch again. The man curled onto his side and groaned meekly.

Jack sat on the logs and watched him gasp like a beached fish in the moonlight. He was an ill-tempered souse off the unlucky Prosperous, a blowhard up from Port Royal. The man clutched at his balls with his single hand, gagged on his own groans and rolled onto his stomach.

Louis and Will were considering whether to give him another kick. Jesús was listening down the alley.

"Hurry up," Jack said, standing up. "Get the pearl. They'll be missing him sure."

Jesús scrambled back and straddled the pirate's head like a pig's, trying to wrestle it still. The old buccaneer rocked and groaned.

"God's shit, someone is going to surprise us soon," cried Will as some brouhaha rose from one of the taverns, died back and rose again.

Finally Jesús grabbed the man's beard, pinned his head between his knees and pulled his knife. Jack and Louis stood ready to kick him again, fore and aft. Now Will listened and peered down the dark alley.

Jesús pried at the ear with his knife, poked it, shook a piece of bloody tallow from the blade's tip and then sighed with delight. The others bent forward to see.

There was a shout of "You bastards!" behind them and at the same moment the old pirate's hook struck like a snake into Jesús' calf. Jesús screamed like a child and jumped to his feet trying to shake his leg free of the barb. Two doors down the cook who had shouted dropped his pail of slops and disappeared through the leather curtain.

Jesús jigged in the dirt on one foot while his hooked leg swung the pirate's short arm in a dance. Louis kicked the old man hard in the mouth, doing nothing to loosen the hook. From the cook's tavern the chanteys and oaths suddenly turned to a roar of shouts and curses that seemed to shake its thatch roof.

Jesús wriggled his leg helplessly. Two street dogs scampered out of the alley yapping and jumping, and then Jesús squealed in terror as a shave-headed freebooter stumbled through the cook's leather curtain and into the moonlight. The man waved his cutlass and roared with glee when he saw the boy caught on the hook. Others were shouting and clanging through the kitchen behind him.

Will ran into the palm shadows and was gone. Louis stood rooted. Jack's eyes raced over the alley like a plague mad rat.

Two steps to the wall, his hand ran across the rough bark, found the axe and jerked it free. He turned and swung it in a high arc, chopping down through the old pirate's forearm.

Louis jumped forward to slice free the last thong of skin and Jesús skipped away fast, running for the dark with the bloody hook flapping in his leg. The old pirate let out a hoarse scream and waved his spouting arm over his head as Jack flung the axe past him into the legs of the maddened pirates and Louis tossed dirt at the freebooter's eyes. The man leaped, dodging both and swinging his cutlass for Jack but slipped on the bloody muck and tumbled onto the bellowing Bristolman.

Jack ran for his life and more. At their heels the freebooter's mates collided with buccaneers dashing pell-mell out of the alleyway and the lot tumbled cursing in the gory sand.

A knife nipped between Jack's elbow and ribs, another past his ear. They dove down the next alley as pistols banged, the wall spitting adobe across their backs. More pistols banged impotently.

Jack ran head down between the dark walls, Louis a step behind.

They turned and ran down a narrower alley, jumping kegs and crates near invisible in the blackness, turned again, and again, twisting through the knotted back ways they knew better than any, past Cayona's taverns, storehouses, brothels and armories.

Finally they halted behind a tobacco shed, leaned against a rain barrel and panted in the dark. Far behind them, by some freak of the breeze, they could hear faintly as the old sea-artist peered at his gory, shortened stump and bellowed a forlorn note that would have struck his mother dead, the hoarse ululation rising over the brawl of the taverns.

"Ach," Louis grunted, shaking his head.

Jack nodded in agreement.

"Aye, what a mewler. He was lucky we didn't slit his throat."

They laughed and struck out in the direction of the beach.

"What of Jesús?"

"He's limped off home to the Tree." Jack shrugged. "Let Will nurse him."

"That was the best prize in Cayona tonight. No one else in that crew has muck. Why a share of the little silver they got selling those poor little barges and that worm-eaten galleon . . ."

"And the coconuts," Jack reminded him of the pirated cargo.

Louis gave a rueful chuckle. "And the coconuts. Those shares won't last a two-day drunk. What did I say? I said let's waylay the Walloon gunner ---"

"No. No," Jack broke in. "Jesús says he saw that old Bristolman wiping earwax off a pearl the size of an eight. I never saw it myself."

They both grimaced and shook their heads recalling other hopeful tales Jesús had convinced them of in the past.

"Someday he'll get one of us killed."

"Aye," said Jack, and after a few steps "But it was a famous escape."

Louis voiced a low mimic of the Bristolman's cry. They both laughed, and then began to trot down the gloomy, stinking alley, looking for better luck.

2 CAYONA

The winds swept over the turtle's hump, verdant, mottled, Ile de la Tortue, Tortuga. Columbus' appellation stuck. The turtle's beak is filed sharp by the whetstone winds roiling past where it hangs in the sea like a pilot fish before the maw of the Passage; the winds come in long, hot silken sweeps off the Silver Banks, zephyrs seeping through Mouchoir Passage, blusters from the Turks, mere scents from Ambergris Key and the Caicos, Mayaguana and even Crooked Island whiffs and wafts blown through Clarion Bank join the rush to pass the snouts of the New World's own Scylla and Charybdis: Cuba hanging in the sea like a shark, Hispaniola frozen in the leap of a spawning Scot salmon, or so fanciful cartographers say.

The winds tumble over Tortuga's empty north and ransack its ribbed spine of mountains where lofty, ancient trees grow close as grass, their mammoth roots tangled like ivy cracking the mountain stone. Above the forests broad clouds of pigeons drift and swerve, then disappear like rain into the leaves. Wild boars rummage through the thick green bushes between the trunks, seeking china root and acajou.

Tradition divides the little plateaux and myriad valleys of the south into four. The Mountain holds the first plantations cultivated by the Brotherhood of the Coast, then Ringot, and Middle Plantation, and last the Low-Land surrounding the great two-channeled harbor of

Cayona. High above its green, glinting waters the tingling, tart mist of a broken orange woke Jack.

He opened his eyes and studied the shadows on the cave's ceiling. It was well past dawn. He rolled over on the palm leaves of his bed. Jesús sat at the cave mouth sucking the wedges of orange. A cloth knotted at his shin wrapped a large leaf of sotweed around his wounded calf.

Past him the sun's shafts blinked and danced with the last of the early morning breeze. Jack reached into his niche for his clay pipe and bag of shag, then went and sat by the coals of the fire across from Jesús. He lit the pipe with a twig and puffed hard on the long stem.

Jack peered back into the cave. Eight of them slept here, kept their pipes and shag, their handfuls of trinket treasure from the Main, camped beneath the roots of the giant candlewood. Their cave and two other warrens to each side among the roots of the great tree were Under-the-Tree, home to half the abandoned, lost, and orphaned boys of Cayona, many once babes who had never tasted their beestings. Far back, all three caves were connected by narrow tunnels and others led to bolt holes and cracks in the rocky bluff. When one of the boys grew too big to crawl between the three caves, the rule was he would ship out on account, or, if lucky, apprentice and sleep on his master's worktable, or, worst, become a buccaneer's valet in the forests of Hispaniola. Both Jack and Louis should already be gone.

None of the younger lads had pressed them as of yet. But if Louis went, Jack himself would follow soon after. To what and where he did not know.

Jesús tossed the last orange rind on the coals and spit a seed past Jack's head.

"What shall we do today?" he asked.

Jack watched the tobacco smoke twist lazily before him.

"I'm not going down to town," he said. "The Bristolman's complaint is sure to be all about. Too many evil eyes 'll be turned on us."

"Could get skewered."

"Just for spite. Where's his hook?" Jack asked.

"I pulled the damnable thing out and tossed it to the lee right quick," Jesús said, gently rubbing his leg. He spit into the coals. "I saw where it fell."

"We can retrieve it and sell it to the chirurgeon," said Jack, then laughed. "And he'll sell it right back to the old fart and we'll all be happy."

"If the dogs don't carry it off for that bit of arm." Jesús smiled, thinking about it.

"Not much arm," Jack said proudly and made a little chop with his hand. "I should be a chirurgeon myself. Where's Michel and Will and Louis?"

"They went with Andre to help him sweep out the baker's ovens. We'll have bread for breakfast, at least."

"There wasn't much in those sailors' purses we cut after your Bristolman was rescued, but maybe it'll

fetch us a small cask of brandy. Then we can hie ourselves down to Skinner's Cove. Catch crabs for supper
and get drunk"

Jack scooted back across the dirt until he could lean
against the rock outside the cave's mouth. He puffed
the bitter smoke and stared up into the green and gold
spangling above him, thinking of the soft golden hair of
Rebecca Van Duyn.

Soon, instead of bewitching himself with her fanta-
sy, Jack decided to get a view of the wench herself. He
tapped out his pipe on the ground, stood, and headed
down the westward path. Jesús called after him, but the
girl's image already had formed in the leafy shadows and
Jack did not answer.

Up slope from Herr Van Duyn's big house he shin-
nied up a small candlewood to peer down into the walled
garden. It was empty. He descended and continued
across the slope, looking into the windows opened to collect the morning's brief coolness. But he caught only the
glimpse of a servant's mop swabbing over a floor. On the
far side of the house Rebecca's window was nearly closed
and Jack could not see past the sky's glare on the panes.

3 JACK'S QUALITIES AND TALENTS

The late summer day became torrid early and they did
not go down to Skinner's Cove. The boys of Under-
the-Tree slept in the cave or along the stony hillside in

favorite nooks among roots twice and three times as big around as them. Some shot taws on the shaded path or played listlessly with their knives, or sharpened them.

Despite the heat Jack decided to climb the long ridge to the small peak that sat far above the Governor's stone fort. From that vantage he could look down on the tiled roof of the Van Duyn's house and their empty garden, on the heat-deadened town, the bay, the sea, far Hispaniola.

A flotilla of brown pelicans dipped and rose gently on the gleaming noon surface of the emerald bay. Jack chewed on a baton of sugar cane and squatted in the tree shade, counting ships far below that slowly turned on their anchor chains as the tide went out. A single barca was tied at the long pier. From it a black horse in a canvas sling was being raised. Its head tossed and twisted. Its whinnying could not carry this far up, even in heat-stilled midday.

The black horse, the figures at the barca's winch and on the dock, were the only living things that moved, except the pelicans.

As soon as the horse's feet touched the dock's planks it kicked a man down. The man immediately jumped up and then fell down. Another figure tossed a white cloth over the horse's eyes.

A bee tickled the back of his hand, touching briefly, then flew off. Jack studied the worried tip of his cane and then chewed it, sucking the sweet juice from its soft quills. It was so hot he had to lean back against the palm tree, forgetting the horse, stretching out his legs and thinking of Rebecca.

Her hair was the color of evening sunlight on straw, he thought. Her eyes were a blue he had never seen in sky or sea. Both her cheeks were lightly freckled with tiny constellations of copper stars. He had made out the Hay Wain on her right cheek.

She had told Andre, when she stopped in her carriage at the bakery with their housekeeper, her uncle, she said, told her not to talk to the boys from the town, said they were no better than dogs. But she knew it wasn't so, so why shouldn't she talk to someone near her own age, except now her uncle said no?

Jack opened his eyes and smiled up at the sky. He knew why her uncle said no. His cock was stiff and burning beneath his dirty pantaloons, warmed by the memory of her speaking lips, and by a bobbing shaft of sunlight that stroked over it.

The whores always told Jack, as far back as he could remember, that he was a handsome boy, that grown he would make many a maiden cry. He was near on full grown now. Would he make Rebecca cry? he wondered.

When he had a chance to look in a pier glass at Madame Pearl's his face always seemed a sturdy, regular face to him, with the deep set, deep brown eyes his best feature. His smile had long teeth, all of them still, and he had a high forehead topped with rough-cropped coppery curls.

Of course the pier glass did show the rest of him. Rags, any rags that were close to pantaloons and a shirt, those were what he wore. His feet were bare, had never known a shoe, boot, or sandal.

He was more long than short, taller than many men in the town, but not a thing to remark. He was not thin or stout. But he surprised with his strength, whether wrestling with the bigger Louis and Klaus, or escaping the grasp of a cook who found him in the larder. Jack's sinews were not so much stronger than most, but strung on a broad-shouldered, well-proportioned frame that gave them strength in leverage, or so he thought.

His regard among the boys of Cayona first came from his speed of foot. None could match him in a dash down the beach or in cutting a purse on the fly and disappearing into the shadows before a man could turn around. Even these days only Jesús could shoot ahead of him in the first ten strides, but on the eleventh Jack was not to be headed.

His only other talent, it growing as he approached manhood, was uncanny, though no one ever seemed to notice or speak of it. Jack knew the daily ebbs and floods, the seasons and the moons of Cayona like none else Under-the-Tree. Unlike Andre, Pedro, or Will, he never thought hard on where to find a drunken sailor, but seemed to follow some signs in the songs in the taverns, the curses in the streets, the lanterns on the ships until he would say "Let's try the Golden Boot" and sure enough a drunk with a jingling purse meandered out for them. More often than not, truth be told. In the same way Jack could judge from the heat of the day that the baker would have a free loaf at sundown. If a copper could be earned turning tobacco leaves, he would wake up knowing it.

This came, perhaps, from his practice of climbing alone to this bluff above Cayona and staring down at the town and harbor. It had been his game since he could remember to while away the torpid afternoon hours remembering and seeing behind his eyes what was held in each and all of Cayona's buildings, and the cargo and gunnery of each ship anchored in the bay that day, who was its quartermaster, who factor and cook, did they drink rum or brandy, gamble, drink, or whore their money away? All Cayona lived in his mind, an invisible city.

Sometimes, as last night when he and Louis escaped the Bristolman's mates, in one part of his head he watched himself running through the black alleys as if he were still sitting on the noon day bluff. But Jack never thought very long on his game. He just knew he did not know where his next meal would come from. He thought mostly on that.

Or did until Rebecca had vouchsafed him a smile at the half door. Now his mind puzzled at the contents of the Van Duyn's house, her room. Her blouse. He smiled ruefully. He would never see any of that, she a high merchant's niece. But his thoughts continued to drift in that direction until he grasped himself and thought of the warm magic laying between her thighs.

4 HOTEL AEOLUS

That night the moon stood high and uncannily bright above the street as Jack and Louis approached the wide flung doors of Old Kit's Hotel Aeolus. They heard the chink and clink of coins, shouts of rage and glee, laughter, and greedy cackling mixed with the clatter of the dies. The Aeolus was famed for its dicing and the half-a-dozen fortunes that changed hands in a night.

The Aeolus had been built and christened by Old Kit, the richest and most ancient man of Tortuga. He owned fully another dozen taverns and whore's dens, and was Cayona's preeminent trader in jewels. Old Kit most often spent his nights at the Aeolus drinking himself into a stupor perhaps little different than the stupor of his ancient mind where, if his conversation were any guide, the day and the past leaked in and out like seawater through uncaulked seams. Still, when sober he was famed for having the finest eye for a pearl's worth in all the Caribbean. Best of all to Jack's thinking, Old Kit had a liking for the boys of Under-the-Tree and would suffer their presence more than most. At times that was good enough for a small coin or a trencher from the kitchen.

Jack peered cautiously through the doorway, making certain he spied none of the faces from the previous night's encounters. This street had many of the better brothels, including Madame Pearl's annex to the Aeolus, so their prey of the night before was less likely to be here. Still, in Cayona men and women of any standing and fortune could be found careening and swaggering in any den of iniquity high or low.

The stools and benches around the great room's eight long tables were packed with men dressed in silk rags and stained velvet, poorly cured hides and lace, their scalps shaved bare or top knotted, hair cascading in perfumed ringlets or lank, greasy twists. They were cursing and beseeching God in every accent of the seven seas, rattling the leather cup, stirring their silver coins with a finger, slapping doubloons to the table, waving their hooks, stomping their peg legs, meeting the snake-eyes' stare with the squint of one good eye and a groan. Scattered through the room a baker's dozen of rouged and painted doxies cooed over the moment's winners.

Jack and Louis looked at each other and nodded. It was busier here than could be expected since half the Caribbean had sailed off with Morgan. There was a chance they could wander in and scoop a fallen 'eight off the floor, if some hawkeyed whore hadn't spied it first, and then slip out no one the wiser.

They stepped over the threshold just as half a man came flying over two tables and landed in the aisle at their feet. And jumped to his own feet.

5 FRANCISCO THE DWARF

It was Francisco the Dwarf. Jack and Louis stepped gingerly to each side of the doorway.

"Filthy, cheating devil-spawn runt," shouted a skinny, black-haired young sailor as he clambered over a back table. "Son of a witch and a monkey."

The dwarf slapped at the dust on his red velvet breeches with one hand and twisted one of his great black mustachios with the other. He spoke softly in the now almost quiet tavern. There were a few chuckles and mutterings anticipating some blood sport.

"Poxy eruption of a sow's womb." The dwarf's voice was low and creaking. "We'll see who's more the man."

The sailor grinned with teeth like broken oar pegs and stepped forward slowly. A dirk was already in his hand.

Francisco drew from its little scabbard a buccaneer's long Flemish dagger. The sailor tossed the hair out of his eyes and went into a crouch, then uncertainly crouched still lower.

"En garde, Scaramouch," shouted the dwarf. His small foot stamped out and he presented his knife like a tiny sword.

The sailor guffawed, then lunged and slashed, nipping a curl from the dwarf's head as the little man whirled out of his path and around behind him, gashing two swift deep strokes above the youth's knees.

With a scream the sailor toppled to the floor at Jack's feet.

"There go his sea legs," Francisco said, giving Jack a wink. He let out a self-satisfied laugh that was echoed among the peg legs and cripples around the room. A cheer went up among the dwarf's partisans.

The fallen sailor shouted in horror when he could not even raise his knees. His mate, a tall Dane who had knelt beside him rose up and turned toward Francisco, his cutlass slipping from his belt. Pistols were cocked in braces all around the room. The Dane growled deep in his throat. Eyeing the dwarf he spat on the floor and let the blade subside, then knelt down to attend his mate who was now mewling like a kitten.

Once again the dwarf laughed, then spat at his feet himself, crouched and back flipped, replacing his dagger in its sheath in the same motion. Acknowledging the hurrahs, he saluted the crowd of pirates and whores. The dwarf strode royally around the pool of blood his victim sat in and was carried out the door by a great gale of cheers.

A few steps out the door, Francisco turned, looked in, and nodded to Jack and Louis who stared after him with open mouths. They stepped back out into the street.

The dwarf dug into a heavy, chinking pouch and tossed an 'eight to Jack.

"I'm off to the Unicorn," he croaked at them. "You keep watch none of his shipmates try to waylay me."

His teeth gleamed in the moonlight.

"And if you think to waylay me . . ."

"No, Francisco," they chorused, a mix of mock and real indignation.

None of the pack from Under-the-Tree were fools enough to pounce on one of Cayona's more or less permanent citizens; would not even cut a purse unless they found them dead drunk.

Chuckling to himself the dwarf turned and walked away with short, rocking strides. When he had turned down Cochineal Street, Jack held the silver coin up in front of Louis' nose.

"That was an easy 'eight," Jack said.

"Let's go in and wager it. I feel lucky tonight."

Jack rubbed the welt on his neck where the adobe spit by the pistol ball had struck him the night before. He was doubtful.

"Our luck's been mixed of late. Let's go in and cock an ear. If the new cripple's mates go hunting for Francisco we could earn another 'eight or even a gold cob."

Louis snorted and shrugged. They turned to go in, but stepped back to make way for three men carrying out the hamstrung sailor.

Both his thighs were tied with bloody rags. He was tossing his head, crying "Chuck me to the sharks, mates. I'll never be a beggar. Chuck me to the sharks!"

One of his mates turned his head to Louis. "Where can we find a chirurgeon, boy?"

"For an 'eight ..." he started. The man slapped Louis hard, spinning him clear around. The boy spit blood on the sand.

"Doc Smeeks is down at the Griffin most every night he ain't here," Jack said quickly. "That's the closest. And he won't be much drunk yet."

The three sailors set off wordlessly under the dull silver moonlight, their burden crying "Chuck me to the sharks" and bawling like a calf.

Jack turned his face aside, hiding his smirk while Louis rubbed the side of his head. Again they stepped into the bright-lit gaming room of the Hotel Aeolus.

6 OLD KIT'S HIGH TABLE

The dice cups already rattled and men were shouting for brandy and rum, but now that the dwarf's victim and his friends were gone half the room was talking of the fight they witnessed and blood they had seen spilled before.

"That damnable cockalorum!" a man to one side cried good humoredly and slapped his thigh. Jack and Louis skirted the gore in the aisle, muttering "bread and butter," while a taverner shook an armload of straw over the bloody mess to soak it up. Everyone was unpacking oft told stories.

" . . . we slaughtered half the village and hamstrung the rest . . ."

". . . popped out his eyes on their roots and let the kittens play with 'em. Then . . ."

Jack considered. He was hungry. He jerked his head toward the other side of the Aeolus.

"Let's go up and see Old Kit. He'll tell the cook to give us a trencher and a mug of wine."

Louis shrugged and followed Jack into the Aeolus' taproom. Here things were far quieter. An African tuned a mandolin, some planters diced at one table, and in a corner six men huddled over a portolano argued compass points. Gino the cook's boy waved to them from where he labored at the spit turning a fat little boar. A scattered handful of dandied, sullen men drank alone.

So few people on the "deck" made it seem empty, but on the Aeolus' taproom "poop," set above the rest at the back of the big room, the master's long table was crowded. Here Old Kit held court, at least when sober. At this table were found the traders in odd jewels and rare medicines, paunched pirates who had retired from the seas before Jack was born, vagabond scholars and sawbones, planters from The Mountain who recalled when Cayona was no bigger than a fishing village.

Even great old Mansveldt, the Main's first pirate admiral, had sat blustering at Kit's table before he died.

Jack could not see Old Kit now, though the big fire that warmed his spine on even the most sweltering nights was burning at the back of the poop. If Kit were up at his great house, the taverner would not even have scraps for them. Jack stepped up on a bench. At the far end of Kit's table he saw the old man's shining bald pate surrounded by a pure white nimbus, his wispy, candent tonsure lit by the firelight. Asleep while the others railed and laughed.

They said he was the oldest man in the New World, likely all the world. Some superstitiously called him the "Ancient One." Some said he had sold his soul to the devil, others that he knew some Carib magic that preserved him. Few on the island could recall when he had not been the old man of Tortuga. But Old Waite, Waite the baker's father, could recall Kit's coming in the long past days. He said Kit's beard and brow were as white as clouds even then, when the Brotherhood of the Coast still held to its compact and pirates from the Mosquito Coast and the merchants from Nieuw Amsterdam stopped at Cayona for boucan and water and little else; little rum and no women were found on Tortuga in those days, the old men said.

Jack turned and nodded to Louis, who headed confidently back toward the kitchen to tell a lie.

Jack climbed the three steps to the "poop" and sidled past the pillars of Cayona, men in ill-gotten but clean lace, satin, and velvet, waving their ruby-ringed hands about in the abandon of a tale, or pulling at their drinks, eyebrows raised in disbelief, or drawing their long pipe stems from their lips to give a derisive snort. Here the best sea tales in Cayona could be heard.

Jack sat on the plank floor next to Old Kit's viceroy chair. The old man lay on the table with his round, small-chinned face cradled in his arms. He snored into his elbow. Jack noticed his pipe on the edge of the table, stuffed and unsmoked. He pulled it down, found a straw to stick in the fire behind him, puffed the shag to life, and listened.

7 SEA TALES

"The Jesus of Lubeck was so shot-ridden that the fish swam in and out through the rents in our hull," exclaimed Bosola. Jack knew most of their voices. " It was blasted ---"

"You've told that before a score of times," Bartholomew the Portuguese interrupted. "Now the greatest danger a ship was ever in and still reached safe harbor was the galleon Santa Maria of Mindanao. We were in the midst of the China Seas, out of Macao bound for the Spice Islands. All morning the sky darkened and the swells mounted till the wind was shrieking and clouds black as the pit mounted over us and we ran before the typhoon.

"The waves had swept four men overboard by noon, and most lay below decks praying to their Maker. I had lashed myself to the mainmast and a half dozen others were trying to tie themselves to the mizzen and taffrail hoping to grab some flotsam if the ship went down, instead of sinking in her like a coffin.

"All of us on deck cried out in terror when we saw the waterspout. High as Babel's Tower and bearing down on us like a wild boar, it was.

"I clung to the mast like it was my mother as it charged down on us and crossed close by our starboard bow. We were capsized in an instant," said the Portuguese with a snap of his fingers.

"Like a gull flipping over a crab, and so hard it seemed we spun almost around and up again. But my heart chilled through when the mast subsided and I hung there, tied upside down in the black water among the fishes."

He paused to look around the table at the brown, scarred faces, each placid at this plight, but attentive.

"I was clawing at the knots that held my waist -- and then the miracle occurred!

"That waterspout wandered right back over us, straight down our floundering keel and sucked us up stem to stern! Our old chamber pot of a galleon rolled over so quick it almost broke my back. The bowsprit dipped down into the spray and rocked back and, I swear, sighted straight down the bowsprit was that waterspout heading off across the black waves."

There were dubious guffaws from two or three at the table. The Portuguese took no note of them and continued his tale.

"Luckily we were battened down tight and took little water in our brief capsizing. It was all pandemonium below decks, you can imagine, but up on deck every man jack had been washed away. Only I remained—and the pilot, who'd lashed himself to the wheel, poor soul. That waterspout must have whipped the rudder back and forth like a fish's tail. The pilot had been spun around like a wheel o' fortune, pounded on the deck like a piece of tough beef.

"We cut him free soon as we could in that gale. The ropes had cut his wrists to the bone, but when we picked him up his legs...his legs, those bloody pants."

He bent his head and coughed.

"His legs were god-awful like muck and sticks and splinters. My hands, Christ, tremble and crawl when I think of the feel."

He raised his hands from the wine-stained table. The flesh did crawl and goose up on the backs of them.

"Pah, what a story," said a grizzled captain at the far end of the table. He spit into the fire.

"Magicians and pickpockets can do that," said one of the merchants, nodding at Bartholomew's hands.

"And mountebanks," the Portuguese shouted in mock anger and slammed his hands on the table. "And jewelers, stonecutters like myself. There are," he said turning up his palms and spreading his fingers. "There are some stones I've cut that bring me goose flesh yet to think of them.

"There was a diamond from a cannibal island---"

"You've told that before. Now I . . ."

Louis nudged Jack and sat down, dropping a steaming yam into his lap. As they ate, a merchant from Plymouth, usually a silent man at the table, clothed all in funereal black, cleared his throat and began a tale, soon interrupted.

"Hieronymo's mad again!" Old Kit shouted, starting bolt upright, staring, alarmed by his own drunken declamation.

The others at the table studied him, some expecting an imminent apoplexy, though Jack and Louis knew better. The old man fell to his elbows, plucked a jug of wine from the table and splashed the dregs into his gap-toothed mouth. Rivulets of red wine joined the bits of pork and yams in the tangled floss of his beard.

"Mad," he said with a satisfied sigh. Kit put his cheek back to the puddled table and slept.

Jack thought Old Kit must have started early tonight.

"He'll wake up screaming 'Gadzooks' and the devil's, too," Jack said to the Plymouth man, who sat in the nearest chair. But the merchant's attention was already drawn away by an argument over the orient of pearls and they did not hear his sorry tale that evening.

The Portuguese held that those pearls purchased from the vast Pacific's ocean nomads were "white as a high winter moon, as purely round as angels' tears" and the finest in all the world.

Maynard, a sort of gypsy scholar that Kit welcomed to his table, claimed the blue-tinged pearls of Persia, plucked by naked men from the maws of sharks, were the pearls most prized by the margaritaril of old Rome.

"White is for the fashion," he proclaimed tipsily. "The discerning eye must have subtle tints."

"Now Old Kit is with us, or will be shortly, and he may have a word on that himself," a black Irishman said and winked at Kit who was slowly rolling his head back and forth. "Well, I was goin' to say I never did see a sky blue pearl, but once when we looted St. Augustine I saw one as gold as amber and shaped like a tear, big as my thumb. But Captain Red Legs, now he . . ."

From Kit there was a low, long groan ending in a scream.

"Gadzooks!" He leaped as if stung by a scorpion and fell twitching and wide-eyed back on the wine-blackened table. That was how he often awoke on such nights.

"What year is this?" Kit asked Jack. He did not raise his head from the table.

"It's the year of our Lord sixteen sixty-nine, Master Kit." Jack looked at Louis and they both raised their eyes.

"One hundred and five today," the old man said gleefully, slowly sitting up. His dark eyes were feverish bright and his grin had but three dark pegs in it. "Yes, I remember singing that. One hundred five, today."

The others at the table raised their mugs and flagons a bit and gave a desultory hurrah. Old Kit was one hundred five today, as he had said frequently for some months, and they had tired of congratulating the ancient liar.

"Mad again," he said and laid his face in folded arms. Jack scooted over and sat on his toes. The old man sighed and was soon snoring.

8 SKY TALES

The Portuguese was in a new argument, this time with barrel-chested Van Oort, a pirate quartermaster who was disparaging the Portuguese's claims in thick, Mokum-accented French.

The Portuguese seemed genuinely affronted. As a poor orphan, he said, he had been taken as a servant by a Jesuit sent to the Court of the Emperor of China. His hands chased each other above his head as he showed how red and gold kites the size and image of dragons fought among the clouds like gamecocks. These flying monsters, he swore, were the Punch-and-Judies of huge armies of yellow chinamen who tugged and pulled at them not with twine, but a dozen ropes as thick as bowlines.

Once he had watched a great contest all afternoon while a thunderstorm piled itself above the Forbidden City.

"The sky was shot with greenish flickerings from horizon to horizon," the Portuguese said. "But I and all about me were so intent on the battle of the great kites that we paid the storm and then the rain no heed, with the generals of each gang shouting and exhorting their men to tug this way and that. I was almost trampled. Of a sudden, a thunderbolt plucked a golden ribbon off one dragon's tail and I smelled burnt flesh on the scream of the man next to me. I turned and saw a line of fifty like him that clung to the line and then the bolt's clap hit, striking quick and dead alike to the ground.

"There was the devilish smell of St. Elmo's Fire all around and much wailing."

The Dutchman merely harrumphed and Kit stirred and blinked open his eyes. "Milvus tremulque voce eh tera pulsat," the old man muttered with a smile and pushed a wisp of hair from his eye.

"Well, as I said," continued the Portuguese. "These Chinee kites kiss and clamber over the highest clouds in the skies. In the Zeeland," he said giving a sidelong glance to Van Oort. "In the Zeeland no doubt the clouds are much lower, too."

"Har! Again it is you who doubt me," said the Zeelander. "I have flown kites when a boy that could be seen by ships beyond the ocean's rim. I challenge you, Bartholomew," Van Oort said raising his tankard and lifting his butt briefly from the chair before falling upon it again. "Ha! You shall fly a chinaman's kite, and I shall show you a Zeeland kite soaring like a hawk above your duck."

"Ten doubloons," the Portuguese said, affecting a sly smile and tugging at one of his long, black mustachios.

"Done," cried the Van Oort. "On the morning after tomorrow we meet here before the Aeolus at the second bell."

Bartholomew nodded, still twisting his mustache.

"The Jesus of Lubeck, as I was saying," the Genoan slave trader at the end of the table said again. "Yes, there was a battle . . ."

And Jack had heard it first and secondhand more times than he could count. He put his chin to his knees and closed his eyes.

"Now in El Dorado," Blind Harry, seated on a stool in a corner of the poop was saying, interrupting a dispute as to how much gold Pizarro had sacked from the Incas. "There are golden ---"

"God's teeth, must we hear about that fairy city every night!" grumbled Bosola.

"It's true! They drink from diamond cups, their children play ninepins with fist-sized emeralds, rubies and golden nuggets---"

"Dream on, blind one," another man called, not stilling Blind Harry's recital.

Jack looked over at Louis who lounged in the corner looking back at him. El Dorado, Atlantis, the Seven Cities, all were arguments they had heard too often before. Kit already snored again, their bellies were full. It was unlikely they would do better at the Hotel Aeolus this night. Jack winked and tilted his head.

They got up, sidled past the disputants and tale-tellers at Kit's high table, and left the inn through the taproom door. Behind them someone leaning against the Aeolus' wall plucked a mandolin and sang of the Duchess of Alba.

9 REBECCA VAN DUYN'S LIPS

In the morning Jack headed down into the town hoping to find Louis and Will.

Remembering that the lower reaches of Cayona might still not be healthy for him today, when he reached

Quartermaster Way he turned and walked along it slowly, peering in the dirt for the glint of a coin. Up here on the Way a copper dropped by some captain leaving the great taverns, hotels, or whorehouses was not always instantly gleaned by the beached, bleached-eyed sailors that scavenged among the rum houses near the water.

Ahead he saw Old Kit's gilded palanquin sitting on its rails before the Hotel d' Aeolus. Its carriers, the two Gascons, leaned on its roof, deep in argument as usual.

Jack looked up at the facade of the great building, the largest in Cayona save the fort. It stood at the center of Quartermaster Way, three stories of adobe, cedar, and pine, nearly as tall as the palms.

There was glass in the upper windows and red tiles on the roof. Its sign was a huge leathern bag sewn from the hide of a whole bull, stuffed, tied and hung from its beam with a gilded chain. A second floor gallery bridged to Madame Pearl's nearly as grand whorehouse, so that the Aeolus' guests – at least those that were merchant and buccaneer captains, the wealthier traders, tradesmen and planters -- could drink, feast and then retire to tup their doxies with a Turk's convenience.

The two Gascons stopped their argument just a moment to sneer at Jack as he passed. He gave them wide berth. They knew that Jack, Louis and some of the others from Under-the-Tree had become casual favorites of their master. A copper tossed to the boys was one less that might come their way.

It reminded Jack of his grumbling stomach. If he could slip in the back of the Aeolus through the kitchen while Kit was still there, maybe he could get a bite. The worst he would get is a whack on the head with the cook's spoon.

He turned to go down the alley, but it was filled with a black horse and a carriage; Van Duyn's carriage. Rebecca Van Duyn sat within it. He stopped and gulped a breath. She was bent over, face hidden by her shining hair. She was helping a young girl sitting with her to straighten the dress on a tiny doll. There was no one else about.

He walked up to the carriage.

"Bon jour, Mademoiselle Van Duyn."

She looked up quickly, the sky glowing in her eyes. "Bon jour."

Jack did not know what to say. He glanced around, down the alley.

He could see the back of a man conversing with someone around the corner by the kitchen's doorway. Jack shuffled his feet.

"My uncle," the girl said and startled him.

"My uncle," she said again when he looked at her. There was a mischievous turn to her lips. Sea-sparkled eyes. "He tells me not to talk to you boys from the town, he said you are all no better than dogs.

"But I know it isn't so because I've talked to the baker's boy . . ."

"Andre," said Jack.

"Yes, Andre, and Jean, the boy that sharpens knives for a pence apiece, and anyone comes running with a message for Uncle, like the day before yesterday, you --"

"Jack," said Jack.

"You at the half door. I've only my older sister to talk with, who crochets hours and hours, and the cook's girl." She nodded at the child beside her. Jack's eyes did not even glance, but were fixed on Rebecca Van Duyn's lips, almost not hearing what they formed; the tiny freckles above her lips and dappling her milk cheek.

" . . . only nine, not company at all, really. So why shouldn't I talk to someone my own age, except my uncle says no?"

Before he could form an answer there was a gruff shout and her uncle's factor came tromping from the back of the alley.

"Get, get," the man called, shooing him away with his hand. Now, suddenly Jack felt more in his element.

He gave the man an insolent smile, then bowed to Rebecca Van Duyn with a flourish of his hand as if it held a great plumed hat.

"You must excuse me," Jack said loudly. "Perhaps I will call on you."

He looked up to her; they both laughed. The factor grumbled "merde" as he came up to the side of the carriage and swung the back of his hand at Jack who danced back a few steps.

The factor began apologizing to the girl for leaving her alone, but she still watched Jack with her almost magically bright eyes.

"Until tonight," he called. She pursed her lips as if to keep from giggling and the factor turned with a livid frown. Surprising even himself, Jack blew a kiss to her and gave a wink to the factor. The girl clapped her hands over a surprised laugh.

"Insolent jackanapes," shouted the factor, raising a fist and stepping toward him. "I'll have you beaten, I'll . . ."

Jack danced back a few more steps, smiling happily, then turned and walked with long-legged strides as tall as he could out the alley.

Without looking back as he rounded the corner he waived farewell to the continued threats and curses of the factor.

Within a few steps his euphoria stumbled into a gloomy, puzzled panic. Did she think he was insolent to her? Just a stray from the street, like her uncle said?

Did she even remember his name?

10 MEANDERING FOR GOLD

That night they had had no luck in the upper town as either beggars or sneak thieves. They drifted downward. Near the Griffin they saw familiar heads turn their way and quickly stepped into nearest break between buildings.

They began to trot, padding down through the tiny quarter of log and stucco storehouses filled with boucanier cowhides, a place both the drunk and sober avoided for the smell. In the alleys half a dozen stray dogs hunted rats. Next they meandered through double-stacked hogsheads of rum and fat pipes of wine, hoping to find a snoring drunk sawing away with a couple of 'eights in his purse.

They had no such luck, finding only the still, scrofulous body of Dick the geek. As usual he had pounded a nail between a keg's staves so he could lay suckling at the rum through the night. They let him be.

They came out of into the moonlight near the eastern cusp of the long crescent beach of Cayona's harbor. The beach was crowded with longboats, gigs, freiboats, pirogues, dinghies and canoes along its whole compass.

The two had to wind through a wooden maze down to the dark-silvered water. Stepping in, little shells and stones were lapped languidly across their toes.

Farther along this end of the harbor three ships lay careened and quiet on the sand; at the western cusp the beach doxies were careened nightly and not so quietly. Jack and Louis stepped out of the water and walked slowly west, keeping an eye cocked to the boats' shadows, watching for a fisherman sleeping in his freiboat. A score of dark shadows out in the bay -- barcas, catches, tartanes, xebecs, flutes and sloops, even an ancient galleon -- were turning in the tide, straining gently at their moorings.

To their right, under the first palms, were ramshackle rum huts crowded three deep the length of the beach, serving the poorest of the brothers of the coast and the most wretched flotsam of the sea.

Behind those started the taverns, armorers' workshops, whorehouses, warehouses, hostels, outfitters, and more taverns climbing up the slope to the tall gabled houses of just as ill repute along Quartermaster Way. Higher still, a few gleams through the pines and palms showed the big houses of the merchants who trafficked in the robberies of Tortuga's pirates, like all in Cayona robbing the robbers at every turn. On its crag, looming and dark against the stars, stood Governor Ogeron's fort. The watch lamps were lit on the battlements.

Jack picked up a flat stone and skipped it ducks-and-drakes down the silver moon path that blazed the bay's ebony water.

A spitting bottle of brandy whirled past Jack's head and disappeared with a splash in the bay. He dropped to all fours and crab-scrambled beneath the hatchet prow of a pirogue. He heard raucous laughs from one of the rum houses.

Jack jumped to his feet and shouted "dog fuckers," then ran up the beach

He heard Louis shout the same and he soon caught up as they trotted to a stop. They could not hear a reply if there was one. Only the soft surf, and men growling, shouting, grumbling, chantying, women screaming or laughing like gulls, clatter, thumps, the clang and tink of cutlass on cutlass, ships' musickers tattooing their drums, tooting bugles, skreeing bagpipes, and bottles breaking in a slow constant rhythm throughout the town.

Louis heaved a sigh.

"No luck down here. What now?"

"Let's go climb the tree behind Van Duyn's garden," Jack said with a sensible air, then grinned.

"Christ's blood. Why you're so besotted on that prissy little wench is beyond fathoming. I doubt you've talked twice with her. Let's try the Wheel. None of the Bristolman's mates 'll be there."

"Rebecca's the prettiest girl in Cayona," Jack said. "This side of one or two delights at Madame Pearl's. And a sight more sweet tempered."

Jack imagined the Dutch girl's bare bosom heaving meekly beneath his gaze. An unlikely event, he had to admit. Her uncle had kept her mostly sequestered or chaperoned all the half year since she had arrived from Nieuw Amsterdam. His encounter with her by the Aeolus had been rare luck, he knew.

Louis just shook his head as they threaded through the boats again and headed up along Armory Street. It was empty except for a yellow dog snuffling at a gory rag.

"And what's more," Jack began after a few more thoughts on the, perhaps, freckled breasts.

"Oui, I know. 'And she'll bring a fine dowry' you say. Ha!" said Louis. "To some merchant captain, yes. But her uncle would hang you by the codsack if you tried to kiss the hem of her skirt, and for good measure ship her back where she came from. Van Duyn will allow no truck with you."

He shook his head. "Ha, to think --"

"Ha, yourself. When I make my fortune--" Jack protested in a mock tone of hurt.

"Ya, oui. But let's be on with getting it."

"All right, let's try the Wheel o' Fortune," Jack picked up the pace. "It's the best place to start."

11 THE WHEEL OF FORTUNE

The sign of the Wheel of Fortune was a wagon wheel with tarnished pieces of eight nailed around its perimeter. Bright light and gamblers' shouts, coos, and imprecations spilled from the door.

The Wheel was always bright. Candles burned in two dozen mirrored sconces to aid the sight of Squint, the proprietor.

The square low-ceilinged room was filled with seamen: sailors from the Dutch, French, and English merchant ships, beached pirates, and small planters who had retired from the sea. But only two doxies worked the room, toothless Angie and Crazy Mabel. No tradesmen or other lubbers were in sight. He and Louis' entrance drew no more notice than would a stray passing in the street.

A ring of men diced on the floor, another cluster diced at the center table. One table hoisted their mugs and sang a song of drinking Spanish blood. At another, all on one bench, were a trio of rawboned young Normans, little older than cabin boys, their faces flush and their eyes set with rum.

Jack gave Louis an elbow in the ribs and nodded toward the three. "Easy pickings," muttered Louis.

Black John the barkeep saw their intention and gave them a wink from across the room. They found a corner out of the way of the gamblers and took up the wait like buzzards. They did not lack for amusement.

Bushy-haired, red-headed Crazy Mabel was laughing and arguing with a short Breton sailor with a blue kerchief tied over his head.

He kept lifting her skirts with his hook, resisting her little pushes and tugs toward the door. He showed the whore an 'eight, then two, and struck her price.

She dropped the coins between her breasts, then bent over the nearest table and tossed her skirts up on her back. This revealed a stern nearly as broad as a galleon's and nearly as ornate.

On her left buttock was tattooed a red and blue leaping royal lion, on the right a rearing unicorn. The Breton, so short he had to kick up a footstool behind her, stood on it, waved his hook in the air, dropped his pantaloons and, with an incoherent shout, mounted the slut with one thrust. His shout was answered alike by his mates.

Jack and Louis turned to each other with amazed grins.

"I ain't seen the like," said Jack.

"Crazy Mabel has no shame," Louis said, gone serious.

At the bar Black John was struck dumb, his own grin frozen on his face. Squint, however, was shouting and jumping up and down beside the coupling couple commanding them to disengage, threatening to toss a bucket of water on them. Squint was quickly shouted down by the whole room and tugged away by Angie, who was enjoying the unprecedented scene as much as the sailors.

The whole company was shouting encouragement to the stubby Frenchman and clapping in rhythm. All, but Squint, guffawed and roared with delight as the whore, face lain cheek against the table, counterfeited a yawn.

Angry, but still humping away at a canter, the sailor tangled his hook in Mabel's red hair and jerked back her head, making her screech.

"Who'll put a spigot in this gaping tap hole?" he cried. "We'll swive her fore and aft."

The room resounded like a barnyard and several volunteers rose.

But before he could be joined the Breton shot his wad and was immediately pulled from the doxie by a hide-clad bear of a buccaneer who kicked away the stool and mounted her himself. Crazy Mabel squealed in outrage as he took her and reached behind her with her palm up for silver, squealing again when she got none.

The buccaneer shot his salvo almost at once with an oddly soft gasp. Crazy Mabel wriggled free, turned and punched the buccaneer peevishly on the shoulder, then smoothed down her ragged skirts.

Squint was shouting again, banning the whole company for life, but no one paid him mind. Tossing the redbush of her hair, Crazy Mabel strode out of the tavern winking and smiling at the sailors who raised their rum and blew kisses to her as she passed.

The three Norman sailors had their heads together, muttering excitedly.

Even through the fogged pane of fresh rum Crazy Mabel had put a notion in their heads, that was plain to Jack. He pulled on Louis's arm and they followed Crazy Mabel out into the street and then squatted in the shadow between the Wheel and the next tavern. Within a few breaths the three deckhands stumbled out.

Jack watched them stop, confused. In Cayona any direction would serve their purpose. They jingled the purses at their belts, exchanged a few words and a laugh, and then took Quicksilver Street towards the harbor.

Jack and Louis jumped up and raced over to Piss Creek Way, then down it, paralleling their quarry's path for a short way, then turned and walked down a narrow defile between two storehouse walls. Louis waited at the inky middle, Jack padded on to the end and peered up the alley.

The three were tripping down the shadowy dirt path single file, babbling about whore-pipe sucking doxies. Jack pulled back and crouched.

They stepped past, one, two, three, four, five, he hooked the last ankle with his foot, then leapt like a tom, snatching the deckhand's purse strings before he had sprawled in the dirt and landed with his knees in the boy's back. His knife slashed the leather thong and he was up to his feet before the other two turned. Jack paused an instant to let them see him dart back between the buildings.

"Cutpurse! Thief!" he heard the two cry.

Jack knew every footfall by heart and ran between the black walls without a flinch, leaping over Louis where he crouched.

As always, he wanted to raise his arms high with the purse, to cry out like a hawk with a dove in its talons. Behind he heard running steps; one of the fools was chasing him, following his murky silhouette.

There was a deep, frightened grunt. He waited in the shadow of the narrow exit. In a moment Louis came up to him with a broad grin, jingling a purse of his own.

"To the Tree?" he asked.

"To the Aeolus?" Jack returned.

"Aye!"

They jumped over Piss Creek and trotted into the blackness of the next alley, skittering and weaving through a secret labyrinthine path known only to the boys of Under-the-Tree, one of whose turns eventually let them out on Quartermaster Way.

12 DUEL OF THE KITES

"Ahoy there, Jack," Pierre called. He opened his eyes. "Come along, you'll miss the kites."

Pierre peered into the cave, shielding his eyes from the sun winking down on him through the leaves.

"Kites?"

Pierre straightened up and put his hands on his hips.

"You hold it on a rein of twine and it flies, lack wit. Van Oort built his last night. I watched."

Jack grunted and sat up. Rebecca's image still warmed his fully awakened roger.

"The Portuguese and he have bet ten doubloons on whose will fly the highest," Jack said.

"Ten doubloons? Then come on." Pierre shouted over his shoulder as he trotted off. "You'll miss it."

Jack tucked his knife in his belt and followed him down the path.

It was half a league along the shore road west of Cayona before they caught up with the party riding along in a one-horse plantation wagon. The Portuguese and Van Oort, matched in their ruffled white shirts, were perched upon large baskets at the fore of the wagon bed. On their knees were perched their flying toys, their kites. On the boards at their feet sat Jesús, Will, Emil and two other boys from the Tree.

Jack and Pierre clambered into the wagon, too. A mulatto plantation hand drove the wagon. Next to him, actually leaning against his shoulder, Old Kit hunched over his cane, snoring.

Jack studied the kites with the other boys. Each man also, surreptitiously, eyed the other's.

Van Oort's was like a large white heraldic shield, a diamond drawn out long at the bottom. A large skull was inked upon the shield, and below it a small hourglass. A tail of rags and ribbons curled on Van Oort's boot tops.

The Portuguese's kite was a much more elaborate construction. At a distance it had seemed to Jack he was holding the model of a watchtower for Cayona's fort, but that its center third had no walls. Van Oort's was made of whittled sticks and printers' paper. The Portuguese, however, had, at no small expense, endeavored to show them a true Chinaman's kite. On each pane of raw silk, eight in all, frowned a fearsome beast, a dragon, he said, painted in red. They looked like boars to Jack.

Where the road turned inland to the Ringot plantations the Dutchman called a halt. The boys jumped out, Van Oort and the Portuguese climbed down and strode through the palms to the beach, half carrying, half pulling their tugging kites out onto a broad, sandy point.

Jack and the others followed close behind. Two boys carried each of the men's baskets filled with bailing twine. Old Kit hobbled along slowly through the sand.

Jack watched the kites wriggle and tug to be free on the gusts. The breeze was stronger than it should be this time of day and had shifted around from the prevailing Windwards' northeast to close due east out of a grayish horizon.

"All the better," Van Oort exclaimed to the Portuguese as the two struggled to tie the lead of twine to their kites' harnesses of net line. "This one will soon soar like a falcon."

"But this, my friend," the Portuguese said, jerking his knot tight, and planting a kiss on his kite, "This will climb like a soul."

Motioning the boys out of their lee, the men stood up and moved apart. Their kites twisted and dodged before them like frightened horses on their reins. With a look and shout between them, they let the kites fly free.

The white shield and red tower flew off down the beach, like flowers on a swift stream. The twine slipped through the grommets of the two men's thumbs and forefingers, which soon closed, easing on the lines and the kites rose, the Dutchman's in darting swoops to left, then right, the Portuguese's in longer tacks, both quickly rising higher than the palms rimming the beach.

Now the little shield and tower caught another stream and blew swiftly away above the shore. Twine whizzed in a blur from the two baskets beside the kite flyers.

Van Oort squeezed and slowed the whirring line and took a dozen steps backwards. His kite swooped up like a white bird, turned sharply as if to dive, and he released the line, almost losing it as it whipped about. The Dutchman's kite luffed about for some moments, then steadied and pulled evenly against the twine. He motioned with his head for some boys to shift his basket behind him.

The Portuguese still let his line play out, carried by his gaudy kite on the rapid breeze. His twine passed more swiftly through his fingers than did the Dutchman's, and it was some moments after his rival took his new stance that the Portuguese's gloved thumb bit down on his own line.

The Portuguese walked backwards up the beach into the wind. The line slipped slowly through his fists and he stepped unhurriedly past the Dutchman, exchanging sly grins, and, with Andrew and Will carrying his basket of unwinding twine, moved several yards further up the beach, almost out of hailing distance in the now blustery wind. His kite too began to climb.

Jack stayed by the Dutchman, hoping to maintain his perspective on the contest. Both kites seemed now a league away, though they couldn't quite be that. Van Oort said there was but half a league of twine in each basket and his was not yet half gone. The Portuguese's kite climbed almost imperceptibly, but its reddish form was gaining to the height of the tiny white diamond.

Old Kit had at first reclined against a palm. Now he struggled to his feet and made his way over the sand to where Jack stood staring upward under the eave of his hand.

"Can you see them lad?" Kit asked breathlessly and grinned, his four yellow teeth gleaming in his mouth.

Jack wondered why the old man made so much of the game. Still, it was a greater wonder that two pirates were dashing about the beach chasing breezes with their children's toys instead of gaming with the dice.

"Aye, Master Kit," Jack said. "But they are the size of flies against a wall."

"You point the way then and I shall follow your line like a gunner."

"They are not close together," Jack said raising his arm.

His eyes widened enviously as the old man pulled from his deep coat pocket a spyglass and snapped out its second length. Its slender cylinders were chased with silver dolphins and its three rings were gold filigree studded with diamonds.

"Where, boy?"

Jack turned his gaze from the spyglass to the sky. The reddish spot of the Portuguese's kite would be easiest for the old man to see against the graying sky. He pointed to it, holding his arm stiff.

"There's the Chinese bird."

Kit shuffled around behind him, crooked his head back against his widow's hump and put the spyglass to his good left eye. Jack watched over his shoulder while the glass wavered around the line his arm held.

"Ah," the old man said at last. His squinting grimace spread into his pink, near empty grin. "Six-sixty-six."

Jack dropped his arm and searched the clouds for the Dutchman's kite.

Van Oort had moved away from them, down toward the rough breaking surf, and turned his back with the wind, which had shifted a few more degrees, now east southeast. The Portuguese had done the same.

"And where's the Zeelander's, Jack?" Kit shouted into the wind, squinting his eyes almost closed.

Jack followed the Dutchman's line as it rose up past the palms, high above their crowns, floating in a long curve, till, shimmering, it disappeared from sight like a bowline to some great sheet of wind.

Far beyond, a patch of dark gray cloud passing behind it caught out the tiny white kite.

Jack raised his arm to it until the old man again found the kite in his glass.

"There is no difference between them I can spy," the old man said lowering the spyglass. "You take a sighting on them."

First briefly turning the ornate optic in his hand, Jack raised it to his right eye, seeking first the Dutchman's small white diamond, then the Portuguese's little Chinese tower. In degree they seemed to him the same.

Van Oort hailed them over the blusters and the rush of the rolling surf.

Jack extended the spyglass to Kit, but the old man waved him down to the Dutchman with it.

The wind had shifted further, now directly southeast, whipping across the straight from the gloomy bulk of Hispaniola. The gray tides of clouds mounting over the island were suffused with a soft glow, a pale pearl-yellow light. Herald of a hurricane.

Van Oort met him halfway. With Albert and Emil carrying his basket of twine he was retreating from the waves that had surged over his ankles.

"What say you, boy, do I win?"

"It's a match to my eye," Jack answered.

"Let me see," asked Albert, but the Dutchman grunted at him like a boar and extended his own hand.

Jack gave Van Oort the spyglass. The buccaneer also turned the glittering piece in his hand before putting it to his eye. While he studied the sky, the Portuguese and his retinue were making their way downwind to them.

"Do you ask for quarter?" The Portuguese called with a broad smile.

The Dutchman lowered the spyglass.

"No eye but a Jew's could distinguish the measure between them."

He offered over the spyglass, but the Portuguese shook his head. His black ringlets whipped about his face and blew into his mouth. Kit shuffled up to the group and took the glass himself.

"What say you," said the Portuguese, "We pull them alongside 'another and then match them in the glass?"

The Portuguese looked into his basket of twine. "The gale will soon carry them away of its own accord and there's no skill in that to measure."

The Dutchman considered this a moment, then frowned.

"I know your plan," he said. "I've heard you talk of Chinese tricks to knock the other fellow down. And then you'd win the wager."

Jack searched the rolling clouds for several moments before sighting the kites floating like distant mates. They were quite close together even now, brought in conjunction by the Portuguese's return.

Suddenly the Portuguese charged right up beside the Dutchman, letting the line run out swiftly between his fingers, then gripping the twine tightly. He smiled mischievously. Van Oort growled and stepped back a pace, confused about how to respond to this tactic.

The six boys, Kit with his spyglass, and the two kite flyers all turned their faces skyward to watch the distant points of white and red.

The two kites crossed in the sky and shortly the white one dipped lower by a degree, then another.

"Arghh," roared Van Oort at the sky. He ducked below the Portuguese's hands and ran up the beach with his line, shouting at the boys to follow with the basket.

Again all eyes watched the distant spots of color. Soon the Dutchman's kite rose minutely and pulled apart from its foe.

Two whoops sounded behind him, and Jack jumped around just as the surf broke over his ankles. He stumbled backwards and fell to his butt, soaking his britches in the brine. The Portuguese's near empty basket of twine was knocked over by the wash and it rolled about till Will retrieved it. All of them retreated up the beach.

"I myself will return to town," Kit announced from a cupped hand. "My old bones will not take the soaking that is soon to arrive."

He gestured to the smoke black clouds mounting above the far main island.

"You gentlemen can do what you like."

The Portuguese and the Dutchman frowned at their kites and at one another, each reluctant to sound a surrender to the elements that might also forfeit his wager.

"What do you say," shouted Jack to the duelists. "At the Old One's shout we grab the twine playing out at the baskets' mouth and cut loose the kites? The man with the shortest line in his basket is the winner."

"Agreed," said the Portuguese instantly.

"Aye," said Van Oort.

Emil and Jack kneeled beside the two baskets and drew their knives.

The old man, looking about the beach like an admiral on his poop, threw up his arm.

"Away !"

The lines were cut. The pirates held their lines for an instant, reluctant, then released them, as if they each dropped a gem into the ocean, fulfilling a regretted drunken vow.

The lines were drawn away up into the air, licked across the madly thrashing palm tops, mounted higher and were gone.

They all looked skyward for the kites, but the white one had disappeared, and the reddish mote of the Chinese kite blinked in and out like a star at dawn and was gone.

13 HURRICANE RAINS

The blusters had become a gale. By the time they reached Cayona rain drops spattered the party, stinging like pebbles. Kit, clutching his seat as if he feared he'd be blown away like thatch, bid them all jump from his wagon at the nearest high street. The mulatto driver turned the frightened horse and gave it the whip, hoping to make the old man's house before the heavens broke.

"To the Black Parrot," Van Oort shouted above the blasts shoving them about like waves of water. He meant to celebrate his victory, or loss, hurricane or no. All but Jack bent low and made for the tavern, whose sign rattled in the wind at the far end of the street.

Jack hurried in the opposite direction to find Louis and whoever else of their cave mates he could find. There would be food and drink aplenty for all today at the Black Parrot. Jack guessed today he'd find his Louis with the Walloon carpenter, but instead of sweeping shavings they'd be battening down the shop's shutters and doors.

At the first cross street Jack put his shoulder to the wind and still was shoved to the opposite side before he'd crossed the way. Lightning lashed over the hills, but the thunder was drowned in the wind's howls. Two more streets and down a few shops and he would be there.

The rain struck before he reached the next street, rattling like grapeshot on tile roofs, across the walls and shutters, jabbing at Jack's head and back like hundreds of angry fingers.

The water fell like a wave on his shoulders, nearly beating him to his knees. He stumbled down the middle of the street, wrenched and shoved and slapped by the storm's watery hands. Barely holding his feet, he staggered to the nearest building. He broke through the waterfall pouring from the eaves and hugged the stucco wall, dazed and coughing up the water he had breathed.

Jack turned and rested his back against the wall. He was in the lee of the wind here, but it did him little good. The drafts and freaks of wind constantly rent and whipped the silvery curtain before him, lashed him with its rains. He stood on the low side of the street, a natural sewer; already the rushing stream following this building topped his ankles and tried to tear his feet from under him.

The stream churned along the wall and gushed out into the torrent of the next cross street. There, near the end of the wall, Jack spied a doorway. As quickly as he could, steadying himself with one hand, sometimes two, he made his way to the already awash porch stone, jerked up the door's wooden latch and pushed inside.

He slammed the door shut and leaned against it, closing his eyes and breathing deeply. The barrage of rain on the palm thatch overhead, though diminished from the watery thunder of the street, frightened him in its ungodly hammering. Jack opened his eyes. He was in a tobacco leaf warehouse. This batch is ruined for certain, he thought. The palm thatch had been torn off in a dozen spots on the windward face. The rain gushed through those holes and poured in little streams from ten times that many leaks. The wet sotweed was already rank to his nose. The rain, for a few moments reduced to rattling drum fire, rose again to a pounding barrage. Water squirted beneath the door at his back, washing over his feet. Curious about the turmoil in the street, Jack opened the door.

The stream rushing by the door flooded past him into the warehouse. The silver curtain was now broken by the torn roof into half a dozen pouring spouts. A hissing, crashing wall of rain thick as porridge wavered up and down the street.

Jack held fast to the door jamb, placed a foot in the stream boiling over the flagstone, and leaned outward for a better look at the corner. Where it joined the mad rush of water down Piss Creek, the stream swirling past him had nearly eaten away the foundation of the building that was his refuge. And the waters of the Piss Creek itself, channeled by the open sewer, were now like a smallish river filled with flotsam--barrel staves, rags, a chicken--that had found its new bed through the center of Cayona.

As Jack watched, the body of a man came rolling down the shallow new river, pushed over and over in the torrents. The body, its clothes soaked black, washed against a hump in the street and halted. The stream continued tugging at the man's limbs, eager to carry the body downstream.

14 A MERCENARY RESCUE

The body, the man, slowly rose on one elbow. Unable to attain the other elbow, he sprawled again and the water churned about his head. A new burst of rain fell in rattling waves over the street, obscuring Jack's sight. Then he saw a new channel of water had caught the man's leg, pulling him around, dragging him into deeper water.

Jack clung to the door jamb. He could easily drown himself if he tried to help. The piteous creature's hands clutched at the hump of over-washed mud that held him. His white face rose up from the waters once more, a final gasp.

Jack started. It was Old Kit.

The jeweled spyglass flashed in his inner eye. If it had not slipped from his pocket, he might slip it from the old man and no one be the wiser. Much later he remembered that thought with a twinge of shame.

Up the churning stream he saw their overturned wagon, the horse on its side, raising it head and splashing back trying not to drown. Beneath the wagon, the mulatto's arm stuck above the water, flopping lifelessly in the churning.

Jack leaped over the stream rushing past the door. Prancing across the slippery mud, he jumped over the roiling channel that cut down the near side of the cross street. When he hit the swift water it nearly toppled him and he went down to his hands, the water to his elbows. The water was tugging at the old man's body, turning it over on its back, pulling at both legs. Scuttling sidewise through the wash like a crab Jack gained the scoured hump of earth and dove to grab the old man's sleeve cuff as he slid into the rushing sewer channel. Jack pulled himself forward with his other hand and grabbed hold of Kit's coat collar. Straining against the drag of the water over the old man's belly, he seized the old man's pants waist and tried to heave him up onto the muddy little island. Instead the torrent dragged his own legs around and dug its liquid fingers beneath his chest and belly trying to flip him over like a turtle.

Jack let loose the pants and held old Kit by his collar. He clawed his right hand into the mud and shoved his elbow hard against the over-washed ground. He grunted with the strain as he tried to raise himself. First he gained his right knee; then, his left. Keeping his forearm braced, Jack held tight and heaved on the old man's collar with a strength he found in a raging shout.

This time the old man helped, kicking his legs weakly, and Jack had Kit's head resting on the hand that clutched his collar. The water churned about the old man's ears. He looked up at Jack's face, but seemed blind to it, seeing only the tumbling heavens above.

"My God," he croaked weakly. "My God, look not so fierce on me!"

"Mad One," Jack said to the old man's face. "Help us now or we're both lost."

Crabbing sidewise on three points he gained a little height and heaved again. Out of the greatest rush of water, Kit's body had little weight. Repeating this exercise twice more, Jack gained the top of the little hump of mud. The water topped its crown by only an inch. Jack was panting and shivering, cursing all God's elements and plans in his mind, unthankful that he could turn and sit where he was. He grasped Kit between the shoulders and pulled him up between his knees, letting him recline his head against his stomach. The old man coughed and gagged. Turning his head, he vomited a stomach-full of water.

Jack stared at the muddy stream rolling past on either side of them.

An undercut wall collapsed into the torrent far down the street. But the water did not seem to be rising, though the rain still fell with a cold, hard drumming.

"We'll be staying here, Master Kit," he said, speaking mostly to himself. "We'll drown for certain if we don't."

The old man retched more water back into the stream.

As the rain and wind slackened, three men emerged from the building next to the one that had collapsed and began to study the shambles. It took a lull in the wind for them to hear his shouts.

They helped Jack carry the old man to the Aeolus. The staff erupted in shouting pandemonium. The frail, dripping body was taken from Jack and the other's arms and carried up the stairs and across the brothel gallery to Madam Pearl's own bed.

In the taproom there was general agreement that Jack would be given a king's ransom for his efforts. The fire behind Old Kit's favored chair had been flooded out by the rain washing down the chimney, but soon as the fresh one was lit they sat him on a stool in front of it, put a blanket over his shoulders and a bottle of brandy in his hands. He called for a pipe and it was brought to him.

An hour later, as he described to Jesús, Emil, and Louis his plunge through chest high currents, the Aft Gascon came up to the table they now sat at and dropped a heavy pouch before him.

"Master Kit says that that is but a drop in the hogshead that will be your reward," the man said glumly. "But I would hang onto it if I were you. Doc Smeeks doubts he'll last the night and that will be all you'll get."

"Then I'll buy drinks for all to toast his health." Jack shouted tipsily, raising his bottle in the air.

The boys from the Tree and hangers on around the room shouted a cheer.

The Aft Gascon turned and slowly climbed the stairs to the gallery passage. Under his breath Jack cursed his luck even as he pulled open the pouch and peered at the hoard of silver 'eights. Far better than nothing. He wondered what had become of the jeweled spyglass. He had forgotten it until this moment.

Near sunset, as remnants of the tempest's winds whipped the clouds to tatters, the old man was carried in his palanquin up to the great house. The next day common word was that Old Kit was dead. Jack, lying in the cave nursing an awful katzenjammer, cursed his miserable luck a dozen score of times.

Part II

AN UNSENTIMENTAL EDUCATION

15 JACK'S LAST 'EIGHT

By the next afternoon the word throughout Cayona was that the ancient one was taking his time dying, but was mad with a death fever. The following day the word was the same. When Kit was not dead in a full week's time, stories about the ghost of an Indian sorcerer and a pact with the devil gained currency.

Jack's hopes had gone up.

But the reward handed him by Kit's Aft Gascon, was --- except for a handsome 'eight --- already gone. He had a buccaneer's Flemish knife to show for it. The hat with the red plume he had lost as soon as he'd had it, dicing with Jean. The rest was divided among the boys of the Tree, their pact, more or less, to share each alike. Still, the fact that the silver had not been some loot, or that it wasn't bread bartered for a bit of work, this division of spoils bothered him more than a little. His reward had been more like a gift. What should be done if Old Kit increased his reward to ten times that much silver? Divided it would soon be gone, squandered by the Tree's boys just like the drink-sodden pirates they all mocked. If he did choose to keep it all to himself they would make him a pariah. But then, it would be a favorable trade. He could build himself a house up the hill and be attended by doxies on every hand. Until those coins were gone.

That night Louis suggested they scrounge for loose pennies around some dicing tables, then go wager the coins themselves in another tavern. They looked into a several doors before they found The Griffin crowded and bustling enough for their intentions. Jack took a seat on the end of a bench at a trestle table, leaning back from the game so that he did not distract any evil tempered gambler. He looked around at the men hidden in the shadows whose faces they could not make out from the street. He did not want to encounter the Bristolman or any of that crew.

Jack turned his attention to the table. Across from him sat Black Angelo, a Sicilian with a gray streaked topknot and a T branded on his left cheek. He was raking a handful of 'eights, a few gold doubloons and misshapen pearls, and a great pile of coppers into a heap before him.

He winked at Jack.

"I'm through with this chamber pot," shouted a surly Englishman at the end of the table. He slammed the leather cup down and stood up.

Jack watched the Sicilian raise his drink casually, but through the mug's glass bottom he kept his eye on the Englishman and the other losers.

In Cayona everyone kept a close watch on the dice, the pot, and each other's hands.

Jack looked around the room for Louis. He was sitting at the end of a table in the far corner. Louis appeared intent on the gaming, but Jack could tell by the way he hunched over that his toes were fishing for some coin on the dirt floor.

The dies clattered on Jack's own table. Fours and a five.

"Threes," Jack said on the next shake, placing the shining piece o 'eight on the rough pine, keeping the tip of his finger on it. The man in the green kerchief matched him. On the toss his 'eight was gone.

"God's hooks," he cursed. That was a week's rum for every boy at Under-the-Tree. Or a fine salmagundi for all. He thought he could feel Louis's stare on the back of his neck from across the room. He did not want to face that sour look.

Angelo brushed more coins towards himself; copper, silver, a gold cob. The Sicilian's hard glance caught Jack's envious eyes. The man rubbed the T on his cheek reflectively, winked, and tossed Jack a fat penny. Jack caught it with both hands.

"Go take a gamble on the pox, boy," Black Angelo said.

Jack grinned. "Merci!"

He climbed off the bench and made his way to Louis, skipping over a coagulating mat of bloody straw in the center of the room. Louis met him with a frown.

Jack shrugged.

"It was your notion."

"What pittance did Angelo toss you?"

"An English copper."

Louis just grunted and shook his head.

"Where now? The Mermaids? Red Jack's? Hung Dog? Black Parrot?"

Jack tried to sound merry, but it was feeble. Louis just looked at him and turned and walked out into the crowded dirt street. Jack followed, back once again to pondering where he would beg or steal his next meal. He heard shouting and the clank of cutlasses, but did not bother to turn around.

16 A CONTINGENT TREASURE

"Shoot! Shoot, damn it."

"Sorry," said Jack. He measured a hand span from the second hole, cradled the taw in his knuckle and shot. It rolled a wobbly course over the hard dirt and went just wide of the third hole.

"Merde," he said.

Jesús laughed and hunkered over to get a good line on Jack's taw.

Six of them from the Tree were scrambling around in the dirt behind DeSale's armory, playing at four-hole poison. Jesús was already poison. The dark, little mestizo cursed when his taw missed by the width of a fingernail and rolled clear over to the armory's log wall. Abel was lining up on the poison pot when Louis came around the building' corner with the Fore Gascon.

"Here he is," Louis said.

The lanky, lantern-jawed man gave Louis a penny. The man studied Jack crouching in the dirt with a dark, disdainful air. Jack stared back.

"Master Kit wishes to speak with you," the Fore Gascon said, then turned and walked back around the corner of the armory.

Jack jumped to his feet, grinning. The others gave a shout, clapping their hands in the air.

"You'll be a prince!" one of the boys shouted.

"You'll have your own barque!" said another.

"A brigantine.'"

"We'll all be princes!"

Jack trotted after the Gascon without a word to the others.

Old Kit's house was the finest in Cayona. Built by master shipwrights out of mahogany, cedar, and pine, two tall stories roofed with red Spanish tiles, it stood higher on the slope behind Cayona than any of the houses erected by rich planters and merchants, higher even than the Governor's fort on its promontory. Jack had never been beyond the high fence surrounding the house, though he had run messages up to the gate for merchants and factors many times.

Today he rode through the gates in the same wagon that had taken them to the battle of the kites. The Gascon had been silent the entire way up the hill. He reined the horses to a halt before the broad, cedar-shuttered porch.

"Climb down," the man said. "Dust off your filthy clothes. Then go knock on the door. The old mulatto woman will take you to him."

Jack did as he was told. The old woman, who seemed clothed in layers of bright aprons, let him into the dark, shadowed house. In the sudden dimness he could make out little in the broad, dark rooms to either side of him. Bent under the weight of her widow's hump, the housekeeper led him up the stairway across from the door. Its rail was one long, sinuous mahogany snake ending in a fanged head at the bottom post. At the head of the stairs they turned down a long narrow gallery.

Its only light seeped through the slats of shuttered windows on one side. Moted planes of light striped the slowly shuffling, wheezing woman.

At the end of the hall she knocked at a door. Jack did not hear an answer, but the old woman opened the door and then stood to one side to let him pass.

"Come here, boy," he heard Kit's hoarse voice say.

Jack entered and the door was closed behind him. There was more light in the room than the rest of the house and Jack felt a breath of relief. Men most often choose to die in the twilight, they said.

The drapes of one high window were drawn back and a large candle burned beside a huge, covered bed. Jack walked forward, trembling with anticipation of a great reward. He could almost feel the deep weight of a gold ingot pressing across his palms, the strain of his loins as he hefted it, the warmth.

Old Kit's round face was blurred in the soft light by the wispy white hair about his ears and patching his small chin. He looked like some sickly royal child propped up by embroidered pillows in the huge oaken bed, carved poster and frame with lizards, pears, and grapes. The bed's indigo canopy gleamed with golden threads. The old man's soft brown claws were folded over an ear horn in his lap.

Jack halted several paces from the bed.

"Good morn, Master Kit."

The old man smiled.

"What were you doing?" his voice rasped with the slow effort.

"Uh. Shooting taws, sir." Jack's eyes strained surreptitiously into the shadows looking for the rumored treasures, one of which might be his. The shadows gleamed as if filled with stars.

"Sheep's knuckles," whispered the old man.

Jack stared at him. "Sheep's knuckles?"

"The Scythians. We are told they used sheep's knuckles for their taws. What ---" he coughed, hacked, hawked, leaned over the side of the bed and drooled a pale glob into a bowl on the floor. Then he sat back up slowly. "Playing taws you said?"

"Poison. Four-hole Poison, sir." Jack shifted his feet. Old Kit was off on one of his famous tacks against the wind. He damn well might not get a thing, Jack thought. Not ever.

"In my day boys went to span-counter for French Crowns."

"I don't know that one, Hieronymo." Jack used the name Kit called himself when he was crazy drunk. Sometimes he smiled at the jibe, but today he did not seem to notice.

"The sacristan of St. Gall's. He lays the cat-o-nine-tails on boys like you that shoot under the fish stands."

Mad again, Jack thought.

"There is a stool at the foot of the bed," the old man said. His voice was smoother with a little use. He gestured with the ear horn. "Bring it around and sit beside me."

Jack did as he was told. As soon as he had perched, the old man's hand rose shakily from the ear horn in his lap and extended toward him.

Jack's cupped hands darted out just in time to catch five gold doubloons. He drew them to himself.

"Thank you, sir," he muttered. He had expected one of Hieronymo's great pearls, or an emerald.

"That is all your reward," the old one said, pursing his lips in a small smile. Jack's last great hope sunk beneath the waves. "All you can hold."

Jack cupped his two hands together in front of his chest. "I could hold much more if you were so kind."

"I might give you a hundred times as much, even a thousand, but what would you do with it?"

"Uhh--"

"More than likely your friends would help you drink it and whore it away in half a year," Kit said, then chuckled as if at the thought.

"No, I would--"

"Would you go into trade? I doubt you can factor or read a score of words. And a youth like you'd be cheated blind on any account from jealousy and general principles."

Jack had indeed thought to establish in trading one thing or some other. One where he could meet on even footing with Herr Van Duyn, perhaps.

"I can factor, Kit. McRae the chandler showed me two years ago when I started helping when the supplies come in. I can count all the hundreds and do sums. His assistant never finds an error and puts them right in the ledger. McRae says I am right smart with numbers and I'll learn ledgers, too. I'm sly about who cheats who and how in this town, and I won't be cheated."

Old Kit managed to both frown and raise an eyebrow on his wrinkled face. Jack decided to try another tack.

"I might, well, with a greater reward I could use it for the purchase of a sloop."

Jack shifted on the stool, studying the veined old face, the wide-apart, dark, steady eyes. The old man was playing him, and not for cruelty, though that certainly wasn't against his nature.

"A sloop?" Kit finally said. " And sail on account? Worse than dicing it away and more likely a whelp like you'd have his throat slit some midnight and tossed to the sharks in any event. You and your mates have waylaid half the sailors in port one time or another."

"I am bigger than half the sailors and buccaneers that come to town, and I'll say better with my knife than many, too."

He had Jack's back up now.

"I shouldn't even be at Under-the-Tree by our articles. And I have tupped more wenches -- some more than a half dozen times in one night – tupped more than most of those freebooters, I'd wager. At least ones that ain't paid for."

The old man began to laugh, but it barely broached his throat before he fell into a brutal hacking that continued for some seconds. A few flecks of blood dashed the coverlet across his chest. When he had finished he drew a lace kerchief across his mouth.

Jack had no wish to catch whatever plague the old man had caught in his Piss Creek dousing. He jumped to his feet.

"Thank you in any event Master Kit." He shook the coins in his palm. "This is a just reward for the little life that's left you."

He was across the room before the old man could cry "No, no, boy. No, no boy. I want you to have a greater treasure."

Then he was coughing again. Jack walked back quickly, afraid the man would cough himself to death before he had given him his reward. His own small treasure.

When Old Kit had recovered he said "Now, let me see your purse."

Jack drew the leather bag out of his sash.

"Put your doubloons in it."

He did, greatly increasing its heft.

"Tell me," said Kit, leaning back and staring up at the dark canopy. "Could your purse hold a hundred doubloons?"

"No," Jack said warily, tightening the leather strings.

"Jack," the old man said turning his head to look him in the eye. "You are like your purse. You haven't the scope to hold a hundred doubloons. First, near man or nay, you are too young still and unproven, no matter your size or slyness about back door cheats, or how many kitchen wenches or doxies lift their skirts for you."

He paused. When Jack said nothing, he continued.

"You say you are still one of the Tree boys?"

"You know it, Kit." Jack tucked the purse back in his sash and sat again on the stool.

"If I gave them to you would you keep a hundred gold doubloons in your cave? Would you divide it in shares?"

Jack said nothing. The old man's small mouth pursed in a smile.

"That doesn't sit well? I thought not." He dabbed at the spittle at the corner of his mouth with his lace kerchief. "You saved my wretched life; none of them did. And I mean to give you a great reward for it."

Jack straightened on the stool. "Truly?"

"But first, first you need a great chest to hold it."

Jack looked around the room for his treasure chest.

"As a conceit, boy. I mean only that I will give you a treasure when I can see you have the powers to keep it."

Jack clasped the stool seat with both hands and leaned forward. "How is that, Master Kit?"

The old man rolled his head back and gazed again up into the gleaming shadows.

"I am the margaritaril of Tortuga. In fact, if not by appointment, no Caesar being at hand to anoint me.

"Every pearl of worth that reaches this port finds its way to my hands and coffers. Whether it's stolen on the Main, the Malabar Coast, the Spice Islands, be it fresh from the sea or from the ancient crown of a Hindu prince on the far side of the world, no great pearl is offered in this port that does not in the end find its way to me."

Jack thought of the pearl in the Bristolman's ear. He wondered if it merited that distinction.

"I will teach you every orient found in oyster's flesh, Jack. And much more.

"How to pick flaws in an emerald by moonlight. How to whet your sight eagle sharp with an opal's gleams. There is more, so much more!" he cried and then coughed, though not hard as before. Kit bent to his bowl again, drooled something into it, and then lay back. Jack was afraid to speak; the ancient man might lose track.

"When you have been my apprentice for three years, I will have fashioned in your mind a chest equal to the treasure you have earned in saving me. It is a double reward."

Three years seemed an immense span. But in less than five he would be a man at his majority, though that not a mark of much account in Cayonan's dealings. No gathering crabs from under the tide pool rocks, or racing for his life through the dark alleys, then drinking palm wine and laughing around the fire --- he had to cut those meager adventures, that scrabbling life loose like those kites on the hurricane. In a moment they were gone. Only the wish for the jeweled spyglass remained.

"I will." Jack fell to his knees and grabbed the coverlet prayerfully, almost sincerely. "I will. With all my heart I'll learn all your wisdom."

"No reflection? No weighing," Old Kit said with a chuckle.

A triumphal heat was rising inside Jack. He wanted to jump up, dance, shout at the birds in the sky. A treasure worthy of Pierre Le Grande was falling into his hands. But he held hard onto the coverlet and let it come out in tears.

"I am no fool," he said. "I feel like Pierre Le Grande!"

The old man laughed weakly. "Good. Now get up. Tell---"

There was a knock at the door and the old mulatto housekeeper looked in.

"Get the boy new clothes," said Kit. "And have the room next to the Gascons' cleared out and a cot put in for him. He's apprenticed to me now. Aren't you boy?"

Jack nodded.

"Yes, Master Kit," said the woman and motioned Jack toward the door.

"Monsieur Van Duyn and his daughter Rebecca are below enquiring after your health."

Jack looked back at the old man sinking down beneath his coverlet.

"Tell them I'm too weak as yet. But tell them I'll send this lad to ask their return on the morrow, or the next, if they will be so good, and I'll receive them."

Jack raised his eyes to the dark ceiling. The wonders of fortune.

17 KIT'S CLOCKWORK CHRIST & OTHER CURIOS

Jack found his first weeks of apprenticeship to Old Kit were not arduous.

Some days he spent a few hours listening to Old Kit's disconnected reveries that were sparked by the oddities and treasures that abounded in his magnificent house; or reminiscences and anecdotes that were drawn from the air and fabric of time and drifted back into them as he talked.

But it was the ancient man's tales that Jack later remembered on his journey, tales told in the alchemist's clutter of Kit's library or the cool crepuscular lower halls that they walked as slowly as meandering tortoises.

Kit told of haunted jewels, fatal jokes, and sword fights beside stinking ditches. Even more, the old man delighted in showing him his own treasures.

"Yellow ivory also," he said as he stood staring into a small cabinet in the corner of his bedroom. Jack had not followed his line of thought.

"Still I do have the one piece of ivory I treasure most. See the unicorn horn? The ivy relief spiraling up its flutings? No unicorn horn though, but a narwhal's tusk. It belongs to a vicious fish that uses it as a sword to slash and pierce its enemies in the icy seas of the north."

Jack reached for the latch.

"Don't open the cabinet. The glass falls out of the doors."

"Now look at this." Kit opened the door anyway. No pane fell. He drew out a small box and opened it.

From the suede pouch inside he extracted a chamois rag and pulled apart its folds to discover a gold egg. With one aged thumb and forefinger he lifted half the egg away. Within was a chryselephantine crucifix,

Christ's white ivory body hung on a cross of gold, the tiny face anguished in fine detail; the loincloth, nails, thorns and His blood were of gold.

Kit smiled to himself, seemingly oblivious to the boy. He replaced the golden shell, gently wrapped the egg, placed it in the pouch and returned the bag to its box.

"I have one other crucifix," he said. "A clockwork Christ."

The old man shuffled toward the door. Jack rose and followed.

Kit drew a watch from his pocket and opened its lid. Its single arrow nearly touched a numeral.

"Hurry now," he said over his shoulder. "Give us a hand."

Jack took the old man's elbow and they shuffled into the next room.

It was a little used room. Kit grabbed his shoulder and when the boy looked up he nodded to one corner of that room. Carved all in linden wood, a foot-high Jesus hung upon His cross, which itself was affixed to a small house at Christ's back.

Jack started as the clockwork Christ raised its head slowly heavenward to the Holy Father and its chin dropped open, the mouth issuing a groan of despair. The mouth shut and the wooden chin dropped to its chest.

The Son's head rose again and cried out. Kit chuckled. Jack stared, his own mouth wide open. Christ groaned once more and then fell silent.

"Perfect," Kit said, replacing the pocket watch he had again extracted. "He cries out the hours, a dozen times at twelve, once on the halves. I don't like to hear the squawks though, so I keep it in this little purgatory." "

Jack smiled at him uncertainly as they left the cluttered little room..

On a broad porch enclosed with fine net, Kit had an aviary. Shutters kept out the night winds. Prismatic birds would flash, dart or brood, sing; emerald and scarlet macaws, acute, jabbering gray parrots from the Afrique coast mimicked human words; he saw toucans, cockatoos, two birds of paradise, a raven. They perched on bare peeled limbs propped in barrels of sand and short trees in barrels of dirt of their own. Blind Alexandrian canaries had their own cages outside the nets where he walked with the old man.

But there was only one bird in the house proper.

A gray parrot Kit called Fool flew to them and perched on the netting near their faces.

"Well, bark, ye dogs," the bird said in a true mimic of the old man's voice, "I'll bridle all your tongues."

"Mock me will you?" said Kit in a sudden anger, and swiped weakly at the bird, striking it down to the floor. It immediately hopped to its feet and flew off.

"In Old Rome there was a hedonist, a wise man I deem him now, who at some revelry delighted his guests with a giant boar stuffed full of fluent talking birds of every description and then roasted on the fire."

Jack shrugged. He had heard the curses, chanties and ribald ripostes of enough parrots to stuff a dozen boars.

"Gathered from every palace on the seven hills, I suppose," the old man murmured to himself.

18 GEMS OF EVERY HUE

In the kitchen each morning Jack had a breakfast of porridge, milk, and a mango with the two Gascons, the old housekeepers, and the even older cook. If they were not boon companions around the table, at least the fare was regular.

At first, he spent the hour after breakfast with a clerk who instructed him in the mysteries of numbers and ledgers. But for Jack the mysteries proved slight and he picked up ciphering and columns quickly enough to make the clerk exclaim and congratulate him. Then, often as not, Old Kit would call for him to observe his dealings or judge the cast of pearls, emeralds and such that were being offered him that day. The old man examined every facet and flaw and had Jack note every hue and blemish. By noon Jack's eyes ached and his brain pulsed.

Kit's tutoring in the art of trading gems was compounded of keen judgment of a stone and rich smatterings of legend and lore.

"All of which falls onto the scale in the final measure of a jewel's price," he advised.

To aid Jack in learning the various cuts a gem might have, the old man created a pyx of bijoux to hold one crystal of each cut, filling it from his deep and unusual coffers. There were single and brilliant-cut sapphires; Lisbon, French, and table diamonds; a fat Swiss tourmaline; a pharaoh's Portuguese peridot; and, last, star and rose-cut rubies.

Opals the old man claimed to hold in awe.

"No other stone is so inconstant. It will love one man, hate another, and change like the seasons in the fate of the last."

Of the scores of opals in his treasury he held one very dear.

"Here," he said holding up a gleaming milky oval the size of a hen's egg. "Gaze."

Pink, rose, green, vermilion lights ran over its surface, beneath it, turning and shifting like iridescent shoals of fish, suddenly breaking the surface with a flash that hurt the eyes, then scattering over the surface, reforming in swirling shoals . . . Kit closed his hand and Jack blinked.

Jack looked at Kit, who stared back at him. Jack took a deep breath; here was something frightening, but intriguing. He reached out to pry back the old man's fingers --- Kit quickly pulled it away and put it in its special wooden box, slamming shut the tiny lid.

Jack shook his head to clear his thoughts of the iridescent swirls that still played like a daydream before him.

"Good for the eyes," said Kit. "Not so good for your mind if you are caught unaware. I promised I would show you how to sharpen those eyes of yours, but later, after we practice with some other opals. Better ride a gelding first, before the stallion."

He himself stared back at the walnut box and laid his hand on it.

"I've had that stone for some four score years, Longer than all else I own. I purchased it for a princely sum in haunted old Kirschweiler, a little town where they know opals like nowhere else on earth . . . Kit was drifting into his past again. His lips moved silently.

"What, Master Kit?"

The wizened face looked up.

"Patron of Thieves, I said. Ancient Bishop Marbodus tells us that certain opals will make those who know their secret invisible." His eyebrows rose quizzically. "Something a boy from Under-the-Tree might like, say I true?"

Jack smiled.

"I brought this stone to a great master in the alchemical arts, my tutor in those arcane sciences, Doctor Dee. A great master of illusion and delusion," Kit gave a soft, wry laugh. "Invisibility can be of great use in many trades and I had vaunting ambitions in mine. Odds Blood how we labored!"

After a few moments he shrugged his thin shoulders.

"Opals have other uses too. Sweeten foul air. Pass one over a head of golden hair and it will be more radiant than any. Mayhap you'd like to caress young Rebecca's hair with one?"

"I would fancy it."

"Use one of these smaller ones from Kirschweiler. I'll find one, should you ask. Those black opals from Brazil, and the Aztecs' fire opals ---"

He set one of each on the table before Jack. Their living light gleamed in brighter flecks, but moved in deeper, slower eddies.

"I deem them poor for golden hair. Different spirits and tendencies make their homes within."

Kit picked up the reddish fire opal, peering within it.

"Dear Dee forgot that fact when he spoke to his stone mirror."

The old man smiled to himself.

"An Aztec mirror, I know now. But he thought it the work of some Alhambran magician. He spoke to it in Arabic, Greek, Spanish, Latin, what have you. It was blackest obsidian polished so smooth it shone clear as a silver mirror, so smooth dust would not settle on it. He spoke his incantations into it but never could understood what that mirror returned."

Kit shook his head, then spoke of the varied meanings of gems. Gnostic, zodiacal, alchemical and vulgar lore all seemed to cross and mix within the gleaming crystals. Sapphires ruled by the house of Virgo, courageous and cruel ruby, Piscean amethyst symbolizing the Hebrew tribe of Gad and the cursed apostle Judas. Each strange meaning was a clue and point of value to someone who might desire any certain stone.

But for all Kit's instruction in other jewels he spent fully as much time on pearls alone. These were the pride of his knowledge and possession. Pearls, he said, required the truly subtle sense and measure.

The nacreous globes challenged the eye and faculties with the most precise gradations, infinite variation, and eccentricities of taste.

"Every pearl holds a tear," he said, raising his forefinger.

"Therefore do not expose them to the glaring sun. They will dry up, their colors will fade."

He set a moon-white pearl the size of a pistol ball on the table, beside it its mate as black as charcoal. He had Jack gaze deep into the luster glowing up beneath their shining skins.

Once he had Jack unshutter the windows and lay a black velvet runner the length of the great banquet table that set unused in a lower hall. Placing the huge white pearl at one end and the black ball at the other, he preceded to range between them a nacreous rainbow. The orients began beside the moon pearl with a tiny pearl holding a gleam of sky, and ran through a half dozen others to the color of amethyst and further still to a shade like turquoise. Then, from the palest sea froth, twelve pearls grew to a green as brilliant as the sun's disk glowing through a palm leaf; next, one the size of a pistol ball and tinged a yellow soft as babies' down was followed by another of hurricane yellow, then butter, amber, gold and bronze; pink as soft as breath, rose-pink, and rose; then white so hard it set your teeth on edge, wet-gleaming white, silver, dusky, gray, black, and the great black pearl.

Jack learned to swiftly roll a pearl between the tips of his fingers so he could see the whole surface with three sure turns. Kit measured his speed with an egg glass until he could find the one dimple in three score perfect white pearls before the sand in the little glass had run out.

Jack wiped the salty sweat of his fingers from the pearls with flannel, or with chamois for the truly prize ones. The perfect spheres claimed the greatest price, as a matter of course, but those that were "tears shed by the stars" had a great many fanciers in the courts of Europe. A flawless black glowing tear the size of his thumb was the one Kit said was the pearl of greatest price. Unless, perhaps, it was the rosy-lustered lump he held in his palm. It looked mightily like a woman's bosomy torso and, miraculously, had a dimple right where her belly-button should be.

"A connoisseur's delight! I have had offers from the Vatican."

The pearls with fine grain and a banded gleam were judged best for rings, and best of these were the flaw-less round pink "Hanadama" that Jesuit priests smug-gled out on their Black Ship from the forbidden port of Hiroshima. Even Old Kit had seen only one in his life, greatly increasing his wealth with the acquaintance, he claimed.

Kit also tutored Jack on how to effect a sleight-of-hand in nacreous weights on the unwary, trading in Persian abas or Roman carat as the advantage dictated.

At first Jack had no hope of ever being Old Kit's true apprentice. But as he warmed to the challenge, the tales, and the always palpable beauty of the gems, he found he could place each element in a town laid out by his mind's making. Just as he could close his eyes and see, as if from above, all Cayona, recall each street, and then each building, and door, and those that passed through each door, in the same way there was a Ruby Street, with hues, cuts, attributes, and even some of the greater rubies in Kit's caskets placed in the warehouses bordering that street seen only in his inner eye, and a Diamond Street, and Emerald Way. One whole quarter of his mind's-eye town, the most richly built and peopled, was the one reserved for pearls.

19 THE TWO GASCONS

Old Kit soon tired of telling Jack how keen he was. And Jack was feeling very smug about his evident prowess, so that finally Kit had to caution him.

"Knowing your wares is the smallest part of trade. You cannot live in Cayona and not know that well. At best the treasure chest I am helping you build has a frail frame, part built at that. You have a long way to go before you have nailed iron bands around it."

Old Kit's soaking continued to vex his bones and lights, so he took to his bed to nap in the afternoon. Then, if he was not studying with Maynard or shadowing Kit's factors, Jack was free to go down to Cayona proper, or visit Rafael, Louis, Jesús, Andre and the others at the Tree.

His only complaint with his new condition was sleeping in the room next to the Gascons. It was worse than the cave, even with the soft-padded palette they had given him. The two Gascons argued more than eight boys together: about each other's habits, the time, about the color of the moon on a night years past; about transubstantiation, horses, palm wine, disease, cloth. Every night there was a brief scuffle, thuds, shouting. They seemed evenly matched, victory depending on who was the drunker.

In addition, neither had a liking for Jack. They saw him quite correctly as a usurper of Kit's largesse. The Fore Gascon stepped on Jack's toes given an opportunity;

the Aft Gascon would less subtly put an elbow in his ribs if Jack did not give him the whole passageway when they passed.

The two old women of the house were no more congenial between themselves, a matched pair to the Gascons. Their enmity was not as apparent or deep, their bickering not constant, but when it erupted Jack found the Gascons' spats seemed mere tomcat spits and mewlings.

He made the mistake of lingering over his noon meal for one last bite when Mary, the housekeeper, arrived late and complained not enough had been set aside for her dinner.

The cook, a Parisian who claimed she could barely understand the Gascons' croaking French, just turned away muttering "You'd be twice the sow you are now if I filled your trough at every squeal."

Mary slammed her spoon to the table and turned to Jack.

"Sow, she says? Squeal? Why Grace here squealed a dozen times a night when they swived her in Paris. King Louis swept the city clean of her and all the other quails and sent 'em to Tortuga to work their trade, you know."

She gave Jack a wink.

"Quail!" screeched Grace, rounding on the house-keeper, who smiled back poisonously. Jack kept a blank face and made ready to duck beneath the table if pans and bowls began to fly.

"Quail? Dear Grace," said the wrinkled housekeeper. "I truly meant whore!"

"You sow, you gaullefretiere!!"

"Say you, Tess Tuppence?"

"Bas-cul!" shouted Grace.

"Frisker" retorted the other.

"Consoeur!"

"Trull!"

"Friquenelle!"

"Backscratcher!"

20 HERR VAN DUYN

Otherwise Jack was delighted with his lot, even though with his new chores he was kept so busy he barely had an opportunity to celebrate his fortune with the rest from the Tree. Each day he learned his ciphering and letters. Or nodded as he listened to Kit's twisting catena of memories, trying his best to winkle out whatever lesson might, or might not, be meant for him. Or peered through Kit's lens to find the flaws in a ruby's heart.

He studied each day with one of the factors who ran Kit's various enterprises in Cayona. Today the bloated, yellow-eyed sotweed factor and Jack strolled the sheds. Jack watched while the man crumpled, rolled between his fingers, and sniffed the leaves of fine Priest's Tobacco. The next day the pinch-faced armory factor took Jack to the stone powder houses set three hundred yards east of town. Jack made hash marks on a tablet while the man counted casks in the cool, dim light. With the rum house factor and a wagon driver Jack helped deliver the morning barrels of rum and brandy to the huts and shabby taverns Kit owned along the beach.

The little he saw of his Under-the-Tree friends allowed for just a few words as he rode by in a wagon. They admired his boots, but they shook their heads in mock pity at seeing him work each day.

"You're no better than an indentured servant," Will said, pleasing the indentured driver not at all. Jack's shirt stuck to him with the sweat of wrestling the day's rum barrels. "Tell Old Kit you expect a richer reward for his bony carcass."

"Aye, I'm expecting a richer one," Jack replied.

That clipped Will's tongue. They all expected he would have a rich reward and hoped to share in it, as always. But, except for the Spanish boots, Jack seemed no better than the other boys that time had turned out of Under-the-Tree. In fact, they could see Rafael, who had grown too big for the Tree just the year before, unloading barrels at a tavern at the street's far end. But Jack, sweating every day, snoring on his pallet while the rest of his friends prowled Cayona's noisy dark streets, had prospects.

Another prospect he had, but had yet to see fulfilled, was meeting with Rebecca Van Duyn on a footing where he was more than diverting rabble, more than a clever dog -- though she knew he was no dog, she said.

He had missed the visit she and her uncle paid the bedridden Kit the day after Jack was taken into his house. After two hours of totaling ciphers, the most fatiguing two hours he could remember spending, he had asked the housekeeper if he could help by conducting Kit's visitors up the stairs for her. He found the Van Duyn's, Ogeron, and DeBasco had all arrived and left in the space of an hour. His offer did her scant good now, she said. For the rest of the day Kit had banned all visitors except Madame Pearl, and she was a friend who knew her own way.

Now Herr Van Duyn and several others of the high and mighty in Cayona made daily solicitous calls. Depending on Old Kit's mood they were received or not, and on occasion Jack was there to escort Van Duyn. The man did not speak to him, but Jack could tell he was watched sidelong, the rumor of Kit's favor making him one to keep an eye on. Twice Kit had had Jack sit in a corner while they discussed an exchanges of opals and molasses and bolts of linen.

Van Duyn was a round-faced, clean-shaven man; the lack of mustaches or beard where most sported extravagant foliage gave him the air of being younger than his years. That his ruddy and round, heavy cheeks had not yet sunk into his jowls added to the effect. But his fat lips always seemed pursed, ready to scowl beneath his hard blue eyes and bristling white-blond eyebrows. It was the look of a man who had seen years of hard trading and lost ships. The braid at the back of his neck was ash gray.

Jack had thrice run messages to him. His manner was gruff and short, the same Jack saw as Van Duyn conducted business at the docks or outside his warehouses. At a distance it seemed to Jack his manner with Rebecca was kind, but shallow; she was pleasant and blood kin, but still an obligation and distraction from the business of trade.

Van Duyn saved his smiles and good cheer for the chief denizens of Cayona: Old Kit, Governor Ogeron, DeBasco, and few others. This fawning veneer fooled none, but was appreciated and regarded as their due by some. It had not hurt his trade. The grand house he had built a year before not far below Kit's own was ample proof of that.

Van Duyn habitually wore coats of blue damask, black pantaloons, and white linen shirts whose cuffs were over ample with lace that almost hid his pudgy hands and ruby rings. Except for the ornate silver buckles on his square-toed shoes, the rings were his only jewelry. In all, an unremarkable merchant trader. But, as Rebecca's uncle, Jack was determined to study Herr Van Duyn as closely as Kit's pearls or his lessons in ciphering.

Jack was practicing his totals one morning when Mary the housekeeper stuck her head in the library door. Her face and hands were begrimed.

"Your Van Duyn's carriage just pulled in the gate and I'm no sight to greet 'His Majesty' and the Gascons ain't here neither."

Jack ran to the door, pulling it open at the first rap of Van Duyn's silver-headed walking stick.

Herr Van Duyn, alone, strode in as usual, then looked at him and nodded.

"Jack," he said pleasantly, though he did not smile.

Jack was taken aback. It was the first time Van Duyn had even indicated he knew his name. He turned to hide his surprise and closed the door.

"Sir," he said, not knowing what else to reply. Should he have said 'Your servant' or some such? He led the Dutch merchant, who wheezed slightly as he climbed the stairs, to Kit's rooms.

The old man was sitting at a table under the window. His ear horn rested before him, hiding whatever jewel he examined. He folded it in velvet as he bid Van Duyn good day and placed the jewel in a little majolica patch box.

"Stay and listen," Kit said as Jack turned to go. The boy took his usual stool against a wall, not far from the table, but not at it.

"A fine boy," the merchant said, seating himself on the cushioned chair.

Kit smiled and glanced at Jack.

"I mean," the Dutchman said," By all report he has shown your factors some industry and good sense. More than one might hope from his, ah, upbringing."

He turned to Jack. "I hope you are properly grateful to the Lord God and Master Kit here that he has put you in his employ."

"Aye, sir." The braying ass, Jack thought.

"You are teaching him some skills of your eye, too, Master Kit?"

Kit smiled.

"It is a trade he may be able to follow. But I have him sit with me to learn from others, not myself."

Van Duyn's smile faded in unsure steps, as he attempted to fathom Kit's meaning.

"About your pearls," said the old man. "The five hundred escudos would be theft from the blind. Make the purchase. I will take the two largest for the same amount. The others . . ."

Jack listened, Jack watched. Jack was soon lost. Commissions, ship leases, and the juggling of logwood, emeralds, slaves, and brandy left him bewildered. And a little frightened to sail into this battle where speed of foot and knife were nothing.

When Van Duyn left he nodded to Jack and said his name again.

21 BESTIARY & BIBITS

The next day Kit brought in the gypsy scholar Maynard. He was to tutor Jack further in ciphering and reading, so he could attend to the books and business that would one day be his. Jack learned his ciphering even more quickly, but Maynard averred it would be two months or more before he was able to read or write a simple letter.

Thus Kit's library amazed him all the more and he came to imagine it held the greatest treasures of the house. Its shelves were lined with books and the floor was a maze of stacked columns of dusty tomes. Jack recognized only a few score of words and they did him well enough, but here there were so many other words it dazzled him to consider it. What could they all be for?

On the long, littered table in the middle of the room only one book lay open. Jack stared uncomprehendingly at the groups of letters that he knew must be golden words. Old Kit shuffled up behind him and looked over his shoulder. After a moment he snorted softly.

"Shakespeare," he said, turning away. "I taught him everything he knew. "

Then he paused looking back at the open book.

"Still, he's been dusty bones, bones and dust these many years and I . . . almost the same." Kit shook his head and shambled away.

Jack's favorite book in the library was an illustrated bestiary he discovered on his own. Here man and beast were made one: First the beast with two backs and then other chimeras: woman and minotaur; and a sailor conjoined with a mermaid--his mouth sucking tiny nipples slippery with a coy wreath of seaweed, hands on her barnacled hips, his cock thrust disturbingly low into a slit in her scales. A common ewe was tupped by a shepherd on one page, a griffin by a knight on the next.

On another, frightened storks were held like bellows by randy chimney sweeps; on the next a young, lithe Cyclops girl straddled an astonished man while in the cypress forest background two Cyclops voyeurs peered. A she-bear in shackles united with a gypsy; a pack of wolves circle while a woman, whose placid face rests on a coil of her braids in the snow, is mounted by their leader; a blinkered giraffe in a stable stall ravished by a blackamoor on a tall stool; ape and woman, man and sow, harpies and armored heroes.

When he had flipped through every page Jack closed the book and held it, grasping both boards tightly, as if afraid it might burst open.

Jack saw that Kit did not allow Maynard to browse among his books, or even enter his library. He thought Kit must have treasures there that perhaps only Maynard in all of Tortuga would recognize and be tempted by.

But after Jack's lessons Old Kit had more than once invited Maynard to sup and drink with them. On those nights, especially after the second and third round of wine, he could not follow their conversation at all, even nodding off like the ancient one himself.

On one such night wine splashed on Jack's shoulder starting him awake. He scooted sideways in his seat, out from under Kit's swinging cup. The old man and Jack's tutor loudly sang a song in the priests' tongue, though it were no priests' song by the evidence.

"Bibit hera, bibit herus,
bibit miles, bibit clerus,
bibit ille, bibit illa,
bibit servos cum ancilla,
bibit velox, bibit piger,
bibit albus, bibit niger,
bibit constans, bibit vagus,
bibit rudis, bibit magus."

They clanked mugs and drank and joined in again in
even greater voice.

"Bibit pauper et egrotus,
bibit exul et ignotus,
bibit puer, bibit canus,
bibit presul and decanus,
bibit sorer, bibit frater,
bibit anus, bibit mater,
bibit ista, bibit ille,
bibunt centum, bibunt mille."

Kit and Maynard drank once more and went on to the
next verse leaning their heads together attempting some
harmonious precision.

"Parum sexcente nummate
durant, cum immoderate
bibunt omnes sine meta,

quamvis bibant mente leta.
Sic nos rodunt omnes gentes,
et sic erimus egentes.
Qui nos rodunt confundantur
et cum iustis non scribantur!"

Kit and Maynard tossed back the last of their wine and, laughing, pounded the table for more. The cook came scurrying in with a pitcher.

"I've not sung that in a dog's age," said the old man to the younger. "We were merry with that at Corpus Christi."

He leaned back chuckling and shortly was lost in some faraway.

22 An Unsentimental Education

Most importantly, Kit began Jack's instruction in the character of those that ruled Cayona.

"Gold and blood are the law," the old man said sipping at a milk punch on the twilit veranda. "And for some, but not all of us, the Governor's whim."

"Aye," said Jack, leaning back in his chair. He was tired. He had spent the afternoon with the rum factor and his rum kegs and felt the victim of the old man's whims.

"Already Van Duyn has sniffed out my broader plans for you. His little courtesies to you prove that. And if he has the scent, then DeBasco and Ogeron do, too. Bosola and the Portuguese will have their eye on you soon. Madame Pearl I have already told.

"Those are the ones you must attend to. My trade is greater with or through them than all others combined. All may be allies, all enemies. Even Pearl, who is like a daughter, and never gave me doubt. In my life I have seen more intimate bonds than that betrayed."

He shook his head slowly.

"In some few years you may find it good practice to smother me in my sleep."

"Master Kit!" Jack sat upright, banging down the front legs of the chair.

"But for now we have bonds. Yours are gold and mine is blood --- my wretched juices that you saved." He raised his cup to Jack and drank.

"Master Kit," Jack began then stopped. He had no idea what to say.

"Just listen." The old man proceeded in his meandering style to note the foibles and fangs of Cayona's citizens.

Madame Pearl was, as he said, his greatest intimate. Her house and the Aeolus were conjoined and likewise were they partners in Madame Bernard's house at the east end of Quartermaster Way. Also shared in three taverns farther down in the town, and a large estate in Surrey outside London that neither expected to ever see, except in rents.

Her woman's eye appraised the stolen laces, silks, and satins that crossed Kit's docks. And most important to both of them, she oft-times had her doxies glean a few golden words of negotiable advantage from the pillow talk of her bawdy house.

Bertram Ogeron, Governor of Cayona and all Tortuga, demanded women to praise his beauty and was aroused only when they begged him to deign to roger them.

"Or so our Madame Pearl tells me," Kit told Jack. "And she must supply our Governor his worshippers. Keep his vanity in mind if you ever need deal with him. But as a man, do not play to it too openly. He is too shrewd for that. Honeyed compliments serve Van Duyn no better with Ogeron than DeRuyter's bluff and bluster."

The Governor was, of course, a familiar sight to Jack. Ogeron was a short man, thick as a side of beef, but with fine features: a straight nose with small nostrils, thin, dark lips that parted over strong white teeth, something almost unheard of in Tortuga. He parted black, shoulder-length hair in the middle and had it brushed glossy every morning.

Gold earrings set with small emeralds decorated his ears. His black eyes were set deep, looking out without sympathy, expecting none. He fancied two thick but precise mustaches above his lips and just drooping at the corners of his mouth. To Jack they seemed like little leeches set there to relieve a swelling, and Ogeron petted them frequently.

As vain as Governor Ogeron was about his countenance, he was erratic in his dress, sometimes parading on the pier in just stripped pantaloons, a linen shirt and broad-brimmed Spanish cloth hat. Other times he would hold court at the Aeolus arrayed in red satin from hat to slippers, his chest puffed with gold-threaded lace, a diamond and gold headed ebony walking stick held across his lap like a scepter.

"He has no enemies and he has no friends," said Old Kit. "That is the most dangerous kind of man."

Bartholomew the Portuguese was chief, second only to Kit, among Cayona's gem traders. Emeralds were his greatest love, as high with him as pearls with old Kit. Rubies, opals, and diamonds the two of them would exchange like boys' taws, though Kit preferred loose stones and the Portuguese found profit in gem-encrusted jewelry and crucifixes. On occasion they had combined to purchase with one sum every gem from a treasure ship.

"More than a week of arguing it took us to divide the last time. He knew my vigor would wane and I fear I let him press that advantage. You will help me the next time."

Kit winked.

From Van Duyn he bought French brandy and muskets, and sent back rum to New York --- which Van Duyn testily still called Nieuw Amsterdam --- and then tobacco, indigo, cochineal, and paprika to Amsterdam or St. Malo. Most importantly, Van Duyn's captains were trusted to transport Kit's gems to agents in the Amsterdam markets, and hand off cryptic letters that would travel farther.

"But that last is a traffic I doubt you will inherit." Kit said no more of it.

"Now Bosola, he serves me well. I take but rare interest in his slaves. Those new pens on the ridge are an affront to the Brethren of the Coast, if I am asked.

"And though Bosola may play the renegade from his clan, he still has, ah, friends in the Company of Negroes. Those Genoese may have their franchise from the Spanish Crown, but . . ."

Kit's thoughts seemed to carry him off before he spoke again.

23 BLACK THESEUS

"Bosola tells a tale about when he first came to the New World. Received his position in the Company as a favor from his distant cousin the Doge of Genoa. But instead of a grand villa and factotums to order about, he was set to watching over the coffles of slaves paraded over the isthmus to Panama City. They have a great warehouse or stable there for the Africans, to hold them until they send them up the coast to Salvador and Acapulco or south to Guayaquil and beyond. A huge place, Bosola says, with pens for three hundred or more, but sometimes twice that if storms kept his ships in port. Then the Negroes would fight among themselves, they being from many different tribes that hated one another or took offense from another's tattoo, and kill each other or break an arm so they couldn't be sold. Once they revolted and they strangled their guards and some even escaped into the hills before soldiers put the riot down by killing scores of 'em. They were weeping over the Company's ledgers that night, I'll wager.

"But a man of some learning struck upon a plan. At the back wall of this great slave stable they have cut a door which is always open. It leads into an annex. And this is a labyrinth of unlit hallways leading to a kitchen. There they placed the most giant negro of the many hundred there. A great monster with teeth filed to a point. And they said to him 'This is your home and you will never toil in the fields and you will never know the whip on your back. A woman will be given you for your pleasure at every full moon and new. But for this boon you will have but one sustenance: The miscreants who offend the company's guards will either be hung or forced into your labyrinth. You may eat those who enter or they will eat you and take your place.'"

Kit slapped his thigh and drained the last of his punch. There was a brief green flash from the western horizon and then the light was gone.

"A clever stratagem," Kit exclaimed.

"It sends a shiver up my spine." Jack rubbed the goose pimples on his arms.

"Aye, Jack. And those benighted Africans, too, I doubt not. But they have had less trouble in their stables since, Bosola says. No black Theseus has come to slay their Minotaur. Or if one has, he becomes the Minotaur. I wonder if Bosola will try that here."

The old man held his hand to his forehead. In the dimness Jack stared at him.

"Ah, yes." Kit remembered his purpose. "Bosola serves me well, Jack. I will not give you an instance now, but know that his ties among the Spaniards and his own people are not entirely severed. There are times a trinket may get a better price in Havana or Veracruz. But more of that anon. Let us go in and eat."

24 A VERY UNSENTIMENTAL EDUCATION

Jack sat in the place of honor at Kit's dining table. It was a broad, gleaming mahogany slab long enough to seat twelve on a side and carved so deeply around its perimeter Jack could lose his fingers in it like stiff, gnarled gloves. Golden candelabra ranged the center of the table, but only two places were set, with plates and bowls of gold, and clinquant flatware.

The cook was setting a gold rimmed tureen on the table as they entered.

"What is the occasion, Master Kit?"

"None. A fancy."

Jack helped the old man into his chair while the cook dished up a fish chowder for them, then left. Jack seated himself. The cook brought out one of the double-necked wine bottles from Peru, both corks pulled. Jack smiled. As she poured, the upper neck gave a soft warbling whistle.

Kit smiled, too.

"We've not had any from these vineyards in a dog's age. Came as part of my share in a sloop DeBasco and I leased to Lendos and that crew. Poor haul they brought back, 'cept these."

As they ate, Kit told Jack what Jack already knew. How he and other traders of the town might buy a captured boat or ship from its pirate crew so they could divide their spoil and drink and whore their wealth away.

And then some new crew anxious to sail on account, but with hardly enough for their powder and ball, would come to beg the lease of a ship on the promise of shares in their loot.

The going rate was twenty shares. Less for a leaky ketch, more for a brig with new sails. Being a dicey venture, with fully a third of every crew to sail out of Cayona never seen or heard from again in any port, a ship's lease was an investment often divided.

In such contracts Kit relied on Michael DeBasco. The old pirate was wealthy as a count long ago from his plundering with Mansveldt. Then he shrewdly came out of retirement to help the madman L'Ollonais raise enough men to sack Maracaibo, and near doubled his wealth again with his own shares and shares on half the leases in L'Ollonais' fleet.

Now DeBasco was Major of Tortuga, the Governor's chief military officer in name, but in reality it was a sinecure that gave him his share of the French Governor's tax on Cayona's commerce.

"Michael can measure the quality of a crew at a glance and there are none in all the Caribbean that would dare cross him. Not even Morgan. For this keenness we share the risks at six for myself and four for him, and split our profit in halves.

"It is an arrangement I have no complaint of, and, if it falls to you, have no complaint of it yourself. DeBasco will treat fair once he was settled terms, but he holds grudges and superstitions. If he ever thinks you've caused him ill-luck it will be to your woe."

Kit was silent a moment. Then he lifted his bowl and slurped the dregs of the chowder."

"Truly, old one," Jack said shaking his head. "I don't see how an Under-the-Tree boy could treat with DeBasco."

"You will!"

The old man set the golden bowl down with a heavy clunk. He was suddenly angry. There was a fierceness in the dark eyes set in the leathery, wrinkled face.

"You will indeed treat with DeBasco! And with Ogeron. And soon. I am not rewarding you for just my miserable life, damn you. I'll not have them divide the spoils when I die, like beggars stealing shoes from a corpse.

"No! Long ago I was cheated of one place of eminence in posterity. These 'hijos de puta' won't divvy my substance here and forget me. No, you will hold my house together, you will divide the spoils of Cayona. You will be my ghost to haunt them!"

His last words croaked in his throat and he fell into a wracking cough like Jack had not heard since the first days Kit had taken him into the house. Jack jumped up and held the old man's bony shoulders, but they jerked free. Kit pushed away the glass Jack offered, leaning first on one side of his chair, then the other. The old cook hurried out of the kitchen and slapped him feebly on the back until Kit pushed her away.

Finally, the hacking diminished. When the cook offered him the glass again he took some wine and at last quenched the coughing.

Kit sat his elbows on the table and his head in his hands, breathing swiftly and shallow.

"Shall we help you upstairs?" asked the cook. "Shall I call the Gascons?"

"No, no. I'll rest here." Kit looked up at Jack. "Sit. We'll continue. More wine!"

After several long minutes when he seemed to have lost his way in his memories, he began again.

"However, you must be careful when you collect what's due you in Cayona. Whether it is DeBasco or old Long John that rents that tumbledown rum house on the beach. It is sometimes better to lose a sum than dun a man. When you press a man so far that he must sell himself into your service, be quite sure of what he is made."

Kit pressed his thin lips thinner and nodded to Jack.

"I've heard a tale of ancient Rome that is good instruction. A moneylender had given out a goodly sum at usurious interest to two Captains of the army, centurions they called them 'cause they led a hundred men. Well, these gallants had lost their money in gambling or some other misadventure.

"And no matter how much they begged for time or relief the moneylender would not hold off or give quarter. Even followed them into the public baths and berated them in front of their friends and foes to their great humiliation.

"These Captains resolved to pay their debt despite all, and sold all their possessions to gain the sum, which was several talents in gold. They waited by the goldsmiths street where the moneylender was in a habit to pass by and they seized him. Saying 'Here is your gold, our debt is quit" they pulled back his head, lifted up a smith's crucible and poured the molten gold down his throat."

Kit raised his hand in the air. "Chrysostomos!"

Jack nodded and smiled. "I like that story."

"Just let the factors dun those lesser than you. Those greater than you will keep their word as policy, or roger you right good for the same. Comprende?"

"Oui."

25 ADMIRALTY COURT

Down the strand, past the huts of the beach doxies, a dozen or so ragged pirates gathered where some mangroves, palms, and other trees stood thick enough to make a deep shade, but thin enough at their edge to admit a breeze if any rose. They were moving about waving their arms and laughing, something strange in the heat.

So Jack and Louis went to take a look.

The men passed a small keg of ale among them, but they were not drunk. One, pulling a tarpaulin with him, climbed into the crotch of a tree and tossed his leg around a branch. It was Jack Dann, an old freibooter who had not left port in three years. He lived by collecting old debts that some remembered, some not, or on telling old stories, and free drinks for the telling. He was handed up a shaggy cap that he lay on his shaved head, a tall black hat that went atop it, and a handspike as his symbol of authority. He pulled the tarpaulin over his shoulders and banged the spike on the branch he straddled. Jack and Louis grinned at each other. Admiralty Court was in session. They ran a short way into the shade and settled in the sand at a respectful twenty paces off.

Elias Match, his pants held up with rope and the tops of his ears trimmed off for theft, stood with his arms sternly folded as the Attorney General. From behind the milling, lounging jury two bailiffs led the accused: bowlegged Red George with a yellow kerchief tied over his skull.

George was called Red because his skin never went brown from all his years in the tropic sun, just grew a deeper and deeper red like an Indian they said.

George tried to look grim as well, and glared at the hoots and shouts of "Keel haul 'im!" from the jury. His left hand, that only had the thumb left upon it, he wagged at the jury to quiet them. The bailiffs smirked. But not Elias Match.

"An't it please your Lordship," he said loudly. The judge banged on the branch and the grove fell silent. "And gentlemen of the jury."

Match began to pace a semicircle behind Red George, shaking his head as he eyed his prisoner, declaiming to the jury, addressing the judge in the tree with dignity.

"Here is a fellow before you that is a dog, a sad, sad dog; and I humbly hope your Lordship will order him to be hanged out of the way immediately. He has committed piracy on the high seas, and we shall prove it, an' it please your Lordship, that this fellow, this sad dog before you, has escaped a thousand storms, nay, has got safe ashore when the ship has been cast away, which was a certain sign he was not born to be drowned.

"Yet, not having fear of hanging before his eyes, he went on robbing and ravishing man, woman, and child, plundering ships' cargoes fore and aft, burning and sinking ship, barque and boat, as if the Devil had been in him.

"But," he paused to swallow, as if aggrieved to tell it. "But this is not all my Lord. He has committed worse villainies than all these. For we shall prove that he has been guilty of drinking small beer, and your Lordship knows, that never was a sober fellow but what was a rogue!"

He ended beside Red George, studying him, his arms folded again and a very unforgiving look in his eyes. George, who had chuckled a bit at "small beer" seemed genuinely to quail next to his prosecutor.

"Heark'ee me, Sirrah," shouted Judge Jack Dann. He pointed his handspike at the prisoner and intoned "You lousy, pitiful, ill-looking dog; what have you to say why you should not be tucked up immediately and set drying in the sun, like a scarecrow? Are you guilty, or not guilty?"

His jurors chuckled as Red George hung his head and toed the sand.

"Not guilty, an't it please your worship." He smiled sideways at a bailiff who hid his smile in his palm.

"Not guilty!" exploded the judge from the tree, rattling his handspike in the leaves and branches until he almost tumbled backwards. Jack and Louis and all the pirates except one bailiff, the prisoner, and prosecutor rolled in the sand laughing.

But after straightening himself and the hat on his head, the judge said in a cold, even voice of authority that brought the masquerade back to its solemn mockery, "Not guilty? Say so, Sirrah, and I'll have you hanged without a trial."

His friends stayed quiet to hear Red George plead.

"An't it please your worship's honor, my lord, I am as honest a poor fellow as ever went between stem and stern of a ship, and can hand, reef, steer, and clap two ends of a rope together, as well as ever as he that ever crossed salt water. But I was taken by one Captain Jack Dann, a notorious pirate, a sad rogue as ever went unhanged, and he forced me, an't it please your honor."

"Lying rogue," the barefoot Attorney General exclaimed, pacing again. "Your honorable Lordship, this man has defiled old mothers with his filthy prick and all of his own accord."

This made the jury merry again.

"He burnt a troop of the King's soldiers in their barracks and skewered them as they begged for mercy in the flaming door. He swore to gut and smoke any judge dare stand him for trial."

"A pox of sties on you," shouted George at the glaring Match, seeming truly afraid. "Your Worship, it was not I, it was that cowardly Devil, Jack Dann, a foul and evil ---"

"Lying dog!" Elias Match interrupted. "A pox of chancres from scalp to heels, that will be your reward in Perdition. You are the heinous, savage Red George known for cruelties on every sea!"

"Hold! Hold!" shouted the pirate judge pounding the mangrove limb.

This time he took care to grip a branch. The prisoner and prosecutor held their tongues.

"Is my dinner ready?"

"Yes, my Lord," replied the Attorney General.

"Then heark'ee, you rascal at the bar." Dann squinted down at the prisoner whose arms were now gripped by solemn bailiffs.

"Hear me, Sirrah, hear me. You must suffer for three reasons. First, because it is not fit I should sit here a judge, and nobody be hanged. Secondly, you must be hanged because you have a damned hanging look. And thirdly, you must be hanged because I am hungry. For you must know, Sirrah, that it is a custom that whenever the judge's dinner is ready before the trial is over, the prisoner is to be hanged of course.

"There is a law for you, ye dog! Take him away."

The bailiffs pushed Red George forward and followed by the rest who laughing called for hanging and twirled two bowline nooses in the air above them, they surged around behind the judge's mangrove tree. George jumped up and tumbled Jack Dann off the branch, but rescued the tarpaulin to proclaim his own judgeship. The ale started 'round again, and Elias Match was hugging his ribs with laughter.

Louis and Jack walked back toward town, staying beneath the trees.

"An excellent pantomime," Jack said. "Best I've seen since ugly Dowling was so drunk he thought he was 'bout to be hanged and chopped off the Attorney General's arm. That was the finest."

He shook his head.

"Those fools. They'll sail on account and bring their spoils back to drink until they don't have a shirt, or be drowned, or stand up for hanging."

"You won't hang," said Louis. "But I've got a fortune to make."

Jack looked at him sideways. For the first time he could remember, Louis would not meet his eyes.

"I'm a loyal friend," Jack protested. "There are plenty of enterprises in Cayona to make a man rich if he has the ear of the right personage."

"Personage?" Louis glanced significantly at Jack's new boots that he awkwardly trod in through the sand. He knew the look was meant to include his indigo and red striped pantaloons, the woven leather belt, the lizard sheath for his old knife, and the linen shirt without a rip or stain. Jack was glad his purse with the doubloons was hidden in his room. Louis' clothes were as well ventilated as Jack's own had been two months before.

"I'll be proof of it," Jack said. "I don't have the compass now, but I will."

Louis looked at him as they entered the town.

"I just remembered DuRusset and the other armorer across the way from him need hands to stuff bottle grenades. You want to come? Jesús and I . . . "

"No," Jack excused himself with a lie. "I've got some work at the Aeolus, to run something up . . ."

Louis raised a hand in salute and turned up Armory Street.

Jack had never felt this way. He did not want to be with his friends.

Part III

Christmas 1669

26 A Philosophical Dispute

Late Christmas Day Kit had not even left his bed. Jack
was morose.

In the months since he had rescued the old man
from the flooded stream, Kit's health had never completely returned. He was far too old. The decline was
slow yet steady, with only a few curious, even mysterious,
recoveries to break the drift.

Jack's good fortune was going to be short lived. He
doubted the old man's factors and merchant friends
would let him see a doubloon of Kit's riches. Rebecca
had told him she had heard as much discussed by her
uncle and his cohort.

The sun had just set and Jack was preparing to sneak
off for a night with the other boys when the old housekeeper, coming down from Kit's rooms, whistled at him
and jerked her head up the stairs.

Jack found the old, old man standing in his green velvet coat and satin breeches leaning on his stick and clutching his ear horn in his other hand.

"Get me my hat, boy," he said. He smiled, showing his four little stubs of teeth.

Old Kit was amused by the constant bickering of the Fore and Aft Gascon, called so for their relative positions manning his palanquin. He mockingly called them by the names of fools from old stories he and they seemed to know: Fancy and Folly one day, Nano and Slipper the next. "But I know not which is which," Kit would say and then laugh.

The old man also liked to stir them up when they fell silent. As they carried him down to the town that evening, he gave a wink to Jack who was walking along beside the palanquin, and then called to the Fore Gascon, "Which came first, the chicken or the egg?"

The man snickered.

"The egg, of course, master. A chicken grows from a seed in the egg."

"What say you, Aft Gascon," Kit asked over his shoulder.

"Hah," the Aft Gascon said, tromping flat footed at the rear. "Hah, is what I say. The egg grows in the chicken. Before that it is part of the chicken. Besides, God created chickens."

"As always," the Fore Gascon said and then made a derisive laugh.

He slowed his pace as he spoke.

"'God created chickens. God created chickens.' The child's catechistic response. No. God created only one Bird, and from where it perched all birds flew away -- with a cataclysmic chirp! Hah! God! Mon Dieu!"

"The Word of God has nothing to do with it," said the Aft Gascon.

"Socratic good sense, not sophistry, is the way to decide such an issue.

"An egg could not --"

"Hog shit. Your high soaring thoughts have left your head behind again. We both agreed that the egg came first months ago."

The Fore Gascon's voice growled menacingly on "ago."

Jack walking beside Kit, looked at him expecting a frown, but caught instead a wink.

"But didn't you pummel that creed out of the Fore Gascon," he asked the Aft Gascon. The Fore Gascon looked at Kit over his shoulder.

"He was so drunk I had to beat him to his senses," said the Aft Gascon. "That was all. Then it became clear to him."

"He could not win his argument any other way," the Fore Gascon said bitterly. "For not to believe that an egg ---"

"Enough, enough," cried Kit with a feeble laugh that choked into a cough. "Thrasymachus and Lysias you're not."

"Indeed, we are not," the Fore Gascon said sourly.

27 BLIND HARRY

The Gascons turned off the road onto a dark path between two thick bushes and soon came out behind Quartermaster Way. They passed the kitchen door of the Aeolus and stopped at the back door to Madam Pearl's.

The Gascons sat down the palanquin, drew out one of the poles to let them open the little door, and then lifted Old Kit out onto his feet. The Aft Gascon stepped over to rap on the brothel door.

"Hold off," called Kit. "I'll stoke the fires first with a tot of brandy. I haven't sat on my poop deck in a fortnight."

Leaning on his twisted stick the old man headed back toward the Aeolus' kitchen door.

"Come, Jack," he called.

Jack went to take the arm Kit stuck out for balance, but the Fore Gascon elbowed him aside and took hold of the old man himself. Jack followed, muttering a curse on the man. Quickly he looked behind to see if the Aft Gascon was overtaking him with another blow. But he was leaning with his arms atop the palanquin, scowling at him.

Kit's entry into the kitchen created a hullabaloo. The serving wenches curtsied and the cook doffed his hat. Dobry the taverner was just coming in from the common room and threw up both his arms in greeting.

"Master Kit! You've come to grace us once more."

TORTUGA

From the back kitchen larder Angus, the second cook, came out and saluted with his butcher knife.

Escorted by the taverner and Gascon, Kit made his way out into the tavern with Jack following behind. Additional shouted greetings came from every corner, which Old Kit acknowledged with a beaming, gap-toothed smile. The cheer he had suddenly been imbued with earlier that evening showed no sign of slackening.

Even greater shouts of welcome greeted them in the teeming tap room.

The poop's table was filled with a familiar cohort. As he was helped up the steps Jack thought he had never seen the old man happier. Michael DeBasco rose up from a seat at the head of the table and pushed aside the stool he had sat on, so that he and Belleau could pull over from its corner the tall viceroy's chair reserved only for ancient Master Kit.

Jack could see Kit needed no attention from him. He would join him later. At the moment he would feel ill at ease following him like a dog at heel, hanging on his shoulder like some bastard prince eager for acknowledgement of his place in the succession. That would come later.

Instead, he made his way to the end of Kit's table, where a fire was lit in the small hearth. The night was cool, despite the press of men and doxies.

117

Apparently also feeling the chill were the black-clad Plymouth merchant and Blind Harry, who sat close by the hearth. A brilliant blue and yellow macaw on Harry's shoulder shifted from one foot to the other.

"Ahoy, Jack. Ahoy, Jack 'iggins," it said as he pulled a stool under him.

"Ahoy, Arthur," Jack said to the bird. "Harry."

He nodded to the Plymouth man, who returned the same.

"Evening, Jack." Harry sat up a bit in his chair. He grimaced a little as the bird re-set its claws. "I knew it was you, 'course. I don't need Arthur here to tell who's about."

Jack did not doubt it. It seemed Blind Harry could tell every man and woman in Cayona by their foot step, even in a crowded tavern. Some said he could hear a stifled sneeze at the far end of a busy street and call the man's name out, telling him to loosen his belt, it was too tight about his gut, and be right on all accounts.

"Blind men know more secrets than any man with eyes," he often said. "And they'd trade 'em all for one day in the light."

Jack had never heard anyone tell how Blind Harry had lost his eyes and so he asked.

28 THE HORSE LATITUDES

"I lost my eyes in the horse latitudes," Blind Harry said. "We'd sailed out of Nieuw Amsterdam bound for the

Malabar Coast. One dawn in mid Ocean, not that many days out, there, not half a league away, was a small prize, a Portuguese slaver --- stank so you could smell it from upwind. We took it with ease. Just peppered the man at the pedrero with musket balls. 'Course the cargo merited their weak defense, just a three score miserable blackamoors bound for the Main, chained in their own filth. Just as many 'ad already died and been fed to the sharks."

He settled back in the chair and stretched out his good and peg leg.

"Well, we tossed the officers overboard and split the crews between the two ships. I went to the Portuguese barque. And we continued on 'fore noon, but next forenoon a storm was running us West and separated us. When it passed, our barque was becalmed in the Sargasso Sea.

"In a whole fortnight not a breeze was felt and soon after those horse latitudes claimed their sacrifice. Only a dozen of the Africans was still alive though we took pity and doused 'em clean and fed 'em nearly as much as ourselves, there being precious little. We ran three horses out of the hold and off the deck into the water --- they'd have starved, dropped, and rotted below decks if we hadn't. We saved one to butcher and eat. Them horses whinnying and crying most pitiful, thrashing in the water and weeds. One even tried to climb the side of the ship and rolled over, took water, and choked and drowned first. It took all afternoon for the last to go under."

Harry's wooden peg rested too close to the fire's coals; Jack could smell the scorched varnish.

"But that wasn't sacrifice enough. No. No, three days later the blindness began. I'd heard tell of it, but none I knew believed in it.

"Some say it rises from the dead air of those parts, or the sea grass, working like a slow poison. But if you smell the bilge of a slave ship you know.

"I was one of the first to wake into this blackness." He sipped his mug of brandy.

"The last ones with eyes took down the main sails and rigged some jibs, knowing blind men couldn't handle more should we be so lucky. We's all blind shortly and the melancholy mewling and crying went night and day past remembering 'til all was silent. Except when one would stumble and curse, feeling their way to the water barrel. It was black and silent and the sun beating hot down upon us. I'll always remember the first luff of that sail and we cheered and wept. The steersmen just kept the wind to their backs, soft and uncertain though it was. It was a day more before we thought we should die anyway, the fresh water soon gone, or wreck on a reef. We prayed for another ship, good Lutheran and Papist together. A dozen times a day we fired a signal shot on the pedrero, until one day, the sun was burning high, we heard an answering shot."

A tear emerged from his filmy left eye and coursed his stubbled cheek.

"A musicker blared on his trumpet and we heard an answering horn!

"We all fell to cheering and pounding the deck and rails. Our trumpeter kept hooting and so did theirs. They were bearing in slowly along our starboard side until finally there were shouts of Ahoy! Ahoy! and we were hugging each other. And I don't know which ship it was, who called first 'We are rescued, save us, we are all struck with the slave blindness!' but in a few breaths both ships were silent with despair."

Another tear followed the same course down Blind Harry's face.

"You were cursed," said Jack.

"Aye. We were two plague-blind ships, should have been flying black flags. Two ships passing in blackness under the noon sun."

The man's wooden leg was blistering and starting to smoke. Jack tapped it with a poker; Blind Harry shifted it thoughtlessly.

"But you were rescued?"

"Our ship broke up in the surf of Antigua. Five of us washed up alive. Three got most of their sight back within the month. But not I. I make my fortune with this."

He touched the side of his nose. It was Cayona's premier arbiter of tobacco leaves and stolen perfumes.

29 "BURN THEM ALL . . ."

The merchant from Plymouth, usually a silent man at the table, cleared his throat and began a tale himself, soon interrupted.

"Now when I was a boy," he began, "I and my father ---"

"Never heard a word of the other blind ship, The Beatrice. Not a word," said Blind Harry.

"Now," the man said again, "I was a deer skinner as a boy, where I met greater peril than ever on the high seas. For two years my father and I tramped the dark forests where only bear, deer, and Red Indians lived.

"At times we would be joined by other hunters. One of these precipitated me out of the forest and onto the seas with his cruel, but justified, end."

He cleared his throat again and drank from his silver cup. Maynard and a few others sitting near moved closer. The usually laconic Plymouth man's story would be one of those rare ones they had not heard before.

"One warm September night, after the fire had died, my father and I were attacked by Pequot warriors. My father was killed in the fight, accidentally I think, as they had other plans for us. I asked them in their own tongue, as best I could, what we had done to deserve this and was told we had raped and murdered one of their women. In a sudden rage one of them beat me near senseless and I was dragged away into the black night.

"A gray dawn was breaking when we reached their village. I saw they had captured another white hunter, a tall man with a ruddy face and a great brown beard, a foul-mouthed, surly man named Bainbridge. He was hung naked on a tree like a crucified thief, both arms tied to branches. Dogs yapped at his feet that dangled just above the dirt and his fingers were broken and twisted all which away. I shuddered to think of my own fate."

The Plymouth merchant took another pull at his cup.

"Bainbridge, " he said. "He screamed to me for help when he caught sight of me though I was captive, too, and just a boy. The Pequot braves who'd captured him on the other side of the forest had found a telltale trinket of his victim still in his pouch. I was released on the spot, without apology for my father's death or my own distress, and thereafter I was ignored."

The merchant cleared his throat again and stared down at the table as he told his story.

"The vengeance they took on Bainbridge is horrible to tell, but in some measure I delighted in it, still do, God forgive me, as retribution for my father's needless death.

"The Pequot warriors left him to the squaws and children. Sharp stones and dog bones pelted him continuously all morning, nicking and cutting his face, ribs and legs. Soon enough the bolder ones were using pointed sticks to jab his cock and balls and to worry the wounds the stones had opened. He cried out for God's mercy, but none was his due.

"For hours this game continued, all morning as I've said. The squaws showered him with rocks, spit, curses, garbage, poked and stabbed with sticks. By noon his cock and culls were unrecognizable gore. He writhed on the tree, screaming blasphemies, mad with fear, begging me to help him."

The table was quiet, reflective. Several had seen, or done, worse.

"The Pequot men stood far back from this, laughing and talking among themselves. A small fire was built before him, the crucified hunter. In its flames the squaws' bloody sticks were turned to brands.

"The smoking points they jammed with an ugly sizzle into the bloody gouges in his legs, his armpits, his side. It was horrid to behold and his gagging screams more horrid still.

"Soon his body and limbs seemed to belong to some hellish mottled monster. The man was a mass of charred and bloody holes, his face scab-crusted and beard singed half away by brands held to his face to revive him when he fainted. So much blood had thickened and dried upon his feet that they were hidden as if Bainbridge were a melting candle.

"Finally, a large stone was rolled over by two braves till it rested against the tree. A Pequot warrior and his squaw, the murdered girl's parents, approached Bainbridge solemnly and the other women and the children drew back a respectful distance. The girl's mother knelt beside the fire and the father stepped up on the rock. He grabbed the hunter's hair and jerked his face to his own, drawing out a knife.

"The Indian spat in Bainbridge's eyes and then quickly drew the knife blade from one temple around his forehead to the other and lifting, with short, shimmying strokes pulled the bloody scalp from the man's skull. He managed no scream, but only a hoarse, uncertain cry.

"The Indian turned to his wife and she dug into the fire with a shovel of bark, scooping up a glowing orange pile of coals. She handed up the smoking bark to her husband and he dumped the fiery coals onto Bainbridge's naked skull and laid back his hair atop them. His stark mad eyes rolled back into his head, his gaping mouth uttered no sound but a sharp, clucking gag in his throat. His scalp and hair began to smoke and curl.

"The brain baked. Who knows what his eyes saw inside his head?"

The merchant looked around the table. "His bloody body wriggled once like a hooked fish. Then he died."

Someone coughed. The others who sat or stood around the hearth took deep drinks of whatever they held and contemplated the man's sorry end.

"A stern tale," Jack said finally.

"That was the beginning of the Pequot's antipathy to our colony," the merchantman said, staring blankly into the air. "Most of that tribe perished by fire also, though it was not so much their due. Our militia trapped them in their longhouse.

"The Captain had it put to the torch."

The man nodded to himself and smiled.

"'It is God's work and it is glorious in our eyes,' Captain Mason shouted when the flames had drowned their last cries."

"Just as the famous bishop instructed 'Burn them all, God will know his own.'" Maynard said brightly to the Plymouth man, who nodded dourly and drank from his cup.

Blind Harry rubbed his sightless eyes on his sleeve. The other listeners were drifting away. After a moment Jack shifted on the stool.

"Ahoy, Jack 'iggins" the macaw creaked to him. Even for a macaw it was dim-witted.

"Ahoy, Arthur," said Jack. "I'm going to fetch me some ale for myself. Can I call over a wench for you, Harry?"

"I'm fine."

Another tear coursed down to the corner of his mouth. He took a gulp of brandy, then wiped his cheek with the back of his hand.

30 THE LEGEND OF PEDRARIUS

Dobry was behind the bar and gave Jack a wink as he handed him a mug of warm ale. Up on the poop Old Kit seemed lively and bright-eyed, in no want of him. So Jack just leaned back against the bar and listened to the talk of the motley crew of seamen, buccaneers, fish pirates and ne'er-do-wells at the big trestle table next to him.

Treasure, as it always did, entered the talk. This time it was old treasure: the King's fifth from the sack of the Aztecs, with its six hundred pounds of pearls, with enough gold dust to swamp a longboat, and much, much more in glistering gods melted and cast in rough ingots. Spaniards though they were, those conquistadors were to be admired with awe: Cortez' destruction of Moctezuma's empire, Alvarado's rapine from Guatemala to Panama. Pizzaro capturing an empire of loot with a hundred-sixty men.

"But who conquered the Maya?" A Cornishman looked about the table.

"Last year we ran aground on the Yucatan and when we climbed the bluffs for water there was the great temples, big as any church I ever saw, all sacked and empty. Twas the old Mayan's, the quartermaster said. So tell me. Who got their treasure?"

"Ha!" shouted Gutierrez, a renegade Spaniard from Havana. He raised his cup of brandy. "He was an ancestor of mine. We will drink to him. The mighty conquistador. Pedrarias!"

The company looked blankly at each other; most shrugged and downed a gulp. That Spaniard must be long dead, Jack thought.

"Aye," said Gutierrez. "When Alvarado sailed off from Panama to scrabble for the pickings Pizarro had left, he left benighted old Pedrarias behind. Then Pedrarias heard the rumors of the Maya's hidden empire, an empire of giant temples wearing golden crowns, an empire with few warriors and many priests.

"Fire, sword and a king's ransom," Gutierrez bellowed. "That was Pedrarias cry when he marched three hundred men into the Yucatan jungle.

"A second expedition found the handful that escaped to the comfort of a Christian burial."

Those conquistadors stabbed and stroked as they approached three buzzards who were tearing at what little was left of some dozen men. Jiggling their wattles the birds turned their blue bead eyes skyward. Then they mounted the air with three or four flaps of their sodden black wings and rose through a rent in the canopy of vine shrouded trees.

There before the conquistadors were their comrades in rusting coxcombs of steel, breastplates and halberds, their corpses had bloated, been torn and deflated by vultures, corroded by ants; scabbed tendons, bones porous to insects, knees where hummingbirds sucked the sweet suppurations of new flowers. The conquistadors' Indian slaves buried the remains and their Franciscan priest blessed them.

"Great Pedrarias, conqueror of the Maya." The Spaniard rose and swung his empty cup in the air.

"He had not reckoned on those forest Indians' allies. The Maya can call every animal of the jungle to do their bidding. Every poison snake and toad, every taloned bird, every savage boar."

"Bah! You must think us drooling dotards to . . ."

"No! What he says must be true," exclaimed a bald headed man with long reddish mustaches and a T branded between his eyebrows.

"I have seen the like of that power myself. I was wrecked on the Yucatan, south of Campeche, and lived with those Indians in the hinterland for nigh on two years. They have no gold in any great quantity that I have seen, but they do worship the powers of their temple gods. They name their children right after birth, rushing them from their mother's womb to the pinnacle of a temple where they've readied a shallow pit of ashes to receive the infant. They leave the child there for the night.

"At dawn the priests examine the ash for spoor. Be it the track of a leopard, bird, or lizard, that beast is the child's Holy Ghost for life, his magic name and avenger of his wounds.

"They have a story of a young warrior ambushed in a clearing and ringed round by eight stags come to avenge his murdering of his enemy that the stags were bound to avenge. The stags charged and leaped at him all at once, crashing together and locking antlers about him in a wreath of horn.

"The man, seeing his good fortune, dove under the antlers and escaped the ring unscathed, but for a kick from an angry deer. That deer stumbled and snapped its neck and fell, bringing down all, each brother around the ring breaking its neck."

There were a few harrumphs to that story.

"Birds are subtle assassins," someone chimed in with good cheer.

"To be sure," said another.

"Have you seen sloth wounds?

"Anteaters, too."

The men laughed shortly and pulled at their cups. The old Spanish renegade turned his Indian tales to another tack.

31 Honey with Flies

"All the virgins of those coasts are perpetually crowned with flowers, flowers awaiting the bee." He raised his cup and leered.

The men at the table chortled at that and Jack thought of the bee that touched his hand on the hill above Cayona.

"Ho! That reminds me of old Jean-David!" cried a Frenchman with trimmed ears.

"We was raiding on that same coast and had captured a Spanish village with many hives and a great store of honey pots. Well, L'Ollonais took a fancy to a young wench we'd captured there, probably still a virgin, or so she said in her pleading. He stripped her bare and had the naked girl rubbed all over with honey, then bound her to a macao tree and let the sand flies, blue bottles and verdigris swarm upon her. In the time it takes to quaff a tankard she was buzzing like a beehive, all speckled and gleaming with flies and honey, and wincing and writhing, choking and whining.

"L'Ollonais began slavering as he watched her twist and cry and presently opened his pantaloons and pulled out his roger. He marched over to the girl grunting like a warthog, like he did. Well, she was too terrified by her predicament to even see him, let alone his frigger."

The pirate paused and raised his tankard and called to a shipmate now standing by the fire next to Blind Harry.

"You know how he loved the sight of his own roger." They both laughed uproariously. "Had a hand mirror--"

After a few more guffaws he recommenced.

"Ha. Mort Dieu. Ah, alas." The pirate cleared his throat and wiped his eye. "This will tax your credence, but L'Ollonais swived that girl standing there, belly-on, crushing and smothering hundreds of flies between them, having at her like a mule."

He laughed again.

"When the girl finally became sensible to what he was doing she screamed anew and L'Ollonais crowed and laughed and kissed her fly-black lips and shot his wad in his frenzy, ha, chewing and worrying her lips bloody, then nearly bit off her nose, poor child, would have 'cept he sucked a fly down his throat and choked."

The storyteller stopped, caught on the reef of his own memory. "That saved her. She's a whore in Port Royal now."

"Yes, yes, a mad man," someone said.

But the storyteller's companion by the fire was himself coughing and laughing, saying "Flat on his back on the sand and gagging, flies stuck all over 'im, squashed and buzzin'."

"Aye, that was a queer voyage in all points. Not long after that our ship ran onto a sandbank among the islands called De las Pertas. We were stuck so fast that nothing could free her, so we were forced to tear the ship to pieces and with the planks and nails to build ourselves a long-boat.

"The Indians of those islands are properly savages, never having spoken with a European, nor even have bows and arrows. They use only a very long lance fixed at the end with a crocodile-tooth . . . But I was recollecting that the bees aided us there, too. In those parts there is found a great abundance of a pitch which can be gathered. There is so much of the pitch that it melts in the heat of the noon sun and runs down the beaches and congeals in the sea water into great heaps shaped like small islands. But it is not truly pitch, in my judgment, but wax manufactured in huge quantities by the bees in the surrounding territory. They make their honey in trees and when a tempest racks the forest it tears the honey-combs from the trees and strews it over the beach and the sea and even carries it from the mainland or washes it down river to the sea."

Gutierrez, becoming drunk, muttered "In my honeycomb of bees are small grains of salt."

"Yes, I think that is it. It mingles with the sand, but then the saltwater separates the honey and wax to make this pitch or amber. It does have the smell of black amber like we have from the Orient. Well, we caulked our new boat with it and that is how we got away from that island."

"In Brasil the bees in our forests make black honey," said La Roche.

"Perhaps the hurricanes blow their honeycombs all the way to . . ."

"Nonsense. Yes, we have all seen tempests that even far out of sight of land fill the air with leaves and flowers and toss lizards on the deck. But Brasil? That is much too far to ---"

"Honey and wax will not make pitch," said an old ship's carpenter.

"But there is the black lake of pitch on Trinidad Spaniards call La Brea."

"I have heard of it," the Frenchman said irritably. "But I doubt it is large enough to fill the wind like black chaff, nor do the hurricanes blow across the sea on that tack--"

"Yes, yes, it was ridiculous, a jest. Honeycombs."

"Get on with the L'Ollonais story," the man growled.

32 BLUE HONEY

The story teller turned to La Roche, ignoring those who wanted to hear again of Jean-David Nau, the famous L'Ollonais.

"Black honey, you say? How does it taste? Is it made from black flowers?"

"Orchids. Orchids of every color, I think. And in Brasil those flowers grow heavy, heavy as a king's scepter. Petals like some goddess's cunt formed of lapis lazuli velvet. They smell so sweet the bees stagger and weave in their flight back to the hive. Orchids that are violet, rust and peach, and butter yellow, or white as apple blossoms. But the honey is black and smoky."

"Swamp honey it sounds like to me. Like you get at Guadalupe, more bite than sweet." He pursed his lips in distaste.

"You try it," said La Roche. "It goes to your brain like brandy."

"Heady, maybe, but in France we have a sea-green honey concocted by the bees from gooseberry flowers and sycamore. One spoon will delight you an entire afternoon."

The whole table fell to arguing over the merits of honeys, from the Magyars' acacia honey to the lotus honey got from the Malabar Coast. La Roche held strong for his black honey while another reminisced of the snow white honey of Siberia that sometimes found its way to Stockholm at the price of its weight in silver. The French squabbled among themselves over the jasmine honey of Grasse and the crystal rosemaries of Narbonne and Languedoc; Captain Hayes held forth on the purple highland heathers so thick they will not flow from a jar turned upside down; and a slaver claimed that the African kings delighted in a clear green honey dripping from red combs.

"Honey! Honey!" They were soon shouting. The serving wenches brought all they had, two small crocks and a larger one from the kitchen, with wooden spoons for all. They dipped, spun, licked and laughed, dripping the sweet golden, sticky amber across the table, their sleeves, laps, shirtfronts, chins and beards, and called for brandy to wash it down.

Jack took a spare spoon himself and got a dip of honey. In the middle of the laughing and raillery no one seemed to mind the intrusion.

The first licks tasted fine, but the sweetness quickly cloyed and soured with the ale in his stomach. He felt suddenly hungry and off his feed at once. Nothing he saw on the tables appealed to him, not fruits or greasy meats. Cheese came to mind, substantial and mild. As the queasiness in his stomach was growing, Jack decided not to ask a serving wench, but went straight back to the kitchen. The word was out to all of his new place with Kit, so he did not fear he would get his ears boxed or a spoon broken over his head as in days past.

33 PLAYING PEEPING TOM

Going in, he passed the cooks and two serving girls carrying out steaming pots and skewers of chickens. There was no one in the kitchen to help him, but he knew the cheeses were hanging in their twine from the back kitchen's rafters.

No one was in the back kitchen either. But he spied the round balls hung over the back rafters. However, the one that seemed just right to his uneasy stomach was in a cluster above where the floor was covered with waist-high, ranked jars of wine.

"Damn," Jack muttered.

He climbed up on a barrel at the other end of the rafter, clambered up on to the wide beam, and began to shinny across it.

Just then he heard a grumbling command and the Aeolus' mestizo scullery girl stumbled into the back kitchen. Her blouse was pulled off one shoulder and one breast hung naked, covered by her hand. She did not see him. Behind her came Angus the second cook. He leered at her and shoved her again with one hand. She stumbled back into the middle of the room.

Jack held stock still. Angus had a devil's temper and he did not want to be thought spying on him. And besides, this looked to add some excitement to a dull evening.

The mestizo girl had turned her back to Angus and was trying to pull up the shoulder of her blouse. He stepped up to her and jerked the blouse down clear to her waist.

The cook curled his arms around the scullery girl, grabbed her breasts and ground his lips into her neck. She whined and shifted her shoulders.

He let her go and slapped her across the side of the head. She yelped, then fell quiet when he raised his hand again.

The cook turned away, went to the table. He scraped chunks of yam off it into a bowl, stepped over and dumped them into the steaming soup pot hung over the coals. The girl still stood where he left her. Except for her raven hair she had no beauty. Her teeth were bucked, her peculiarly thin nostrils looked awry in her Indian face, her eyes were small and dull.

The cook tossed the wooden bowl on the table and went back to her.

He took her hands and guided them into his pants. He kissed her little breasts, like brown mangos, and sucked on her dark brown nipples till they stuck out long as she-goats. He reached around her, untied the skirt, dropping it to the dirt floor. With his hands on her hips he pushed her back against the table and squeezed her bush. His hand jerked away. The cook bent the girl backwards over the table with a hand on her shoulder and stooped to sniff her crotch.

"Damnation and Christ's foul blood," he growled and stood raising a hand as if to hit her again. From his perch, Jack could see it was her time. A blood tinged rag peeked from her wem. "Turn over girl," the cook said menacingly, his hand still upraised. Though the girl moaned, she did as bid, resting her arms among the scraps of meat and yams and her face on her arms. The cook immediately squeezed her buttocks in his fingers and kneaded the brown flesh like dough, then squatted down to pepper them with smacking kisses. Straightening, he unloosened his sash and brought forth a cock straight as a pistol and primed. Seeing this sight over her shoulder the girl whined, her grimace baring teeth like a horse.

Gentle of a sudden, the cook said, "Not to worry your sweet bum, darling. We'll slip in like a thief."

Laying one hand on her back, he reached beneath the table and drew a wooden cup from the shelf. He dipped his big finger in and came out with a white dollop of bacon drippings.

"This should do it," he said, spreading her bum with one hand and wiping the finger-full of fat on the girl's bum hole. He tamped and poked it in.

"Now it won't hurt a bit," the cook assured the girl, whose face was buried in her arms. He grasped his member and leaned over her.

Jack would have laughed at the porcine grunts and squeals the two soon were making but he crouched and breathed quietly as he could through his open mouth. The cook would not take kindly to his spying at all now, though any serving wench or the taverner himself might have wandered back to this rough, thatched addition to the main kitchen. Jack's legs were aching and his balance was beginning to wobble. He did not like being so close up under the thatch. The rustling of cockroaches as long as his finger made him think of the crab-sized tarantulas that loved the thatch as well.

When the cook groaned and had finished with her he wiped his roger on his apron and tucked it back in his pants. The scullery maid was massaging her violated fundament, then pulled her skirt and blouse back up. She turned at the door, tears on her cheeks, but still silent. She twisted her face in a horrid look of hate, stuck out her tongue --- and saw Jack in the rafters. She turned and ran.

"Why you little Peeping Tom," growled Angus.

Jack stared down at the livid face below him and shrugged.

34 TOES FOR THE SOUP

The cook moved two wine jars aside and jumped to grab Jack's foot, but his bulk barely left the floor.

"Scadraddling, sneaking spy!" He looked around him, grabbed an empty gourd, and flung it at Jack, missing wide. "Gods blood, I've got you!"

Jack scooted closer to the post and hugged it. The cook grabbed a cleaver.

"No!" Jack shouted, cringing to make himself smaller. But instead of flinging it, the cook swung high and chopped into the beam next to his toes.

Jack jerked his foot back and the cleaver bit next to them again. The cook was laughing now and aimed for his other foot. Jack jerked it away just in time.

"I'll have your toes in my soup," shouted the cook. Jack half stood, clinging to the post, and jumped with both feet as the cleaver hacked a splinter from the beam. Desperately he clawed with his right hand at the thatch above him, trying to tear a hole to crawl through. He leaped on one foot as the cleaver thudded the beam again, tore again, looking --- three hand-sized, wriggling spiders cascaded over his arm onto his face and neck. He fell with a shout, grabbing at the scraping wood!

He hung from the beam with his right ankle hooked over it, his hands grasping the splintered beam.

Angus kicked a tarantula away with his toe and laughed into Jack's face. The blade of the cleaver was turned upward directly under his chin.

"Who have we here?" the cook smiled with his dozen scattered teeth. "Why it's peeping Jack, not Peeping Tom.

"All set to butcher up, too," he said, then turned and drew the edge of the heavy blade over Jack's cheek. "Or maybe just a barbering. Could use a little shave here."

He set the blade across Jack's upper lip. Jack could feel the sweat beading and running over his face. The cook scraped a bit, as if the cleaver were a razor.

"Or maybe," he turned the blade then again, setting it between Jack's eyes.

"Maybe just split your nose and leave done with it, fair and square."

Just as Jack was about to let go the beam, turn his head and drop, hoping he could scurry away, the cook turned and walked away laughing loud and long.

"You rascal, Jack," Angus exclaimed, and sunk the cleaver into a block where he had been butchering a large turtle.

"A man gets his blood hot and he's ready for most anything."

Jack unhooked his ankle, swung and dropped to his feet. He pulled a splinter out of his palm and rubbed the little wound against his hip. His knees quivered.

35 CALIPASH AND CALIPEE

The cook walked over and pulled a bottle of rum from the shelf where he had had the bacon drippings. He pulled out the cork with his teeth and handed it to Jack. Jack took a long swig.

The cook nodded. "Another."

Jack took the drink and handed it to the cook, who took one himself before replacing the cork and bottle.

"I was just hunting for a cheese."

"Well, you can gather up those that came down." He gestured at the floor. Jack looked up and saw the cook had slashed loose a bunch of them.

While he gathered the white, coconut size cheeses from the corners and put them on a table, the cook returned to the turtle on the butcher block.

"Don't seem to be able to be done with these beasts," he said.

Taking the cleaver and gripping the rim of the shell he chopped two quick strokes at the belly. Setting aside the cleaver he pulled the stomach shell up, then used a long knife to cut the rest of it loose. He tossed the white plate on the floor. He sighed. "I'll wager I've served up more of these than any cook this side of Camaguey."

"Another?" Jack asked reaching for the rum. The cook raised his knife without turning, so Jack pulled the cork.

"The first two times I sailed on account, those of us who signed the Articles was so poor we could barely scrape and beg our powder and shot, much less provisions. So we sailed for the Caymans, it being the season the turtles come to nest.

"It's a sight, boy. Scores of thousands filling the water, coverin' the beach so' you could walk a league on their backs and never touch sand. More'n once a ship lost on a cloudy dark night has steered by the splashing of their herds that swim there all the way from the Costa Rica. It's a wonder. And no lack of provision and fresh meat."

Angus set some strips of pale meat on the block, then came back over to Jack, who was enjoying the rum rising in his brain. The cook took a swig and put the bottle back deep on the shelf. He pulled out a wooden bowl, plucked a spoon from a bouquet in a dry crock, and went back to the turtle. Jack walked unsteadily over to watch and leaned against a post.

"Much turtle as you could ever want. Feed all Cayona. Feed an Armada. We loaded our ship below decks from stem to stern, every foot of open planking.

"Course you turn 'em all on their backs so they don't wander about. All of 'em could head off in one direction or humpin' one another and they could capsize the ship! Strange, them all there in ranks on their backs, swimmin' like, and blowin' bubbles. We splash 'em with sea water every nonce to keep 'em from dying too quick. Holds 'em for weeks."

Using the spoon he scraped out the jellied, yellow calipash and tossed it in the bowl, and then scooped some crab-butter soft, greenish calipee.

"This is a good one," he said to himself.

"When you first sail a turtle provisioned ship it can grate on you. Hang your hammock up over 'em, and them paddling the air and making their little bleating noises --- it spoils your dreams. But they'll quiet down after a few days.

"And fresh turtle be a damn sight better than nothing but boucan, or salt pork you got to soak the saltpeter out of in the barrel just to eat.

"Better except for the cook," the cook said pointing the spoon at himself. "Butcher four or five of these every day and cook 'em up and a man starts wishin' for a larder of boucan and biscuits."

The scullery maid stuck her head in the doorway. Megan the barmaid's face appeared above it. They looked like they expected to see the cook mopping up blood. Seeing Jack leaning with his ankles crossed and arms behind his neck seemed to make the scullery wench furious. When the cook looked up she drew her finger across her throat, then bolted backward sending Megan flying. They heard the women screeching at each other and laughed.

The cook squinted at Jack, a little of his first anger in his face.

Then he smiled.

"That wench's bum ain't no sailor's dream," he said. "But once I got my blood up, well, any port in a storm, I say."

He laughed and Jack grinned and nodded. Not some ports, he thought.

"You know, a voyage can be long and tiresome. Especially if your becalmed in sultry waters and all's asleep 'cept you. Sometimes I'd be getting set for the evening meal, bring an arm-size turtle up to butcher and set it on its back in a coil of rope so it don't go no place. And it'll be layin' there in the sun awhile, gettin' warm, and its flippers start rowin' the air trying to turn over, till it starts getting real warm and slow, and it's panting, sort of, and even its quim is panting like. And you say, hell, I've rogered worse."

The cook looked at him. Jack realized his mouth was hanging open and closed it.

"Lad, it was tasty." Angus gave him a lopsided grin and winked.

Jack swallowed. Nodding, he edged away. "Thank'ee for the rum."

The cook laughed and dug into the shell with the spoon. "Godsblood, my first was the family goat! Yours, too, I'll wager."

He laughed louder as Jack quick-stepped out of the kitchen, shaking his head to rid it of the cook's notions.

36 SAUSAGE CASINGS

Out in the common room Jack realized his stomach felt back in sorts. The scare and rum seemed to have been the medicine. Even more men were crowded into the Aeolus than usual, many that were rarely seen. They gambled and drank and fought; blows were being exchanged in the far corner, but Jack saw no blades. Jack decided they were just getting an early start on the festivities.

From the talk at one table it seemed he had just missed Francisco. He pulled a stool up and sat at the end of the table to hear an oft told tale.

"My mates and I were the ones that brought that Francisco here to Cayona," declared a pirate with a green kerchief tied around his head.

He tugged at one long mustache while he regaled a weary doxie with the tale. Jack had heard a half dozen different versions of Francisco's story, all good.

"We'd captured a high-pooped, gilded galleon with a viceroy's brother and his wife, a fat Don and his whole retinue, a glorious ransom.

"When we let the sailors out of the hatches and 'who was going for the Brotherhood?' this dwarf, Francisco himself, all done up in harlequin comes out from behind the Don's women's skirts, we hadn't even seen him, and says he'll join up with us." He broke off, smiling and shaking his head.

"We all laughed so hard the Don's crew could have taken the ship back if they'd had their senses about them. We thought he was playing the Fool, like a right royal dwarf is supposed to do. Even though his master the Don was cursing him like a dog that pissed on his boot, we still had a mind old Francisco was playing us the fool, but none of us liked that fat Papist's arrogance so we tied the Don to the mainmast to have a little play with the dwarf and gave this fool a cutlass and told him to prove his word. We thought he would make some brave gibe and offer the blade right back to us."

"Ha! Francisco made short work of our wit and the Don. And our ransom, too! Walked right up to him dragging the cutlass on the deck, stared right at the Don's belt buckle, and gives this big, two-handed sweep like a man felling sapling."

The man demonstrated with his mug, dashing the whore's dirty skirt with more rum.

"You should have heard the Don and his women screech. Belly just opened up and dumped his sausage casings on the deck."

The pirate made a long flatulent sound with his tongue and cheeks.

Jack laughed.

"Ha!" The man pounded his mug on the table and roared with delight.

The doxie twittered and fluttered her eyes. Jack knew she spoke only French and a little Spanish and did not understand a word. He got up and went to rejoin Old Kit.

37 MULTITUDINOUS SEAS INCARNADINE

The tap room now was tight with stinking, drinking, exclaiming men, parrots, and whores. Musickers tooted and drummed while the rest at their tables sang songs and chanties. Sweating wenches carried trays of mugs or meats on their shoulders, or the shorter ones overhead, and they waddled from the bottles they had precariously stuck in the sashes and pockets of their aprons.

Even the poop had been set with three small tables in addition to the usual long trestle held by Kit. Kit was being helped across the tap room by Dobry, probably returning from his private "head" behind the tap room bar. Jack replaced the harried taverner at Kit's side and the man hurried back to his kegs with a thanks.

At one table Azzopardi, the Maltese, half rose from his stool as he told a tale to two compatriots in their strange native tongue. From the listener's wide eyes and his awful tone, Jack thought it must be a ghost story. He and Kit paused while the old man caught a few breaths.

"Minn gos-sigra tal-bajtar," Azzopardi said, drawing his hand slowly across the air before him. "Tliet nisa hafjin hargu jirfsu l-lejl!"

The mouths of Azzopardi's small audience opened wider. Jack almost wanted to listen to the story he could not understand, but he turned to some new words.

"If Cuba is a shark and Hispaniola a salmon, then Puerto Rico is a flounder."

Four navigators, deep in their cups, sat on stools around a great portolano that covered their table. They grinned foolishly.

"St. Kit's a whale," said another brightly and raised his mug from between his legs to quaff the rum.

"Guadeloupe a butterfly."

"Eleuthera is a barracuda eaten to the spine by wasps," observed Dieter the Bremener.

"Hog Island is a Mogul's elephant," a third man called as if he had spied a treasure mark.

"An elephant? Is what?" the fourth asked. "Never mind. What are the Virgin Islands?"

He lay his finger slowly on the parchment as if he had discovered a riddle to stump them. Kit did not object when Jack stepped closer to see what he could make out.

"The Eleven Thousand Virgins of blessed St. Ursula?" Dieter smiled contentedly.

"No. What looks it --- " began the man, but the Bremener was off, reciting a story every child, at least in Bremen, should know.

"Ursula was a beautiful princess who, betrothed to a pagan king, begged her father to let her sail on a long voyage to escape marriage to a man who was not a good Christian. She invited ten maidens to accompany her," he nodded sagely.

"But so many more begged to join her holy voyage that at last she sailed in eleven ships with a thousand virgins in each vessel.

"These were the old, chaste days you must remember. After three years they all returned and landed back at Köln, from whence they came --- on the very same day the city was sacked by the pagan Huns. Eleven thousand virgins defiled," he chuckled. "Quite a flow of blood, ja? Slain, too, those sainted virgins."

"Multitudinous seas incarnadine," Kit said with his own chuckle. He winked at Jack, who did not understand him.

"The Virgin Islands," Dieter said raising his glass toward Kit and wavering a bit. Jack could not tell if he were toasting the islands or the women. "Such beauty. The dearest blue water, gentle waves . . ."

Old Kit turned away, leaning on Jack's arm as they walked and nodding to himself.

"Pulchritudinous seas aquamarine," he muttered, and smiled to himself. They continued through the crowd, which parted respectfully when they saw it was Aeolus' master.

38 GHOST TALES

"Will he join us?" Bosola asked Jack as he helped Kit up the steps to the Poop. He was pointing across the room at Azzopardi.

"He's deep in some tale."

Bartholomew turned from his place at the near end of the table and peered at the gesticulating Vallettan.

"A ghost story, I'd wager," Jack said with a shrug. "He tells it in his own odd tongue."

"Ghosts," Bartholomew said with something like satisfaction. He looked at Bosola.

"When I was a boy those Chinee told ghost stories at every banquet, it seemed. They see spirits everywhere. Why the eunuchs that mind the concubines and treasuries, when they're gelded they dry their balls and put them in a special box. Sixty years later when they die, they take down the box off the shelf, blow the dust off, and put their parts back where they belong. They'd be shamed to be in the spirit world without them: the other ghosts might laugh, I suppose. I saw the palace's store-room once, hundreds of those boxes. I switched the little paper tags on two. I wonder if they will notice."

"There is something to that notion, I'll testify," old gray-bearded Jameson interrupted. He held up his hook and turned it in the lamplight.

"At times I think I have a ghost hand. They may say the soul is not the image of the body, but sometimes, when a storm is rising, I can feel the ague in my knuckles ache so that I just reach out to rub 'em, and they ain't there."

"I've wondered whether souls be stunted myself," said a trader who dealt in pirated indigo and cochineal. "My father, rest his soul, delighted in sports of nature, took me to every one presented in the tents close by the theaters. He said, my father did, said James IV of the Scots had a jester was truly two jesters, their chests and hips all one. When one of the two died, the other took up the most pitiful moaning and crying all through the halls and gardens till the rotting corpse he carried poisoned and killed him, too.

"But the question, friends," the merchant looked around. "Was they one soul or two? Are their souls entwined for eternity? And come the promised resurrection, what then?"

"Questions too deep for my wit," said Bartholomew. Most of the others at the table nodded or just stared into the rafters. Jack helped Kit settle in his chair. He was not as spry as he had been just a short time earlier.

"Now, as you asked how I came to Cayona ---" began Bartholomew.

"That man has left," interrupted Van Oort, but the Portuguese continued.

39 THE MOTHER OF EMERALDS

"It was, as I said, the Manila galleon brought me to the New World to trade my diamonds and topazes, sapphires and pearls. Speaking of spirits, the Chinee peasants in the hinterlands believe a pearl comes from the brain of a dragon, its very nut and pith of its spirit. They'll let you use their daughters, their wives ---"

"Yes, yes, you've told that before and I ---"

"But, but, but," said Bartholomew loudly, regaining his listeners' ears. "As I was saying, I had filled all my coffers for the return to Manila. Mostly chests of Aztec fire opals, very prized in the East. We set sail from Acapulco, but one day out we were attacked and grappled by English pirates, the first since Drake to raid those seas. Fierce fighters."

He nodded to Jameson, as if to placate him for some reason Jack could not fathom.

"But in the end I myself filled the pedrero on the poop with golden chain and raked a swath through their last reserves --- Oeuf bruise! They were bloody eggs.

"We fired their ship and cut them loose and watched them jump, them that could, into the water like roaches, both man and rats, pummeling in the sea till they drowned.

"We'd lost our masts fore and aft, the mainmast was cracked by a cannonball, and we had contrary winds. Took two weeks to tack back to Acapulco and as it seemed it would be a half year until a ship and the winds were right to attempt the Pacific, I decided to see more of the New World than High Mexico. I sailed down to Panama City, a sanguine port. But their trade is mahogany, slaves and such and soon I followed my nose." He tapped his forefinger against his bony bridge. "Followed it to Arica and took the road up into Alto Peru. You can guess what I sought."

"Emeralds," Jack, standing beside Kit's chair at the head of the table, said quickly. He looked down to see if Kit had noticed his recall of the lore, but the old man slept on his folded arms.

"Not just emeralds," the Portuguese said with a wink. "The Mother of Emeralds!"

After a pause that even Van Oort did not break, he continued.

"A gem sought by the likes of me and many more this century past. An emerald big as a cabbage, big as a boy's head. Before Pizarro it was kept on an altar in an Incan shrine. The priests dictated that offerings to the holy spirit in their emerald be in emeralds, too. Bowls and baskets and troughs of gleaming green emeralds, generations upon generations of worshippers vying to honor the Mother of Emeralds by returning her children. When the conquistadors came the priests grabbed the holy gem from the altar and disappeared into the snowy peaks.

"And those soldiers." Bartholomew shook his head and blinked his eyes as if he had been kicked by a horse. "They thought to prove the emeralds as if they were diamonds, using the alter for an anvil and striking them with hammers. Green dust and shards were all that was left of ten thousand emeralds."

He laughed, but everyone else at the table looked glum at the thought of such idiots. Jack thought of

Kit's treasures that might be his, of how the very men at this table would gladly steal it from him if they were given the chance, and he would be left with pitiful fragments, or nothing.

"My plan was not to buy emeralds but to sell them. To follow the Indians' tales and the Indian thieves who stole the verdant crystals, to go from city to town to village to hamlet seeking the refuge of those Incan priests.

"Their refuge was El Dorado! That is plain," Blind Harry cried. He, too, had made his way up on the poop.

"God spare us," exclaimed Bosola. He got up and left while the blind man ran on.

40 Blind Harry's El Dorado

"Gems and precious metals are their glory in El Dorado, but still common as logwood and mahogany to us. They would welcome the great emerald's priests with brotherly love and build a shrine of silver for the nondescript emerald those poor exiles held so peculiarly dear. I have heard many tales.

"Why the gold and silversmiths of that hidden city are the greatest in the world. And the streets are cobbled with bricks of gold, the aqueducts are built of pure silver inlaid with ivory mosaics portraying each step of the city's own Romulus -- the Son of the Sun -- each step from birth to the founding of the city.

"In all the surrounding mountains there is barely enough water to fill these aqueducts. They are tall, they shade every golden street from the rain and the noon day sun, running from house to golden house and over each house like some Moorish tracery spider's web or the leading of a great cathedral's rose window, all rings concentric and all streets running to the king's palace.

"The people, though, say the whole city is his palace . . ."

Blind Harry ranted on, thinking he held all in his spell. But Jack concerned himself with filling his clay pipe, and others relit theirs, or picked their teeth, or waved to the taverner to fetch more wine, brandy, or rum. Blind Harry was well liked and pitied, and he sulked for days if his phantasy of the golden city was shouted down.

"The silver aqueducts empty their thousand score trickles into the palace moat from which the servants draw their water in crystal buckets and from which the sewers proceed in golden troughs diademed with pearls and emeralds. But the king's palace, that my friends, is the most magnificent, with four great wings like a cross, with each wing ending in a mountainous pyramid like hold the royal mummies of Egypt, one at each of the cardinal points. The pyramids have many terraces where the priests sleep and cook, and they worship within. But at the center of the palace, the center of its wings, is an enormous dome of gold, dwarfing the pyramids, of such height and breadth it would swallow a half dozen petty cathedrals. And at the dome's top most peak is a slender, shinning spire of pure silver, as high as ten mainmasts!"

At this penultimate point, Bartholomew finally interrupted.

"Yes, Harry. Magnificent. It must be a magnificent vision."

The blind man was nodding his head, seeing it. Looking up and down the table Bartholomew continued his tale of coming to Cayona.

41 A Screaming Head

"High up in Alto Peru is a region, you all know, they call Potosi, the Mountains of Silver. At twilight it seems as if the mountains burn within like volcanoes, like they have burnt to a shell and the fire breaks through like a pox. But the pox are the coals of the Incan firepots that cover the ridges in ranks of thousands, each one stoked and fed day and night by an Indian slave. The pots themselves are like small volcanoes sending up smoky plumes that the fires turn orange above the twilight mountain sides, then, higher, lavender and gray as the smokes trail away like tresses on the wind. At night the shadows of the slaves dance before their hearths as they rake out their pitchy globs of melted silver."

One single glimpse was fixed in Bartholomew's memory. They had descended from such a ridge of silver and the trail rose to the crest opposite. He had turned and in the near dark the mountain seemed like the head of some storied duchess, her hair caught up in a ruby-faceted net trailing gossamer in the twilight zephyrs of a promenade. But that same image was chained, coffled with memory's inexorable links to another, as, two days later, still on the same trail, he had pondered the conceit of that ducal coiffure when a distant scream brought him from the reverie.

"I was more startled than my horse. A cry can be heard at many turns in the Alto Peru. After a brace of twists the trail brought us upon a screaming head at the side of the road. An Indian buried to his neck. His eyes were alive with ants; they streamed from his nose, his bellowing mouth, his ears. I would have delivered him from his agony, but I had no pistol -- trusting our guard and the Viceroy's justice so evident before us as my protection. And if I had dismounted to slit the man's raw throat the soldiers escorting our tax inspector's caravan would have restrained me. We rode on at a canter till the screaming head could not be heard. No one spoke of the screaming head."

He paused a moment and swallowed.

"Eventually that long road descends to the northeast and I traced its whole length, arriving at last, without the Mother of Emeralds as you may guess, on Maracaibo Bay at the little town of Gibraltar."

"Oui, on Maracaibo," the resplendent Belleau said, seating himself at the table. The Portuguese did not try to regain their ears, still brooding on the screaming head.

42 THE SECRET OF FARMING FEATHERS

"On Maracaibo," Belleau said. "By the time we entered Gibraltar with Morgan every man, woman and child had fled. The town was all silent, except for a scraping sound none of us could place. We found an old man hoeing the dirt of the main square. He was dressed in foul-smelling rags and his eyes jumped and rolled in his head when he spoke. He explained to us like we were children how he was planting eggs to sprout birds and how the moon sang to him."

Belleau smiled sadly.

"It was high humor to most of us, but others thought he was feigning madness and the rags were a disguise. So he was put to the rack. His ravings as they stretched him were most extraordinary; I don't believe I could recall them now. But each time the question of treasure was put to him his teeth would lock shut till they stretched him a notch more and a new cry of agony broke them. I thought we would snap his spine, but at last he broke and promised to show us his treasure. It was hidden beneath the roots of a tree: two pieces-of-eight and six clay pots!"

Belleau roared at the thought and slapped his thigh. He took a swig from the bottle of wine in his fist.

"Of course, the ones who had tormented him the better part of the morning did not laugh like we others. They were mad as devils for being fools. The crazy old man was strung on the rack again and they tied huge miller's weights to his feet. His neck, too. He was pulled taut as a bow string, so that a whispered word brought him agony. But our mates, to hurry the event and since there was looting to be done and Morgan was becoming vexed, they took burning palm leaves and laid them on the old fellow's face one after another. He screamed and shivered on the rack, but it took him half the hour to die.

"It was a pity," Belleau said giving a wink to Jack. "For he took to his grave the true treasure of that place, the one I promised to tell you before."

He paused. "The secret of farming feathers!"

The table laughed and others started new tales. Jack slumped on the arm of Kit's chair, staring into the fire. In his mind's eye he saw vast fields running over the hills, bobbing plumes divided in wide swaths of turquoise, of white, and scarlet, fields wavering under the waves of the wind. On a far, bare slope a horse and man ploughed under a stubble of broken quills.

43 PLAGUEY LONDON

"Gadzooks!" Kit screamed, scaring Jack off the chair arm. The old man rubbed the sleep from an eye with one hand and groped for his mug of brandy with the other. He mumbled to himself and cocked an ear --- he had forgot his ear horn in the palanquin --- to hear the rest of tale. Jack sat back down on the arm of the chair.

"Twas a good thing London burned. I'll declare it," the Irishman Reilly said. "Burned the awful plague right out of it. It's a horrible thing the plague; it makes my skin crawl just to think on it. And I, I was trapped, surrounded by it, almost murdered by it!"

"I weren't in London a fortnight 'fore the sickness erupted again. Spread like a fire in a sleeping house. I come to town and could afford no better than a tumble-down room on the London Bridge, leaning out o'er the river and creaking like a ship during the day time, with half the city's thieves crowding the pawn shops in the morning, and the taverns filling up, and the wagons crossing back and forth, and the whole damn thing like to crumble in the water .

"I'd been sick meself, but not with the plague. Slept two whole days and woke up trapped." Reilly shook his head. "Woke up and it's strange quiet and I go down to the street and its morning, but the shutters is closed on both sides and then walking at me is a giant damnable raven, and the other way it's a wagon loaded clear to the staves with stinking corpses. I run back up the stairs and find an unlocked room lookin' on the road and far the length of it there's ibis-headed, toucan-headed, and raven-headed physickers wandering and poking corpses and knocking on doors. And common folks, ones that are dying, they are robbing the dead or pulling them in carts. The Plague had run up along the river and crossed on London Bridge while I slept. Left me no escape at either end.

"Starve, I thought. Starve rather than put one foot in the street.

And I was damn near starved, not eating for two days. I was sitting there listening to my stomach when I heard more stirring in the next room. I tested its door from the hallway, but it was barred. I got no reply to my knocking and shouting, but I knew no rat could make that noise, and anybody thought they was bigger or better armed would have ordered me off to my own business. So I broke it in with a bench from my room."

"It was a maid. Deaf-mute, I found after cursing her cringing into a corner. When she saw no plaguey sties or such on me she seemed less afeared and understood my mime of eating. She pulled out a bit of cheese rind and a crust from her apron for me."

He paused and spied around the room. He pointed to a doxie with light brown ringlets that fell to her bare shoulders.

"She was a comely wench, much like Molly over there in a plain way. After staring all afternoon at the plaguey death on London Bridge she looked all the better, made me randy, and I forced her right there after a bit of a tussle.

"They make odd sounds when you tup 'em. Mutes, I mean. Not quite a cry or gasp. Did something to me, me thinkin' on it after. I got all randy and swived her again, rogered her real good just to hear it.

"Well, she could have escaped after I shot my wad that time. I was gasping and giddy. But she must o' feared the poison streets as much as me. She just lay there on the side of the bed raining her tears on the boards.

"That night those bird-headed doctors crossed the bridge with servants carrying torches, some going one way, some the other, and the dead carts were creaking past. But all I could think on was rutting the mute girl the third, then the fourth time. I haven't had it in me like that since I was a lad. I lost count, but in the middle of the night she warmed to it, too, finally embraced me with passion, her skin was hot, her cries, like, like, like a strangled cat."

"Not the sound I think would make me swell," said Belleau.

"I am no poet. Well, the last time, in the creeping dawn, she kissed me for the first time, kissed me all over my face between those gasps, the most fervent coupling I have hope of knowing. I was spent and satisfied. But when I looked upon her in the new light I found her staring back with the most horrible smile I ever hope to see.

"Her skin was flush and hot, and not from love. Then she coughed, was the first cough, I knew it in my soul, of the plague! I should have killed her then and there--- she meant her kisses to kill me! Murder was the heat of her passions. But I fled, mindless, running from London Bridge, from that corpse-littered quarter of town, running until I dropped, then walking until I dropped in a country lane. A saintly old dam nursed me through the plague, then died o' it herself."

The Irishman gulped his milk punch until it was gone.

"Plaguey London burning," he murmured. "Wish I'd seen it."

Kit rose, leaning on his two hands. By the evil his eye held for the Irishman, Jack thought he was going to curse him or have him tossed into the street. After the first ship had docked with news of the conflagration Kit had had arriving crews queried for any who knew more of what lanes, taverns, churches, and great houses had been consumed. Jack had run the reports up to the Kit's table at least twice back then, been there when others did. Those nights Kit would start raging, or tearing, or even laughing ruefully when told those landmarks' fates. But tonight the old man just turned to Jack and gestured for him to bring his twisted staff.

"Farewell," Kit called, and those that now told and listened to different tales quieted. "My old bones are still a bit creaky and I will hie them to bed."

All bid farewell to him; none called for him to stay, all knowing how fragile his health was rumored. As Jack helped him along he noted from the side of his eye a few speculating looks and murmurs directed his own way.

44 KIT'S PUNCH & JUDY

As they crossed the rowdy tap room, Kit spoke in his ear.

"Don't you worry about our sojourn at Pearl's, Jack. I just don't find my old pleasure in climbing stairs and dueling with the ribaldry from below."

The tall stairs were the ones leading to the private rooms above the Aeolus' commons and to the gallery linking the Aeolus with Madame Pearl's luxurious brothel. Many a merry or addled wit flung their darts at those who made their way to Pearl's by that route.

They picked up the Fore Gascon in the common room. He looked more sour than ever, forced by service to maintain his sobriety amid the tumult of drinkers, and, as they entered, frustrated in wooing a serving wench who must dash hither and thither through the noisy crowd of rakehells.

Out in the night air the three found the Aft Gascon sitting propped against the sedan chair, sawing loudly. The Fore Gascon gave him a kick in the ribs. He jumped to his feet with a snarl.

"Rap on the door for Master Kit, you derelict," commanded the Fore Gascon. "You was to do it before, do it now. I'm not the only one that's to work here."

Kit chuckled at them, but Jack didn't dare. Their bad tempers often enough boiled over on to him.

The Aft Gascon rapped on the wood and the door was opened almost immediately by a ragged, pug-nosed serving wench.

"Master Kit," she cried, pulling the door wider. She looked at Jack and frowned. Jack returned a haughty smile. Kit nodded at Jack and gave the woman a wink while they both entered Madame Pearl's. Even before the door shut on them, the Gascons were arguing anew about the chicken and the egg.

"We'll be in the Punch and Judy tonight, Marianne," Kit said. He gave the stringy-haired girl a tweak on her chin. "Tell Pearl I'm here tonight and fetch us some French brandy and two cups. And a second chair."

She gave a curtsy and hurried off down a narrow hall dimly lit by flickering candles in high sconces.

"Punch and Judy?" Jack asked. He had not wanted to show his ignorance in front of the serving wench.

"You'll see. It's the closest thing we have to a play-house in Cayona." They went up the stairs that began just to their right, climbing at the old man's laborious pace.

He took each step with his right foot and brought up the left with a small grunt.

Before they reached the top Madame Pearl was there to greet them. Their smiles always showed she and Kit were good friends. She had come to the house or sent a note every day he was bedridden to enquire of his health.

"Ah, Kit. It's good to see you back in my house again. I was wondering if that dousing had chilled your blood as cold as your bones."

"That'll not happen till I've been buried a full day," Old Kit said.

He paused at the top to lean on Jack's shoulder and catch his breath.

"And here is Jack," Madame Pearl said as Jack stared at her. Her mahogany dark hair was piled high, then cascaded curls about her pale Madonna's face. She wore a red satin gown, and diamonds sparked and gleamed

at her throat and fingers, but most dazzling were her
jet black eyes. Some said you could not look away from
them unless she blinked and let you. She blinked and
Jack looked down at the toes of his new boots.

"Jack that saved your old cockerel," the madam said.
"So you could bring it here where my girls know how to
physick old friggers. "

"This is him, a fine lad," Kit said, resuming his shuffling steps. Madame Pearl grabbed Jack by the shoulder
and bussed him on the cheek. The kiss, the flower scent
of her neck and hair stirred a little serpent in his loins.
He was struck dumb.

Madame Pearl tousled his hair then took Kit's arm.

"He's a bit more than a lad, by my eye. Maybe we
should give Jack a prize. A tumble with one of the girls."
She looked over her bare shoulder and gave Jack a wink.

"That notion has merit, Pearl." Kit chuckled. "But
first we'll warm his lewd humors with a visit to the Punch
& Judy."

"What 's ---"

"You'll see right now, boy."

They stopped before a rough wood door with an iron
padlock on its latch. The old man pulled a long key from
his pocket and handed it to the madam. She opened the
door, went in, and lit a brace of candles.

"Now the evening's just begun," she said coming out.
"So it may be a short bit before we've got some randy

fellow up to the Crystal Room. Our trade has been so damn poor since Morgan went off."

She stepped aside to let them enter. Down the hall the slattern that had let them in came with a tray holding their brandy. Behind her little, hunchbacked Charlotte gave Jack a familiar nod as she brought along a narrow ladderback chair. When both had entered and retreated Old Kit led the way into a room shaped like some pantry, deep, but narrow. Once the door was shut it made Jack felt close and uneasy. Rooms were different than the narrow caves beneath the Tree.

45 CAMERA OBSCURA VOYEURS

Two chairs sat side by side with a small table between them supporting two cups, a bottle, and the candelabrum. The chairs both faced a wall close enough so that Jack could touch it with his toe just by raising his leg. It was bare except for a large, blank square of new parchment tacked to it.

The old man seated himself with a grunt in his stuffed, damasked chair. Jack sat in the straight backed wooden one. The square of parchment was at eye-level on the wall opposite. After a few moments he rose and tapped it lightly. The wall behind was solid.

"A spy room?" he asked. If so its arrangement belied the purpose.

"Aye, it is," said Kit with a wicked smile. "Pour us a measure of brandy now. Aye, it's a special one."

"I don't understand. Is there some panel behind here that the doxies remove for some lewd shadow play?"

"No, no," Kit smirked, a somewhat disturbing sight, though why that was so Jack could not say. He was obviously pleased with the little trick he was about to show him.

"Go around behind the table," he said nodding back over his shoulder.

Jack went around behind his chair and investigated. At waist level on the wall opposite the parchment was a small, square copper plate nailed to the wood. In its center was a tiny hole, perhaps large enough for a sail maker's need to be pushed through.

"I can't see through this," he exclaimed.

Kit sipped his brandy. "Push the plate aside."

Jack did, and a more generous hole appeared. He looked through with one eye and had to blink twice, three times, because it was so bright.

He saw a long, long room of many dazzling chandeliers that hung over a row of white satin sheeted poster beds, one after the other, far down the room like an elegant barracks. It dazzled his eye. Into the room from Jack's left came a woman in a yellow gown--no three women--a dozen.

"It's the Crystal Room," Jack said in awe as he recognized what must be the most fabled boudoir of the Caribbean. The woman turned her head, all the women turned their heads, toward the spy hole and raised her finger, fingers to her lips.

She hurried busily around the room lighting more candles in gleaming candelabra and polished silver sconces. Now that he studied it he could easily see the narrow molding between the eight, yard-square mirrors that made up the opposite wall and the wall he peered through at some interstice.

The mirrors behind the bed reflected the mirrored double doors which stood ajar. They opened on the hall where he saw trollops and serving girls passing quickly on their business.

Jack turned to the old man, who watched him with a small, pursed smile like some ancient cat.

"This will be a great sport, but it seems awfully easy to be discovered."

"Some wouldn't mind," the old man said. "But slide the plate back and sit down." He nodded towards Jack's cup. "Take refreshment."

Jack did as he was told.

"What do you think of our Crystal Room, Jack?"

"It is, uh," Jack was still staring at the woman in yellow in his mind's eye. "It is more magnificent and strange than the tales I had heard.

"It is a room fit for a king's whoring. There is nothing like it on this side of the Great Ocean. I built it to---"

There was a knock and Madame Pearl looked in. "Extinguish your candle," she said. "Louisa has a randy young Dutchman's paid his money to tup in the Crystal Room."

Kit wheezed on the candles until they guttered out. It was completely dark in the room. Jack could hear him carefully pick up the candelabrum and set on the floor.

"Only whispers now," Kit said and proceeded to hack gruffly and spit on the floor.

"I'm afraid I'll knock the table," Jack said rising carefully to go around to the peep hole.

"Shush. Sit down and take up your glass. There is no need to watch them through the spy hole with our noses pressed to wood. I tired of that long ago. Take up your glass and drink; watch the parchment. That is the stage for the Punch and Judy show."

Jack's eyes quickly adjusted and he saw that a bright disk the size of a dinner plate lit the parchment. In its center, as if painted with great care, was the mahogany poster bed, but it seemed still quite odd he could not really make it out; at the bottom of the circle of light were bright speckles that seemed . . . the figure of the woman in yellow came into view, tugging a ship's officer --- and both were turned upside down, walking on the ceiling! Jack stymied a surprised cry. All was reversed, the bed, the chandeliers. But it was quite clear, as if spied through a porthole --- if one were hanging upside down.

"Just tilt your head onto your shoulder," Kit whispered. "And we will watch their simulacra couple at our leisure."

The figure of the man and woman on the paper dis-
robed, the man taking some time to admire himself and
her in surrounding mirrors. They embraced and soon
made the beast with two backs. Jack could hear them
clearly; and before him, upside down on the wall despite
his head cocked to his shoulder, he could just make out
behind the humping images, like a second, then third
rainbow, their reflected phantoms dallying in unison
with the first. The man's face was turned toward them
and smiling as he watched the same.

46 In Madame Pearl's Crystal Room

The little play for the camera obscura voyeurs did not
end until after Punch's third sally against Judy had apparently exhausted his ammunition. The Dutchman was
forced to retire. Jack pulled out his shirt to hide the wet
stain on his breeches, then lit the candles and placed
them on the table.

"A merry entertainment, old one," he grinned.

The old man winked, but appeared distracted and
melancholy.

"I am surprised I've not heard of this device all about
Cayona, this magical spy hole of yours."

"It is for me alone," Old Kit said, staring up at the
now blank parchment.

"What is the matter, master? You look sad. How do
you feel?"

"It is nothing," the old man said ruefully. "I merely fell asleep during that little performance."

There was a knock at the door.

"Open," said Kit and the stringy-haired serving wench looked in diffidently.

"Madame Pearl says the boy has earned a treat." She gave a lewd wink.

"I'm to take him to his own bedding."

"Truly?" asked Jack, jumping to his feet. His cock was turning hot at the mere thought of one of those lovely whores.

"Go, boy. You've earned her and much more." Kit lifted his glass of brandy toward him in a salute. "And don't hurt the poor woman."

He cackled as Jack went out, a cackle that sputtered into a rough gagging cough as the door closed.

The serving girl took him through the main hall, where other serving girls, apple squires, and painted whores rushed back and forth. Around one corner and into another hallway they passed doors holding in growls, laughter, grunts, giggles, whispers, and moans both practiced and unbidden; around a second turn and into a busy but quieter hallway; she stopped him before two plain wooden doors, this one without a sound behind it.

She opened one slightly, peeked in, then reached around behind Jack and pushed his butt on into the room, closing the door behind him.

He knew the bright room before his first foot stepped in. There before him, lounging against a pile of lacey pillows on the fancifully carved bed, her lovely face, her wild, bright, deeply black eyes glowing mysteriously brighter than all the shining chandeliers, the candelabras, and all their gleaming reflections shining infinitely around her, was Madame Pearl. She watched the emotions flash across Jack's face and her laugh was merry and musical.

Languidly she reached out a hand.

"Come here, Jack," she said softly.

Jack looked at the dozens of himself in the mirrors to either side. He tried to make out a tiny copper disk between the moldings.

"Come here, Jack," she said. Slowly she began to unbutton her shiny scarlet bodice while staring into his eyes.

Jack looked back into her onyx eyes, willingly giving himself up for lost in whatever was hidden there.

47 A PHILOSOPHICAL MURDER

He found Kit snapping the iron padlock on his private theatre. The old man clapped Jack feebly on the shoulder.

"Quite a performance, young tomcat," he said. Jack did not reply.

He swore to Holy Jesus himself he would never play Punch again. He had some modesty.

The old man chuckled. "I even got a dribble out myself," he said drawing back his coat to display a small wet stain on his greasy, green satin breeches. "Though I'll be damned if I know just when. Still that's cause to celebrate."

They were clumping slowly down the back stairs. Jack paused and studied the air.

"I thought you couldn't get it up, old one."

"Not up, really. Not like my pikestaff in its glory" He coughed and spit on the stairs. They continued down.

"But sometimes with the help of a special potion I received from the last Arawak I can squeeze out a drop or two."

He laughed ruefully. "But it does take it out of me. I think we'll celebrate later. It's best I get myself back to my bed tonight."

Jack let him rest a moment at the bottom of the stairs. The old man looked drawn and weak.

Jack unlatched the back door and opened it.

There in the dirt beside the palanquin the Fore Gascon lay dead. His head was gashed open, his eyes wide, his cheek resting in a fresh pool of blood, one arm extended toward the door. Next to him lay one of the palanquin's carrying poles, snapped double by the fatal blow. The other Gascon was nowhere to be seen.

Beside him in the loose dirt the dying man had written a word with his finger. The letters had partly filled with blood. OEUF.

Oeuf.

Egg. Jack sighed. The two Gascons never let the other have the last word.

Old Kit shook his head, a wry smile not parting his lips.

Part IV

The Last of the Arawak

48 Jack Higgins Calls on the Van Duyns

Late the next afternoon Kit called Jack to his rooms and gave him a small brass-bound casket.

"The year's choice diamonds," Kit said. "Van Duyn has a ship sailing for Amsterdam on the morning tide. Take these to him. I believe the ship's captain will dine with him this eve. Mayhap you'll be invited to dine yourself."

He handed him a letter sealed with green wax.

"Instructions to my Dutch agents." Kit winked. "I need not suggest you'd do yourself no harm cultivating a Dutch agent of your own?"

"Hay. I've had my thoughts on sowing for some time."

Taking the casket and letter, Jack hurried to his room.

Jack appeared at the Van Duyn's gate with the casket tucked under his arm, but now arrayed in what he hoped was a handsome display. His dark blue damask coat, finer than he had ever hoped to wear, set off his copper curls nicely he thought, and almost matched the indigo that alternated with the scarlet stripes of his pantaloons. He had buffed bright the toes of his high Spanish boots with their broad, turned-down cuffs, and the silver buckles gleamed like his coat buttons and the hilt of the fancy Flemish dagger tucked in his belt. The simple ruffles at the throat of his white linen shirt had wilted a bit from the sweat raised by the short walk in the late afternoon heat.

Jack rang the gate bell and looked at the ring on his middle finger.

The stone was an aquamarine the size of his small fingernail. He had chosen it from his own cache of commissions and the casual cast-offs of Kit's that he was accumulating. His hope was to show Rebecca and Herr Van Duyn that he was now a young man with prospects, but that he also retained the sober sense not to flaunt rubies and plumes like some of the preening piratical parrots of the town.

A squat, pink-cheeked maid came out of the big house and showed him in. Jack pressed the smile on his lips flat. It was the first time had had come in by the front gate, not the servant's back garden gate. It felt good.

However, he was ushered through the shuttered, crepuscular rooms and quickly out into the familiar garden. For a moment the old familiarity coupled with his new circumstances gave him a queer, befuddled feeling. He was not actually in the garden, but stood on the flagging of a tiny courtyard that, like the garden, was hemmed by a high stone wall, and separated from the garden yard by a tall, close-picket fence, "Jack, welcome."

Herr Van Duyn stood with Rebecca's older sister and a tall man dressed in the plain galligaskins and coat common to Zeelander merchant seamen.

Jack strode quickly forward.

"Herr Van Duyn." He bowed to the young woman, a long, bony wench, not nearly as attractive as Rebecca. "Mistress Lucy."

Though they had never been introduced, she smiled politely at him as if she had never chased him from the back door and scolded her sister for talking to him. Fortunes rose and fell so quickly in Cayona it did not pay to stand on previous circumstances.

"Captain Deinum, this young man is Jack Higgins."

He and Jack nodded, each muttering "Sir."

"Jack here is being groomed to assist our famous Old Kit." Van Duyn gestured at the casket, raising his eyebrows.

"Oh, yes. Master Kit bid me bring these for your morning sailing to the Zeeland." Jack was not sure what to do with the casket and letter, but Van Duyn called over the maid that waited on them by the door. She relieved Jack of the items.

"Take these immediately to Adolphus. He is in my cabinet completing the manifest," instructed Van Duyn.

"Master Kit regrets he could not attend your invitation. He is somewhat discomfited."

The Captain and Mistress Lucy had turned a little aside. She fluttered a fan over her bosom, smiling at a murmured compliment.

"Assure him our first care is his good health," said Van Duyn. His voice carried a cautious concern behind the formal words. "I trust his progress is steady, if not rapid."

Before Jack could form his lie, the Dutchman's studying eye rose in a glance past Jack's shoulder, disappointed it seemed. Then he smiled, saying as Jack turned "Ah, Rebecca. Come greet Jack Higgins and Captain Deinum."

Rebecca stood on the flagstone with a demure smile only for Jack. Her short-sleeved gown of sky blue brocade, its skirts puffed wide by petticoats, seemed to reflect the falling light of dusk upward to fill her eyes and glow on the smooth high cheeks she had fully exposed by pulling her gold hair back into a loose bun. Between Rebecca and Jack the evening's first fire flies began to flash their tiny lights.

He was lost for a moment before he managed a not too ungraceful bow. She nodded an acknowledgement toward Captain Deinum and curtsied to them both.

Coming forward through the floating fireflies she asked "How is Master Kit, Jack?"

"Most well, Mistress Rebecca." His throat was dry. He coughed a bit to clear it. "But by day's end he is more tired than was his wont. Before his dousing,"

"Aye, that is easy to credit of a man of Kit's great age," Herr Van Duyn said. "It was a brave and worthy thing to come to his rescue. And now to serve him well in his trade is most commendable."

Jack flushed as much as if his pants had suddenly dropped to his ankles.

He would have been speechless if the merchant had not continued immediately.

"Rebecca, please attend on Jack. I must confer with Captain Deinum about the items Jack brought from Master Kit."

As he moved away Jack turned and smiled through his embarrassment.

"Your uncle now seems to count me better than a dog," he said softly.

The girl gave a quick laugh that she stifled with her hand. They turned and stepped slowly away from the others.

"Indeed, he does." She looked up at him with a mischievous smile that weakened his knees. "At first, when you rescued Master Kit, he deemed you a lucky dog."

Jack laughed this time.

"But the past fortnight I heard him say you were a shrewd young fox that bore watching."

Now her eyes were downcast and Jack gazed on the light freckles scattering on her milky cheek and the shallow but real cleavage of her bosom.

She looked up into his gaze and with a small frown, spread and raised a small blue silk fan beneath her chin.

"I fear a 'lucky dog' strikes me as true to my circumstance. My greatest fortune is to be here in your garden this eve."

He had surprised even himself with such a fancy turn of phrase. Now it was Rebecca's turn to blush, though just the slightest pink rose to her cheek. He had meant to add, should have added "with you." She had, had she understood that? Now he instantly doubted, felt like a fool. This was not like bantering with a scullery wench or a beach doxie. Did she think he was grateful to attend on her corpulent uncle?

"I, ah, I have a good many wiles to learn from Kit and the likes of your dear uncle before any rightly call me shrewd or practiced like some of the foxes of Cayona."

They stopped at the edge of the flagging by the wooden fence dividing off the garden. At this end of the courtyard emerald and crimson hummingbirds hovered and darted in the cooling air. One suspended an instant between their faces and then was gone. Unthinking, both the girl and Jack reached up and rubbed a tingle at the end of their noses. They both laughed.

Jack glanced over his shoulder and saw the two Van Duyns turning their heads back to Captain Deinum, who related some tale in their native Dutch.

"I have gained one or two wiles or skills though, and had some profit in them."

Jack reached into his pocket and withdrew a small bundle wrapped in a embroidered silk kerchief. He had practiced his speech.

"I wish you to have these as a token of my aff ---, appreciation that, uh, before my good fortune you thought good --- Odds Blood!" He had not practiced well enough.

But it did not matter. Rebecca's lips were pursed in anticipation and her eyes fixed on her palm as she pulled back the folds of silk.

"Oh, they are lovely, Jack!" she said delightedly. He had given her two gold-mounted tortoise shell combs with three emerald chips set along each arc.

Now it was her turn to flush deeply. She glanced toward her uncle and stepped to one side to be shielded by Jack. She held up one of the combs.

"It is beautiful!" Her glance kept jumping from the combs to his face, and Jack found he did not know what to put on, to grin proudly, or to barely turn the corners of his mouth in casual assurance that he gave her a petty token of gratitude. Rebecca's face was equally uncertain, wavering between girlish delight in gleaming baubles to an intuition this gift was the first lure, the new initiation into the many rites of womanhood. The semaphore that shimmered between their faces in that instant, the heady play of delight and doubt, plucked small gasps from each of their mouths. Paralysis would have set in, at least for Jack, if Herr Van Duyn had not called out.

"It is near dark out here. I believe supper is set. Jack, pray join us at table. I see you are good company for young Rebecca."

Jack turned to him quickly. "My great pleasure, sir."

When he turned back to Rebecca the combs had disappeared somewhere in her gown. And though she had a demure smile, her eyes were lowered. As they walked toward the house her fingers reached out and touched the back of his hand. Jack shivered and was glad his boots could walk without him.

49 FLEEING LONDON, PARIS, ROME, VALLETTA

Within a handful of days Doctor Smeeks became a daily visitor. A stocky Dutchman with ruddy cheeks and gray-streaked hair to his shoulders, he was more a chirurgeon and barber than a physician, and perhaps favored more for his skills as a boon drinking companion than as a doctor. Each day he sent Jack down to the chemist at the Sign of the Unicorn for some new potion, but the old man never touched the half of them.

Still Smeeks gladly and loudly took credit for Kit's occasional "recovery" for a day or part of one. Others thought the devil might have more to do with it.

When Kit had made his first trip down into the town only two weeks after the hurricane he was hailed on all sides as a prodigy of good fortune and miraculous recovery.

But Jack, walking behind the palanquin saw many a clerk, whore, and pirate raise the two-pronged sign against the evil eye.

He knew they were right, but said nothing to anyone, not even the boys Under-the-Tree. The old mulatto woman was a witch. Yet she seemed kindly enough disposed towards himself. Though Old Kit avoided Smeeks potions, twice a day the old woman would emerge from her room beside the kitchen with an earthen bowl covered over with a damp cloth. He could hear the bar fall on Kit's door and then later, briefly, a voice that belonged to neither he nor the witch.

After the mulatto's visits Kit would shuffle briskly through the house, was eager to talk, even babbled, and for some brief hours he was keen of eye and word. It was then he called Jack into the room where he conducted business with his factors, captains and Madame Pearl, passed on the price of emeralds and judged the orient of pearls, or visited the Aeolus.

But his lassitude always returned and Old Kit retreated to his dark suite of rooms in the big house.

One morning, soon after the mulatto witch had left him, the old man sat on the edge of his bed clutching his twisted manatee-hide walking stick, seeming ready to launch into some soliloquy. So Jack quickly asked him a question he had wondered about many times.

"How did you come to Tortuga, Kit?"

"When I was stripling there were gypsy wagons passing on the road each spring and autumn along with the pilgrims. My father cobbled many a sorry sole," he began, not much to the point it seemed.

Kit rose and shuffled briskly to a chair. He sat, smiling for a moment at some inward thought.

"They camped in the woods beyond Canterbury Cathedral. I learned some chicanery and ... but there was a little gypsy girl, younger than myself, with eyes like a Spanish countess, who wheedled and bewitched me into smuggling her into the great holy building.

"I took my own favor in the shadow of the cathedral. I had shared strumpets with my friends before, but that day I wanted none but the eyes of God upon me." After several moments, he smiled. "I could have lost my stones."

After a long minute's silence, which Jack knew not to break, Old Kit began again, far from where he'd left off.

"After fleeing London I took a sealed carriage to Paris thinking to sell my soul to the French. But I was in such despair that, arriving in the city in a rainstorm, I felt compelled to seek the South. Valletta, its languor and sweat --- ah, cheeks hot and rouge misted," he said, unsteady fingers brushing his own liver-spotted cheeks.

"I left within the hour, in the night coach, carrying two bottles of brandy, both opened. The storm followed me south for three days. I reached Rome in a week, but the cardinal's agents were at my heels --- skewered them both --- and I took ship to Malta, then Cyprus, Crete, I searched for the plains of Troy in the land of infidel Turks, the river Scamander ---"

The old man, well in the throes of the witches' potion, babbled on, rising slowly in his chair and falling back into it arrhythmically as he proclaimed. He seemed blind to all but his memories.

"I sought like Telemachus did his magical father: I saw dark brown horses gallop across a grassy knoll that burned emerald under a white-hot sun; I walked the strand and sought Nausicca's kiss; lived in an orange house on Corfu. I ate lotuses and --- Ha! --- I married a man in Alexandria. But alas I could not stay long after murdering his poor brother in a duel. Yes, I had a sword!" He slapped his cupped hand against his codsack and laughed.

"Under the patronage of a mountain king in Crete I tried to brew a homunculus, but the king's confessor discovered our alchemists' lair and smashed the jar in his holy horror. I took to the winds again and built a house with the excess gold from my experiment."

Old Kit choked on his laugh and spit on the floor.

50 HOW KIT CAME TO TORTUGA

"After two years in the burning sun I was blind enough to write home. I took my letter to the port. After weeks of watching ships and passengers I found a courier of Thurn-and-Taxis to carry my note. Someone betrayed it."

Old Kit brooded for several moments while Jack watched silently.

"The king's spymaster had me kidnapped. I was shackled the entire voyage to Marseille and then stripped and locked in a velvet appointed coach that delivered me to the Bastille. Where I learned my employ was mandatory."

He sighed. "I have outlived all my masters."

The old man grew quiet, though his mouth seemed to work behind closed lips.

"You came here from Paris?" Jack asked as the trailing silence lengthened and the old man stared at nothing. Kit shook his head.

"In those days Paris stunk no worse than other cities and far less than London. Roses grew on the stonewalled courtyards where men played racquets, trading hits." Old Kit swung his right arm weakly. "Pack, pock, puck --- pick! When the ball glanced off the birch racquet and . . ."

Kit's mind drifted on. He muttered about lithe musketeers in blue velvet pantaloons, linen shirts, elbows and knees festooned with ribbons, batting the India rubber ball about. He had wagered on the matches, shouted encouragement to his favorites, plied the athletes with gold for the favor of a smile.

Guillaume was sent to him by an avenging Angel, he murmured. Kit had gone mad at the sight of his face, a madness he fell into often in those years as his own beauty and vigor waned. Still, then, he could still plumb a fundament and make them squeal. True, it was Guillaume's face, the round peach cheeks, dark twists of beard at the chin and sneering lips, the winter sea swept eyes that drove Kit into bumfucking hysteria, but what made him fall in love with Guillaume was -- again, the eyes – that he had cried. Didn't squeal, whine, curse, but cried. Cried when he saw his own young frigger begin to droop longer, like a stallion's. Kit watched the young musketeer's prick rising, the tears falling, saw the pink-framed ice eyes turn to his -- and was taken. Like a fish.

"Counterfeit tears, I fear," Kit said wistfully.

"What?" asked Jack, not really expecting the ancient one's eddying memory to return his words. "Did you play racquets?"

"No, no," Kit said hunkering lower in his chair. "I wagered and bought the favor of fair-favored musketeers."

Jack tried to hide a sour pucker on his lips. He hoped the old man didn't think he could still get it up for such sins.

"No cause there, Jack." Kit said. "That is in my past, alas. At least for the most part."

He gave the him a leering wink and then cackled.

"In those days there was one young man could turn my heart to anything and to almost any sum ... he was a randy coxcomb and he desired the favor of one of the Queen's loveliest handmaidens: a distant cousin of the King's whom Louis avoided as an incestuous liaison . . ."

Guillaume arranged his liaisons at Kit's great house. For his aid in the intrigue, Kit insisted on his own favor.

He was allowed to watch musketeer's jousting from the room above, laying on pillows in a darkened room, peering down on the bed through the floor's ingeniously hidden seam. Watching their candle-ruddied flesh cling and wrestle and pound softly together while he squeezed the life from his own prick. But when the full moon rose into the pear tree in the courtyard before the bedroom window the wench would extinguish the room's candles and lay on the bed sheets letting the tree bar and dapple with black shadow her moon-alabastered skin. Guillaume would groan and kiss her toes. Kit would peer too hard, eyes aching, to decipher their motley lovemaking; but his ears caught at each gasp, yip, grunt, groan and cry, while he stifled his own.

"The Cardinal," he said after a long pause. "He decided to sacrifice this loyal old bumfucking pawn; some gambit to threaten the Queen, no doubt, but I never deciphered it."

Jack had no idea of what he was talking about.

"Guillaume's affair at court was as little a secret as such things always are. But when Guillaume and I were arrested for crimes against nature, when all sundry knew she shared her Musketeer with an old man, why the wench had no choice but to abandon her position at court. And I . . ."

The old man began to cry without a sound.

"But how did you come to Tortuga?" Jack asked, hoping to stop the tears.

"It was the Duc de Richelieu," Kit said at once and bitterly. "As devious a man as ever walked firm earth. Though I had served him well on many occasion. And long before him Bacon, and both were Judas to me. It was to his purpose to conspire to trap me in a scandal at court."

Kit sighed.

"At the time I was already growing old by most men's measure. Still I was not near the ancient one you see before you. I still had a quick step then and with a little encouragement could roger whores of either sex. But old. It was my old man's folly to sponsor a young musketeer. I kept him in Belgian lace, and rapiers with silver-chased bells, and bought him trinkets he would give to his ladies.

"Richelieu! --- He contrived Guillaume's meeting with a lady-in-waiting who was also fancied by a certain prince. The Cardinal encouraged their dalliance, had me encourage it, too. Then," Kit shook his head. "The Cardinal's men, men I knew for years, burst in upon us in my rooms and made to arrest us for crimes against God and Nature.

"It took nearly my entire fortune, all my lands, to purchase my way out of the Bastille that time. And exile into a position with Louis' new West Indies Company.

"I was harbormaster of Cayona during that ill-fated venture." He snorted.

"But, still, Cayona has served me well. In just five years here I recovered twice my original fortune by my trade in jewels, was partner with old Gray in the Mermaid, and three other taverns and twice as many rum huts, and the sun, the sun is good to creaking old bones."

The very old man shook his head and his eyes seemed to clear. He brushed at the white wisps that seemed to float above each of his ears.

"Let's be up and about, Jack." He rose unsteadily and Jack steadied him. "I've got some emeralds to sell Jalyot, a cargo of teak for Van Duyn.

"Not much time for us. Not much time."

51 MADAME PEARL'S MOTHER

Jack and Madame Pearl sat watching over Kit as he snored softly in his chair. They were in the cool parlor off the aviary. The birds' coos and trills, whistles and words seemed to drift into the room.

Jack studied Pearl as she embroidered purple flowers on a lace kerchief, making a border around a monogram of golden threads. It reminded him of the fantastic stitchery that decorated the red velvet and satin gowns she wore in her brothel. This late noon at Kit's she wore a simple green silk dress, her bosom covered. Jack wanted her to talk, to look at him. She had not given any sign she had bedded him not many nights ago.

"Is that for you?" he finally asked, nodding at the kerchief. He could make out a golden H entwined with her P.

She smiled. "No. No, it is for my old mother. She is a true mistress of the needle, much better than I."

"That is very beautiful."

"She is very much better than I. But it pleases her that I follow her in this."

Pearl laid the needle down and looked into the room's shadows with her deep black stare.

"She made me such beautiful clothes when I was a little girl. 'My little Pearl' she would say; I was her only treasure. I remember a gorgeous red velvet tunic gleaming with filigrees of thread of gold. We had nothing else. She sewed for our bread. I still cannot imagine how she did it.

"The other children were jealous of my finery. None would play with me; I played by myself. We would walk down the path, I remember it still, and those little demons would scorn us and call us names and their mothers would look away and not even scold them. I remember hating them for the tears they made my mother shed. It was only later I knew she cried because me.

"They are cold-hearted bastards those Boston Puritans. Back then it was still called Shawmut. Just a village then. My mother names it that still."

"She lives there? Do you ever visit there?

"Yes, she does and no, I do not," Madame Pearl said wistfully. "She would be sad indeed to discover my enterprise in Cayona. No, she thinks me installed in a great house in the city of Geneva. I pay Thurn-and-Taxis a goodly sum each year to . . ." She broke off the thought. "Do you remember your mother, Jack?"

He was taken aback. No one had asked of his mother since he was very small. Under-the-Tree boys did not have mothers.

"I think so," he said. "I think I remember her sitting on the edge of my cot stroking my hair and out the door the sun is morning bright and two chickens are pecking at each other."

"You must have been very young. I do not remember the year the Spaniards raided those Ringot farms where they found you."

"Killed my mother and my father, speared me and left me for dead.

"I still have the scar on my back. I don't know if I really remember because there is no one to tell me what's true and what I used to dream. I was passed around by women who took pity, women at the back doors of all sorts of houses, until I was big enough to run errands for scraps and pennies. Then they shooed me off so they could take in another tottering orphan. I mostly raised myself, like everyone Under-the-Tree."

"You were lucky," Madame Pearl said and returned her attention to the embroidery. Sympathy was the rarest commodity in Cayona. Then she looked up with a smile and small laugh, glancing at Old Kit's slumbering face. "You are lucky. About the luckiest rascal from here to the Main."

52 AN UNSEEMLY SUGGESTION

The old man's vigor rose slightly and ebbed even further each day.

The cough he had caught so many weeks before never left him for long. It was worse this morning. It racketed clearly down from the upper floor to the kitchen where Jack ate his breakfast of bread and tea with Heidi the pig nosed, mole-speckled cook's helper. Each hack and heave Kit sounded put Jack a little more off his simple meal.

Kit had been in his latest doldrums for three or four days. But when Van Duyn sent to know whether he and Rebecca might call on him Kit had replied it would do him good. Jack no longer ran such petty messages; it was carried by one of the mestizos hired to replace the Gascons.

When the Van Duyns arrived Jack led Rebecca and her uncle to Kit's rooms. She seemed very shy and caught his insistent glances only once, very briefly. The old man seemed glib and hardy, certainly with no need to be propped up in his magnificent bed like he was. But Jack knew a secretive visit by the old housekeeper just an hour before had everything to do with Kit's vigor. Whatever medicine she practiced, it was potent.

Kit praised Rebecca's beauty and exclaimed how she had been a girl just one year ago upon her arrival, but now she was a young woman.

"Tropic climes bring all things rushing to blossom," he said.

Both she and Jack flushed at this; he for her sake. Old Kit soon suggested that Jack show her the lower halls of the house and the collection "trophies" and what-nots that she had never seen before.

Of course they ignored Kit's treasures, and ignored the trilling, chirping and jabbering of the aviary where they paced together back and forth.

Just that morning Jack had bartered powder, ball, muskets and half the lease of a barca longa for some pearls Kit deemed worth the ransom of Havana's governor. He felt exceedingly good about himself, about his talents and prospects. He told Rebecca how he would one day travel to Amsterdam, St. Malo, and London as Kit's agent, selling dear what was got so cheap in Cayona.

"And in London I'll dress more grand than any Duke," he said parading with his arms akimbo. "Cloth of gold from head to foot, diamonds at every finger, and a powdered peruke upon my head."

Rebecca laughed, shaking her straw-gold curls.

"Oh, Jack. A peruke is just a snob's name for a periwig. Only great merchants and lawyers call it that, my uncle says. They'll catch you out for sure. My uncle . . ."

Jack laughed at himself, too. Coming close beside her he bent over and quickly stole a kiss. He stood back smiling, cock-proud. But the girl stood there unmoving.

"Rebecca?"

She reached out and tangled her fingers in the netting of the aviary.

Jack stepped in front of her, but she turned aside, her face down. He saw a tear run down the side of her nose and she sniffled.

He fell to his knees in front of her and grabbed her other hand in both of his.

"Rebecca, I'm sorry! I've stolen a kiss before this ---"

She pulled on his hand and he stood. She put her arms around his waist and pressed her face into his shoulder, sobbing. Belatedly he put his arms around her shaking shoulders; his heart pounded to hold her, pounded with fear that he had made her cry, and burned in his chest with some triumphant pride that he could move her like this.

"I feel like a whore," she sobbed.

"What?" Now he felt ashamed. "I'm sorry. I didn't ---"

"Not you, Jack. It's not you. My uncle ---"

Jack stiffened, horrified. Rebecca looked up at him, her cheeks mottled red, wet and streaked, the rims of her nostrils moist and crimson; all of it served only to make her eyes more blue.

"He wants to push us together."

Jack sighed in relief. "He wanted our true affection to bind you to him when Master Kit dies. Even that we should . . ."

She gulped her tears, then wailed "Before we marry!"

Jack held her tight while she rubbed her wet eyes against his shoulder.

Van Duyn's plans for he and Rebecca had recently seemed quite transparent as glass to him. But he was still amazed the Dutchman would suggest --- then he felt a lump in his chest. Before we marry? Marry? Marry was some distant event of his desire for Rebecca. "Before we marry" meant a step much closer, it made clearer his lusty phantasm. A frequent one! He felt it closer than ever as her face and breasts pressed against his chest, as his loins felt the sobbing spasms of her stomach and enveloping rustle of her petticoats.

"Damn his eyes," Jack said quickly. "How could he wound you with such, such . . ."

"He said nothing to me," she pushed herself away, found a handkerchief and dabbed her eyes and nose. "He said it to the Major."

"DeBasco?"

She nodded.

53 "SQUEEZE HIM DRY . . ."

"I heard him and uncle in his cabinet arguing fiercely. I took off my slippers and crept closer to the door to hear.

"The Major said it would be years before Uncle could bind his fortune to Kit's by marrying us and 'twould be too late because Old Kit was dying for sure. And my Uncle said twas true, he was dying, and mayhap I could in a shorter time bind you closer."

The girl turned her back on Jack and put her face in her hands. The birds could feel the charge in the air and were screeching, yammering as if a storm were about to break. Jack put his hands on her shoulders and tried to draw her against him, but she shook free and faced him again.

"Beware, Jack," she said softly, but with a precise, hard edge reflected in the determined set of her delicate features. "Beware of my uncle and the Major and all of them. If he dies soon, they will be after Kit's ventures and treasures, my uncle says, like sharks on a bloody corpse. That's why he wants . . . Listen."

She stepped up to him and put her hand on his cheek.

"They are in fear Governor Ogeron will declare some unheard of tax and take for himself all that stands in Kit's warehouses, and all ships he does not have partners in. They say everything in this house, all his jewels -- all yours Jack, you are his heir now! --- the other traders will try to swindle and steal and claim they are held for appraisal. They count you little more than a youth they can cozen to aid them to steal more from yourself than the others will steal from you. The Major said 'Squeeze him dry and cast him away. He'll count himself lucky at that.'

"Jack," she grabbed hold of his waist. "Tell me it will run a happy course. Say Master Kit will recover; he looks well today. I pray it every night."

Jack held on to her, his mind rolling with hot dreams of anger and fear. Of what she had told him; of what he would do.

"Don't worry at all, Rebecca," he said heartily. "I have more reserves and allies than they guess."

She tilted her head up with a hopeful smile. He
raised his eyebrows, placed his finger beside his nose,
and nodded conspiratorially.

"Great reserves," he said, wishing he knew what reserves he could call on in the event Kit did die. But he
knew. None to any effect against the likes of those who
would descend on him.

Jack went and found the housekeeper. He told her
to tell Herr Van Duyn that Rebecca had felt a bit queasy
and, not wanting to disturb him and Kit, had asked Jack
to escort her back to the Van Duyn house on foot.

He took her on the long narrow path used by the
Under-the-Tree boys that went up behind her house. It
was the one that he once took to see if he could spy over
the wall into her room. By the time they came back the
other way on the broader road Rebecca's tears were dry.
Her face, though still red, was evenly flushed as if she
had walked too long in the heat. They talked very little
the whole way. Jack left her at the front gate and she went
into the house without looking back.

54 MARY'S CALAMITOUS TUMBLE

Kit now rarely left his rooms at all in the mornings, as if
exhausted by the ordeal of waking. But after the long,
hot siesta hours his old servant woman would briefly visit
him in his rooms. Then she retired to her own room
down the hall from Jack's room and the Gascons' -- now

the mestizos' -- bolting her door behind her. Shortly after her visits Kit would emerge from his own rooms, thumping down the hall on his stick, hale as a buccaneer and calling for bearers to carry him down to town, or for Jack to run and fetch some factor or merchant on business he was eager to address.

But still he never went down to the harbor as he had done often even shortly after his near drowning, and he could never hold out at his table at the Aeolus all night as before. Jack sat on a stool beside the old man's viceroy chair and lit his pipe for him, stoked the fire at his back until the others at the table groused and muttered and even made up excuses to leave.

It became apparent that despite the ministrations of the mulatto housekeeper, or even Smeeks, Old Kit would never truly recover from his near drowning. After rising above his first exhaustions he was declining slowly and surely. He began to call for the old mulatto woman's mysterious ministrations three times a day, but then rarely rallied for more than a short walk in the lower rooms with Jack. He needed three or four days between his brief visits to the Aeolus or the receipt of a visitor.

Even when he felt up to the Aeolus, Kit could no longer hold the prodigious amounts --- for an old man --- of French brandy that he could stomach just weeks before. And his stories wandered even further from the mark, and rose and fell to greater heights of declamation and absent muttering than ever, his head declining to soon hide in his arms on the table and rise in a moment with his racking cough. The sputum he dripped through pursed lips into a tacky rag was blood streaked and gray.

The chirurgeons Smeeks and Piron, and Ackley the chemist, attended on him and prescribed. Jack was down at Ackley's Sign of the Unicorn twice a day fetching some tincture, powder or foul unguent, until at last Kit halted all their ministrations. Only the visits of the old lady seemed to help, and those less and less, even when she closeted with him seemingly every hour. Jack saw his promised great fortune draining away with the color in the old man's face.

He did not need Rebecca's warning to know the other merchant's and captains of Cayona, Rebecca's uncle just one, were circling Kit's goods and treasures like sharks. And the port's Governor would be the biggest shark of all.

Then the housekeeper fell into a deep hole in her room and broke her leg.

Mary's squawking brought Jack and the Gascons' replacements to her door. She sounded strange, distant, shouting weakly for them to break in the door and help her. She had just returned from Old Kit's room and her door was barred.

The two man servants put their shoulders to it, but the door did not budge. Finally, Jack fetched a wagon stave to beat it down. But then Kit came clumping down the hall, lively and quick, cursing them for fools and sent them outside to pry open the shutters.

Jack climbed through the window. In the middle of the old woman's sparsely furnished room a trap door had been laid back. Looking in he saw the old woman at the bottom of her secret, little root cellar. Her skirts were askew and a short ladder lay across her moaning form.

After unbarring the door to admit Kit and the two servants, Jack got on his belly and swung his legs over, hung from the floor's edge and dropped a short ways to stand over groaning woman. She looked up into her room and cried out for her master to forgive her. He tied a splint on the woman's withered calf and guided her, caterwauling in his ear the entire time, as the two mestizos hauled her out of the pit with a rope tied beneath her arms.

She fainted before they lay her on the cot.

Beneath where she had lain was a pewter dish the size of a man's palm. Beside it, pressed into the dirt, was a pitted, speckled, greenish stone the size of a musket ball. Certainly not a gem. On a small dirt shelf in the side of the cellar was a glass bell jar sitting on its wooden base. There was nothing else in the little cellar.

Jack looked up to see Kit staring down, frowning but with fear in his eyes, staring past Jack at the greenish stone.

Still not looking at Jack, he raised a trembling hand and pointed at the stone. The other two mestizos now stood around the trapdoor's edge looking in curiously.

"Use the tail of your shirt to pick it up," Kit said with a sadness in his voice.

"Put it in the dish, put the dish under the jar, and bring it to my room."

The old man turned away from the cellar, suddenly walking as if weighted with a heavy yoke.

"Have one of these two get Smeeks to set the old hag's leg."

55 TEARS FROM THE MOON

Jack brought the ugly little stone, now sitting in pewter dish and housed beneath the glass jar, into Kit's library. The shutters were closed tight. The old man sat at his table bathed in the yellow light from lamps that bracketed him.

He stared down at the table and seemed to watch the fingers of his left hand trace out a pattern in the wood's grain. To Jack he looked more frail and withered, more ancient than ever before.

As he approached, Kit did not raise his eyes. Jack saw he was not daydreaming but staring at another stone much like the one he had in the bell jar, except this second one was shaped more like a small fig.

Jack sat the bell jar on the table. The room, except for the old man's rasping breath, remained silent for a long time. Finally Kit looked up with rheum-rimmed eyes.

"Close the door and pull a chair over here in front of me. I have a secret that . . ." The cough came on him and he caught it in a kerchief and motioned at the door.

When Jack had sat down across from him, the old man peered first at the stone in the jar, then the one on the table before him.

"I received these magic stones from an Indian sorcerer, a man from the vanished tribe that once lived in these islands, poor soul. The last of the Arawak.

"He gave me this stone," Kit said tapping the stone before him.

"And the other one much later. Ugly and pored they are, but they are magic --- believe me." He sighed a sigh that seemed to exhale the years.

"These stones fell from the sky, tears from the moon itself," he said, "and lay on altars beneath the gaze of the Arawak gods for more generations than even Homer could count."

The old man studied the stones again in silence. Occasionally he looked up at Jack through the curve of the glass bell. After some time he told Jack the tale of the stones and the man who was the last of the Arawak people.

He had been a year in Cayona when he first heard of the Arawak sorcerer and his medicines. At that time Cayona was a much smaller place. There was no doctor then or for some years after. The old Indian had been a great help several years past when the Spaniards drove the first buccaneers and others of the Brotherhood off Tortuga to refuge on Hispaniola. The old Arawak's poultices and infusions healed wounds and fevers no other could. When Kit complained he could find no relief in Cayona for his aches and agues, one of those first settlers had told him of the famous Indian sorcerer, though it was doubted he was still alive.

After months of searching and inquiry, Kit's servants found the old, old Indian in the hills above the plantations at the mouth of the Massacre River, far to the east along the Hispaniola coast. Kit traveled to the Arawak healer and received a potion that brought relief. After that Kit visited often, though the two day voyage was not to his liking. When the Spaniards raided and burnt the Massacre River plantations, Kit convinced the sorcerer to accept his protection in Cayona.

56 PONCE DE LEON'S DOG

The tale of the Arawak tribe was a sad one, Old Kit said gently, nodding his head. Gentlest of people, completely unlike the fierce, cannibal Caribs of the southern islands, the Arawak gathered fruit and yams, fished, hunted and rarely warred, worshipping their ancient gods, their "zemes," in caves high in the hills. On the alters before their clay and wooden gods they placed thin golden bowls. The Arawaks never mined for gold until the Spaniards enslaved them, but had fossicked the sparkling flakes and granules from jungle streams, beaten the soft, gleaming alluvial metal into bowls, then made earrings and bracelets to fill the bowls placed in the laps of their gods. And nestled like dark eggs in an auriferous nest were the pocked green and brown stones, gifts, signs of favor from the zemes.

"Fallen from the moon or high beyond, a brickbat of a fallen star, no doubt," the old man said. Fallen on a night many generations ago, gathered and passed among the Arawak, carried to their scattered alters.

After three generations in the dark and damp of the holy caves, it was told to Arawak children, the moon stones became dappled with a soft, azure mold not of this world. When the priests touched the stones they soon danced before the gods and heard their holy voices. If the priests kissed the stones they would fall into a deep swoon while their spirit journeyed to the home of the gods on the dark side of the moon, and there the priests spoke with the dead and the unborn. And the priests who spoke with the gods lived to be old, old men, much older than the rest of the Arawak tribe.

But the gods could or would not protect the Arawak.

When the Santa Maria foundered on a reef the Indians welcomed Columbus as a celestial brother.

"More like a cursed Jonah that could never be tossed back into the sea."

Those poor souls helped him build the settlement of La Navidad from the broken ship's timbers and they cut the thatch for the Spaniards, too. From the hills they brought Columbus dozens of water jars, big arrobas of cotton, and their little ear rings and pendants of gold. The Spaniards brought with them to the islands the pox and plague, and the whip, torques and chains, muskets, and mastiffs to hunt the Arawak down in packs and tear their flesh from their bones.

"Ah, Becerillo," Kit shook his head with a wry smile. "Ponce De Leon's war dog helped preserve the secret, bless that cur. It seems the great captain captured a high Arawak priest very near a holy cave. When DeLeon questioned the man as to his longevity and that of the other Methuselah's of his tribe, the priest broke free with a start. He would have been easily re-captured in a dozen paces but this dog Becerillo, a mighty beast and already frothing with bloodlust, broke his own leash and in one bound leapt and tore out the Arawak's throat.

"That was as close as Ponce De Leon ever came to the Fountain of Youth."

Kit sighed.

"Because it is here that you enter those waters, only by the kissing of these stones. You are carried there, at the penultimate moment, to an island below the rising sun where you are bathed in the sweet waters of heaven rising from the bowels of Eden. The magic waters caress and cleanse you in a warm, tossing froth of silver light."

After this Old Kit was silent for some time. Jack nodded his head a bit and broke the spell.

"I wonder if I shall go there again." The old man shrugged and stared briefly at Jack. Then he smiled. "De Leon was so very near. All the common Indians he questioned knew of the fountain, the stream, knew the priests journeyed there. The priests told them of it as if it were a real island far away to the east. The isle of Ananeo, or some called it Boyuca, or Bimini."

Kit laughed a little.

"Perhaps if that old Arawak priest had spent an afternoon on the rack, perhaps not. The Arawak were not great warriors, but they were brave. On the south coast where they must needs fend off the anthrophagi Caribs, they knew how to test a man. They'd strip a prisoner naked, Carib or Spaniard if they got one, and tie 'em to a stake and stick him thick with long thorns, from chin to heels, then skewer every thorn with a wad of cotton till the man was fluffed like a new owlet. Then they lit him into a blaze. If he sang his defiance he was deemed a worthy fellow."

Kit raised his head and looked around the room as if trying to regain his bearings.

"War and disease. Those were gifts Columbia brought them in the end.

"And the Cross," Kit added with a bitter chuckle. "The cross to lighten their other burdens.

"Many just fled with priests to their holy caves and never left. They say the caves are crowded with their skeletons, stumbled through, broken and scattered by treasure seekers."

57 THE LAST OF THE ARAWAK

The last Arawak was born high in the mountains of Hispaniola, destined to take his place in the line of his father and grandfathers, priests that worshipped and served at the most remote and revered of the holy caves. But there had been only seven of the tribe left in the last Arawak's boyhood. He had been forced to take his sister as his bride. Over his long life all the rest had died but him, even his one son and heir had died of a fever none of his sorcerer's skills could cool.

This ancient Arawak had not conversed in his own tongue, except with the gods, for nearly fifty years when old Kit had met him.

"We became what could be called friends, colleagues in our alchemical arts. But it was five years before he told me of the caves and the magic stones, these Philosopher's Stones. The only true ones I shall ever know."

Kit rapped his knuckles lightly on the table and shook his head.

Jack said nothing, just continued to listen. There was a treasure at the end of this tale; of that he was sure.

The last Arawak had not visited his holy cave for a dozen years, too feeble to make the journey alone and fearing any others would sack and desecrate it for its meager trinkets of gold. But Kit convinced the man to let him send him on a pilgrimage guarded and cared for by trusted servants, though the old Arawak had gone the last miles alone to worship in solitude, to protect the secrecy of the place, to worship in his own tongue for the last time.

"When he returned he brought three of these moon stones nested in damp mosses in an earthen jar."

Kit hacked and spat into the cold fireplace behind him.

"One stone I buried with him ten years past." He shook his head. "He said to me that he was returning to the cave of his 'zemes.' Then he lay himself down and put that stone in his mouth . . . quivered just once and was gone like blown leaf."

Jack had said nothing for the better part of an hour.

"These stones are indeed from the gods. His or ours." Kit said shrugged his bony shoulders. "I'd wager my soul on it. Indeed, I may have."

He paused.

"The true Philosopher's Stone they be, spawning the elixir of life on their rough hides. In my life I had tried all the alchemical physicks, the golden-salted potions and glistering clysters. But . . ." He raised the fig shaped stone and kissed it. "The merest brush of the lips on that azure powder has brought the angels down to court me."

He closed his eyes.

"That magic mold has preserved my heart, my liver, lungs, like some infernal, unnatural salts. I'm near a hundred and six, Jack. Have you heard of any man, save out the Bible, to live so long? What man sees even four score without becoming a doddering babe?"

"You're the oldest man in all the wide world. It's what they say in town."

Jack watched Kit pinch the bridge of his nose and a tear drop to the table.

"Age sucks the sand from beneath one's feet with every wave, every day."

He looked up and pointed to the glass bell, struck a sharp ting with a cracked, yellow fingernail.

"The new beard of immortality that these stones grow, it will not thrive in my cellar. At best, it was preserved down there. And now, since you pulled me from the creek, instead of a gentle touch of my forefinger when the moon was full, I must softly kiss the stone each night and day --- and it will soon be bare. I'll be licking the dirt from it . . ."

Jack did not ask the question. Black shadow and golden swaths swirled in a formless adventure, stirring in his chest and bowels. His hands gripped his knees; he stared at the old man's lowered, shining head waiting for him to lift it and look him in the eyes.

"I have a friend whose plantation is not many leagues from that Arawak's cave. After his final pilgrimage . . . or maybe his next to last . . ." Kit looked up, glanced away, cleared his throat. "You shall have whatsoever you desire, whatever can be bought or stolen. I will divide my wealth and give you half.

"I have declared you my heir to all and sundry, Jack. I have affixed my seal to that testament. But you are a

Cayonan. You know the ways of this town. Long pig!" He made a bitter snort.

"They are like cannibals, my compatriots. Governor Ogeron, Van Duyn, Bartholomew, Smeeks, Guez, perhaps even Madame -- no, perhaps not she," he said.

As an afterthought he gave Jack a half-hearted wink.

"Long pig is how they see you, see all men. Eat them or be eaten by them. More cunning and vicious, all of us, than any beasts of the forest. And they are right. In this town's savage commerce there is blood and there is gold. Nothing comes to us that isn't compounded first of human flesh and death. Cayona gobbles up these pirates as easily as if they were turtles turned on their backs. We pluck their pearls from them like open oysters."

Now the old man was nearly shouting, his face livid and splotched in the lamplight.

"They trade us fortunes for tots of raw rum! We devour these pirate long pigs as they first devoured the substance of others -- and we spit their bones back into the sea!"

A cough seemed to rise, but Kit hawked and spit it away as blood and phlegm.

"With my fortune as the prize no one in Cayona will show you quarter, Jack. And you have small defenses, as yet. You can barely cipher, though you have a knack for it. No alliances, no secrets. A sharp eye, though, and . . ." Kit sighed, shook his head and gave Jack a grim smile.

"Little long piglet, that's you. Our comrades would cut your throat and hang you by your heels to drain. Lucky if they let you slink back to Under-the-Tree."

Kit paused, but Jack could not speak, hearing already his own musings vehemently spoken.

"And there would be no little freckled bosom of Rebecca's on which to rest your weary head." The old man chuckled.

"But you must keep my secret, boy." He tapped the bell jar again. "I doubt I'll live out the month without . . ."

He broke into a long ragged cough which Jack could not be sure was real. "And you must leave in the morning."

Jack said nothing. He saw a black cave churning with angry gods waiting to clutch the fools who entered.

"It won't be a hard journey." Kit said after awhile. "I have friends along the way. You will have a map the Arawak helped me draw. I think the cave can be found with it. I hope it is so, for both our sakes. Watch for bats at sunset, the Arawak said."

Jack's mouth was dry. The shadows of Indian ghosts fluttered briefly across his mind's eye. So did the gleam of Kit's golden fortune disappearing between his fingers. Long pig.

"I beg you this, Jack," the old man whined and looked up at him.

Jack nodded.

Part V

HISPANIOLA

58 CROSSING TO HISPANIOLA

Before dawn a soft wind rose out of Tortuga's hills and rocky bluffs.

The fishing and cargo freiboats raised sail. Jack huddled in the bow of one, surrounded by small kegs of musket balls and powder. The pack on his knees held the Arawak's precious map, letters to Master Kit's factors and friends to be found along the way, a shirt, hard cheese and biscuits, a small pair of silver tongs wrapped in cloth, and at the bottom a small, latched mahogany box containing a bell jar harboring an empty nest for a magic stone.

Their small fleet tacked across the bay to pull through the southeast mouth of the harbor and then caught the wind full on, sailing wing-and-wing down to dark Hispaniola.

Dawn first came to the distant high peaks of Hispaniola, peaks that just a moment before had seemed bright stars in the night sky. To the aft, red fringed the shadow of Tortuga, then a burning wire etched it's mountains. The stars disappeared in an instant and the black sea suddenly flickered with gold and ultramarine. Now Jack could see the mainland's far, gray massifs looming over the jade dark jungle, high forests and plantations. Soon after, the warming jungle's evanescent dews, colored saffron, crab-lemon, and mauve, rose like thin smoke and, slowly carried up the slopes by the morning wind, disappeared on the heights.

The sun, already white hot, had not yet cleared the edge of the sea when their beam plunged into the sand a few hundred yards from the river's mouth. He would follow the river into the heart of Hispaniola. The boat's two sailors, Jack, and the three other passengers clambered out and pushed the boat up on the beach. Jack reached in and pulled out his pack. As he turned he saw, just a few paces away, a body awash on the morning sand. What was left of a man's chest and face was already being picked through by gulls searching for a succulent crab.

"Crabs off a corpse can be sold for good money to the witches in Valetta," observed one of the sailors as he unloaded his kegs on the beach.

Another cargo boat beached between them and the corpse, sending the gulls squawking and flapping into the air.

Jack grunted in reply and walked purposefully across the beach. What kind of omen is that? he wondered.

Under the first palms, setting on mats of banana leaves, were rude towers of dried beef stacked as high as his chin. They would go to Cayona on the next tide with the returning freiboats, provisions for the town and the ships in the bay. Jack veered back and forth as he made his way between them and then through stacked pallets of tobacco and kegs of molasses. Past this, in the deeper shade, whole limbs of bananas lay like corpses to be counted. Next ranks of goatskins bloated with wine from the high plantations waited to be traded in bulk for bottles of Oporto.

Back farther from the cargo-laden beach were dozens of buccaneers lounging against the palms. These hunters were fresh from the mountains, crusted with filth, most already drunk, flush with gold for the dried beef and boar and the dickers of skins they had sold the evening before.

Boucan fed half the ships from the Keys to the Main, the half not Spanish.

They laughed and shouted among themselves, eager to be off with the next tide for the annual, blissful debaucheries that would leave Cayona richer and them penniless once again.

Their sleeveless cowhide coats were near rotted through where they tied together over sweat and rum-soaked ragged shirts. Their knee-length leather pants were invariably newer, indeed hardly tanned. Their long, oily locks were all surmounted by tall cones of dark leather, hats whose tiny visors could hardly shade the furrows of their brows, much less keep the sun from their eyes. That little crescent, Jack knew, actually shielded their eyes from falling fire ants their hats often dislodged from some rotting limb during a march or manic, gleeful chase after wild cattle.

The two long Flemish knives, now in scabbards thrust in their pants would be raised like candles as they dashed through the trees --- he hoped he might see them in a hunt somewhere in the uplands, but he doubted he would have that chance. Each of the buccaneers also had his musket propped beside him: a Gelin of Nantes or a lighter, longer Brachie from Dieppe. Hollowed gourds tied to their belts held powder and a large pouch held their ball. Their long manchettes, almost like cutlasses, were sheathed in alligator hide scabbards.

Jack strode quickly past the troops of roisterous and slumbering hunters, giving all a wide berth.

The bamboo and pine huts of the upland plantations' beach factors stood where the palms began to mix into the forest. Here, too, were a few thatch ajoupas and sheds for the tobacco, and various sorts of timber stacked in huge ricks.

Jack found the factor with no ears easily. The man at the hut, who he had shown Kit's first letter to, said he was at the river, and each person there sent him further up the river's beach until a mulatto wagoner nodded toward a man just a dozen paces away. He paced about in the sand, directing three mestizos loading small powder kegs into a beached boat.

His indigo pantaloons and waxed, dagger length mustachios betrayed a man of vanity. Where he once had ears were two gauze patches on a strong cord tied around his forehead and knotted beneath a black, pleated bun at the nape of his neck.

Jack stood to one side until he caught the man's attention. No Ears' black stare was fierce yet calm. Jack stammered a bit telling him the beach factor had sent him for the first boat upriver to the Roux plantations and Bassin Bleau. The man did not answer and just turned his attention back to the powder kegs. Then he reached out with his palm up.

"An 'eight," he muttered. Jack would have been shocked, but he was watching tiny flies whirr about the thin patch over the florid scar and dark hole, a hole large enough for . . .

"An 'eight," No Ears growled, but did not turn his head. Jack hurriedly pulled his purse. He stuck the coin in the man's hand and found his fingers squeezed and twisted sharply.

"Par grace," Jack groaned quietly and then shouted it before he was let go.

No Ears still did not turn his head. He pointed quickly to a long boat surrounded by men calling good byes and insults to others along the river bank. Then he strode over to the men loading the gunpowder and shouted for them to hurry.

59 THE BOATMEN'S INN

Jack helped shove off and clambered in. The four oarsmen dipped their blades into the water and the helmsman said "And heave" once, then let them set their own stroke. One rower propped his peg leg against the rib of the broad, shallow boat. Another started a chantey that no one joined.

Along the west bank a flotsam of boats and rafts were beached every few yards. Cargo was loaded and unloaded by mestizos and buccaneer's valets, or indentured servants who, cursing, shouldered baskets, jugs, and dickers of skins up the bank to storehouses beneath the tall ceibas and palms.

Gradually, fewer boats and men inhabited the banks and after two long bends in the river their signs had disappeared altogether. The rafts and boats were replaced by cayman lying beached in the sun.

Little birds pecked maggots and ticks from their horny backs. Now and then one of the lizards opened its gaping, toothy maw, yawning as the first blanket of the day's heat settled over the river. The rainbow gleam of dragonflies eddied in and out of the shadows where the trees overhung the slow current.

Jack tied a knot at each corner of a kerchief and, laying it on his head, nestled down between a butt of wine and his own bundle, then lay his cheek against the gunwale and stared across the water.

The midday passed slowly. There was little talk. Jack was lulled by the placid river and the dark forest that towered out of the water itself.

Here and there a crocodile lay half out of the slime on a muddy island, or on the shallow side of a bend in the river a baker's dozen of herons and dawn red flamingos waded and dipped their beaks in the muck.

Only at these river bends were there any sign of mankind beside themselves. Far to stern just rounding the previous bend two other boats drew up the river, and ahead another disappeared, swallowed by the shimmering green just as they were sighted. For the rest they were alone.

The oars creaked in the oarlocks, their blades splashed lightly, gurgling softly as drawn through the green water, and were raised, dripping blinding diamonds. The oarlocks creaked. Jack shut his eyes and sank into dreams.

Something brushed his cheek and he grabbed his kerchief as it was tugged from his head. He opened his eyes and jerked his face aside from a branch. The boat slid beneath overhanging boughs into the jungle's shadow.

A small cayman slithered from a muddy patch of bank just before the bow bit in with a bump.

Jack began to dig in his bag, but the helmsman tugged at the sleeve of his shirt and told him gruffly to leave off. He shared the boatmen's meal of smoked pig, flat bread and bananas. A jug of water passed from hand to hand.

The oarsmen lauded the cool shade, but to Jack's skin, so used to Tortuga's almost constant winds, the shadows were stifling and the smell of the mud rank.

The boatmen rested through the zenith's hour. He stared off. He tried not to think of the Arawak sorcerer's cave. A dragonfly glided over the shadow dark water. The giant mangroves stood above the mud and water of the river's edge on huge roots, gnarled columns as thick as a man's thigh. The dragonfly touched Jack's hand, then zigzagged away over the river, over the shadow dark water, entered and disappeared into the twisted arcade of roots. He did not see it emerge.

They beached their boat before nightfall at a small river town. Half a dozen other boats were pulled up onto the mud or tied to the short dock.

Before Jack and the others had covered their cargo with a tarpaulin, two other cargo boats ran up onto the beach next to them.

The crews all cursed each other with good humor, eager to join their comrades already carousing noisily, calling to them from out of the town's two taverns or the rum huts beneath the trees.

At that moment daylight was struck from the sky and dark night raised. The little river town was a huddling of two dozen shanties and ajoupas where the forest had been cleared away from the river's bank. There were inns facing the river. Both had low walls of palm logs and steep, palm-thatched roofs. Smoke rose with barely a twist from the center of the roofs and disappeared among the first stars.

Jack went with the boat's crew into the largest of the river inns. This was The Silver Platter, and a large mahogany board to which a silver platter had been nailed was its sign. A boar was roasting over a pit of coals in the center of the single large room. Tables and benches surrounded the pit and ran along the walls.

An old man turned the spit. Jack's stomach growled. He watched the glistening beast revolve. Its grease ran down along its tusks and dripped from their points with each turn. Chickens and bananas roasted in the gray coals at the edge of the pit. The aromas of bird, boar and fruit made his mouth fill with spit.

The shouts for wine and the calls of the old man brought in the proprietor from an out building. This man had a black-stubbled face that dripped sweat where it pooled in his chin's cleft, a small hump on his back, and carried two slopping full pitchers of wine in his hands which he slammed down on the boatmen's table. His customers dashed the dregs out of the tankards left on the table by the last drinkers and filled up their own.

The benches were filling with shouting oarsmen. The innkeeper bellowed as if to shake down the roof and soon two wretched looking boys trudged in from the way he had come with more pitchers. The innkeeper wiped his hands on his leather apron. He took a platter heaped with bones and fruit skins from an empty table and tossed the remains onto the fire. He squatted, setting the platter next to the coals, pulled a pronged fork from his waistband and stabbed out four chickens and a dozen bananas onto the plate.

He took a jug setting next to the old spit turner's stool and poured some wine over the birds to wash off the ashes. He sat the platter before the men from Jack's boat and hurried off to fill a platter for the next crew.

The men tore the chickens apart. The steersman tossed a leg on the table in front of Jack and then a steaming green banana. Jack bit into the charred meat and then tossed wine over his burnt tongue. The chickens were gone in moments.

Jack chewed clean the leg bone and tossed it on the smoking coals beneath the roasting boar. Wing bones, back, thighs, neck, ribs and shattered wishbones followed. The last chicken leg arched through the air and bounced off the old man's noggin.

"Whoresons," shouted the taverner as he and a cook marched out from the kitchen carrying the largest silver platter Jack had seen in his life.

And he had seen many on the docks of Cayona. This also appeared the finest wrought, as the two men carried the huge platter on its side to get it through the kitchen's door. Its gleaming argent rim and face writhed with men and beasts, serpents and vines.

They set the silver platter on the table behind the spit. Both men groaned as they lifted the crackling brown pig over the coals and set it on the platter. Then, in what was their nightly ritual, the boar was carried from table to table to be torn to pieces by the diners. Passing the old man who stood dumbly by his station, the innkeeper shot out a kick in the pants, growling "More wine, more wine."

A ham was hacked roughly from the pig and set steaming and dripping in the middle of their table. Jack did not speak to his new messmates, just minded his tankard and took whatever pieces were shoved his way on the table with the blade of a knife.

These boatmen ate fiercely, but they did not drink like Cayona's carousing pirates, flush or destitute. There was not a fight all evening. Four men diced, but the rest, bellies filled, pulled slowly at their pipes and tankards. They would be pulling at their oars in the dawn. They talked about their host.

60 A GOD FORSAKEN PARADISE

The Silver Platter was kept by a father and his son. It was the son who had served them. The father had been a tavern keep in Bristol as a young man and there he had many times kicked rowdy slavers out the door at the bell, but here he manned the kitchen, where he kept the stock

pot and worked on the perfect salmagundi, a perfect al-
chemy, the Philosopher's Salmagundi.

Everyone traveling that river had heard of the beef salmagundi at The Silver Platter. The old taverner had rung
many changes on this gallimaufry salad, adding at different season's meat of violet crabs or manatee, grapes, liver,
figs, dressed it with blonde to brunette rums or imported
brandies, sprinkling in tiny peppers like scarlet pupas or
golden phalli. He loved chunked melons of every sort,
and he always finished with a squeeze of crabbed lime before serving it in swift, tossing flourishes --- said he had
had his fingers mauled by slavering men anxious for his
salmagundi.

The son and his helper slid the remains of the boar's
carcass onto a table on the far side of the room where
some men of the town sat, well apart from the river men.
They carried the grease-slick platter back into the kitch-
en. Each night after the platter had been washed, the
steersman of Jack's boat said, the father or son sat polish-
ing the silver platter until the night birds stopped calling
in the darkest hour. The platter was as long as Jack was
tall, a shining, knotty silver oval. It was tedious task and
so, if asked, the father would recount the adventures de-
picted on the plate.

Jack asked, "Has no one ever stolen the Silver Platter?
Or tried to, I mean?"

The old innkeeper, the father, was seated on the spit
man's stool scrubbing the spit with a tattered loofah.

"It's been stolen by many men," said the innkeeper.

The peg leg boatman made a low "Arghh." He rapped Jack's shin under the table with his oaken leg. Every other man at the table either grimaced or glowered at him.

"But it's never been stolen from this tavern, not since I settled here a score and eight years ago. It intrigues all Brothers of the Coast what with our larcenous envy, but none would consider taking it. Unless, of course, he needed it. I'd give the silver platter to any man if he could honestly say he needed it."

He looked up at the men here in his tavern, knowing that no one would claim that the silver platter was needed by anyone on the river more than it was needed by the old man at The Silver Platter. To Jack's surprise no one spoke or interrupted what he could see was to be an oft told tale; twice thrice told tale for most of them. The old innkeeper was held in some begrudged but real respect.

"I'm a philosopher," the old man said. "My metaphysic tells me that I'm foolish to trust any man. But as Brothers of the Coast each man is his own and all he owns belongs to each man. There is no cause to steal."

Here the innkeeper seemed to lose his chain of reason.

"We are citizens of a country without taxes," he said after a pause.

"No, no, not taxes," the peg leg moaned resignedly.

"The Frenchies are great taxers," the innkeeper continued. "Rum is five times the cup more in Tortuga than the clear drippings in your cups tonight. Here you drink and eat for pennies and not cobs and eights, not doubloons.

"If I need a man's ax I take it, and he's welcome to mine. That's a buccaneer's creed. That's the way it used to be both sides of the strait.

"But the Brotherhood is a pot o' rot, ha, it's gone, on Tortuga. And Cayona's a festering sore on the butt of Paradise.

"It's only here, on Hispaniola, along the river and up in high plantations and forests. It used to be there were no slaves, not even indentured whites, here on the mainland or on Tortuga. Ha! I remember Cayona when it was a woman-less village of freibooters and fishermen. There was not a slave down the Windward Passage till it tipped Cuba's snout."

"No female slaves for sure," the peg leg said. It seemed to be his duty. Everyone else passed a bottle back and forth across the table as they prepared to sleep with five or six tots of brandy. But the peg leg didn't reach for the bottle. He just listened to the old man and tossed out asides without any relish. His consternation with Jack was going to be a grudging one, the boy could see that.

"No slaves at all. No servants. Messmates one and all, all for one and one for all. No constables or sheriffs."

The innkeeper spit into the coals.

"No sheriffs at all. If a man's a sneaking murderer there is always two, three good souls around who'll kill him. And if a man's a thief --- well, so many of us have suffered the lash, we'd rather hang 'em than stripe a brother's back. At least that was how it used to be.

"Men tilled soil on Tortuga, men sailed the winged freiboats in the straight between and men hunted beef and boar here in these forests and up in the wild meadows. There weren't no temptress Eves in this God forsaken Paradise . . ."

61 The Shield of Hercules

One by one the boatmen were falling asleep on their folded arms. Some had begun to snore. Some had already retreated to the dozen plank pallets that lined the walls. And it seemed more were lunging out the door to surrounding ajoupas.

The washed platter had been carried out of the kitchen and placed on a bare table for the innkeeper's nightly task.

Jack moved to a bench near him for a closer look at the workings on the glistening tray. The old man's rag-covered finger now wiped lovingly over grooves and ridges that limned dozens of awful monsters and heroes.

In the center of the great silver platter the man polished two large eyes that seemed to gather not light but darkness under the terrible furrow of the brow. Then he buffed the bright, argentine teeth.

"Fear," the innkeeper said to Jack, drawing the rag over its tangled locks.

"And this figure above it that drags the dead youth by his heels is Fate itself. Here," he pointed "is Strife."

The old man named each of the lustrous, allegorically distorted figures surrounding the face of Fear.

"Here is implacable Pursuit close on the heels of terrified Flight, this confusion of limbs" --- he pulled the rag taut over a long thumbnail and dug among them --- "this is Tumult, these stumbling men Panic, and here below the chin is their grim Slaughter."

Jack stared, amazed at the tiny silver-ribbed breasts pierced by lances; a severed head caught between a rock and weed.

"What ---," he began.

"The Shield of mighty Hercules," the innkeeper said "The greatest hero of all the ancient world. This platter was cast for some Neapolitan grandee long ago, I have been told by a smith who should know. It was to have been service for the Viceroy of High Mexico's table, but she never made it past the Windward Passage."

Jack's eyes roamed over the shining figures. Encircling the figures were twelve intertwined vipers, their heads rising from the coils, fangs long and mouths wide to strike. Each white eye glittered menacingly.

Then a grim-face giant in plumed helmet --- "Ares, god of wars" --- thrust out sword and spear with each arm, driving teeming, armored soldiers down each side of the ring of snakes until they transformed into the god's own stallions racing till the herds collided, vanguards rearing and striking with their hooves.

These figures of battle were surrounded, where the edge of the huge platter began to rise, by a sparkling, turgid band of sea. In it fat, shining dolphins swam, chasing tiny fishes through the water. Jack could see glints of gold on the little fins, gilt that had long since been polished from their scales.

Around the broad rim of the shining platter chariots raced with their wheels close together, some overturned, and men fought with spears and bows while women watched from high, gleaming towers set all around the compass except at the peak where, above the face of Fear and the god of War, a woman the innkeeper called the Darkness of Death peered with mournful eyes from beneath her cowl. Only in its shadow did the tarnish remain.

Edging all, the outer rim of the shield or mighty platter, were the broad silvery waves and glimmering spume of the Ocean. Swans alternately soared above or paddled among the metallic swells.

The hanging lantern's light struck the sheen of silver, glaring from Fear's cheeks, scattering scintilla sparking and dying and glinting among all the figures. Light seemed to heap the platter with a palpable luster and ring it one last time with a halo.

"It is a fine platter," said Jack after a long while.

"Aye, it is." The old man lastly rubbed the tarnish from the brow of Darkness.

"The Shield of Hercules," the old man said. "Did you ever hear of Hercules' thirteenth labor?"

Jack had not heard of the first twelve. He considered if he should be snoring like his companions from the river boat.

"It seems," said the innkeeper. "It seems Aphrodite, she was the goddess of love, she took a hankering to Hercules, whose cock was as mighty as the rest of him . . ."

62 RIVER TALES

When the boatmen, and Jack, heard the first town drunk lurch in gagging for brandy they knew it was time to go out and push their boats into the river. As always, the dawn appeared first on the black lips of the river forest, hesitating briefly in a pink, bronzed glimmer, then snapped out to the zenith like a lizard for the last flyspeck star.

They dipped their oars and pulled deeply into the waters to feel it through their shoulders. They rolled their shoulders and groaned, and began complaining about the past night's food. Jack yawned and hunkered down in the bow.

They pulled upstream with three other boats. The garrulousness of the chill morning was soon quieted by the hot morning sun. The curtain of forest, the colossal trees bound, knotted, woven with vines, seemed still as stone.

"My creaking beams."

An oarsman called a halt, raising his oar with a squeak. The boat swerved out of line with the broken stroke. The man leaned out, reached in the green water and plucked out by its whipping tail a tiny crocodile. The man laughed and turned to the peg leg rower.

"This lad's no bigger than your ta --- "

There was a snuffling grunt and a little splash behind them. Jack rose a bit and saw a dark eddy course the river and sprout horny nostrils.

He almost screamed, but it was gulped to a peep. The wiggling lizard was dropped back in the water.

"Heave ho!" the helmsman shouted, the oarsmen shouted a ragged "Uno, dos, tres!", put their heels in the boat's ribs and drew deep.

Jack tumbled and bumped his head on the gunwale. He was glad to hear the laughter on the fourth stroke, a laugh of relief. Jack had seen scores of small caiman on Tortuga, and huge, scaly skins, but none that looked so long as that gliding shadow.

"How's our distance," the helmsman called to Jack after looking over his shoulder. "I can't see its snout."

Jack stood again to see if he could sight the reptile's form under the surface. The wake of its tail would be lost in their own ripples.

"Nothing I can spy."

"Don't stop," the peg leg exhorted his mates. "Ten more good strokes."

One of them lost count and halted at nine, skewing them again. Once they had straightened and begun their common stroke, the peg leg let out a sigh.

He had a tattooed crocodile running from his shoulder to his right elbow, a toothy beast done in blue and green with a red eye.

"Nom de Dieu! Those lizards scare me worse than perdition. Those mother crocodiles are more jealous of their newborn pups than a mongrel bitch."

He blew out another breath, breathing a lot shorter than the others.

"Why if the birds start rooting up their nests in the beach sand . . ."

Now he pulled the kerchief off his shaven head and mopped his brow. "Why those lizard's swallow up their eggs and keep 'em in their stomachs 'til the danger is passed. Then they bring 'em up out their belly and bury 'em again. "

He chuckled a little and retied the yellow-dotted kerchief over his skull.

"The little beasts must take some lesson in it," he said as the helmsman motioned with his hand and all took up the stroke again without a word. "I've seen 'em all fresh-hatched, sporting and playful like whelps with their dam, and run in and out of her throat like rabbits into their hole."

"Bah!" said the peg leg's bench mate.

"God's truth. They've got prodigious big stomachs and stretch 'em further by swallowing stones. When they grab some salvage cow or boar that's crossing at a ford and drag it under the water the stones give 'em, even the not so big ones, the extra ballast to stifle their prey."

"Bah," the man said again. The oarsman who had pulled the infant caiman from the river spoke up.

"They may not swallow rocks, but I have seen them carry great quantities in their jaws." The helmsman nodded his assent to this.

"We used to lay cow hides in the fields to dry in the sun and the crocodiles would come a hundred yards up from the river to steal them and drag them back. We could see our stolen hides on the river bottom, well loaded with stones." He nodded in agreement with his own story. "The lizards left them there for days, until the hair fell off and they had rotted to what taste they most enjoy. They fought over those hides like dogs over tripe."

"Nom de Dieu" the peg leg shouted and dropped his oar. Everyone else looked about the boat for a furious caiman. "These beasts, they swallow stones by the score"

His bench mate drew in his lips for another Bah! then thought better of it.

"I myself have seen it," the peg leg continued, looking challengingly at everyone in the longboat. "I was washing my tent one day at the riverside.

"I'd just begun when a crocodile fastened his jaws on it, shaking it with a fury and pulling it into the water. An't, it being my only tent, digging in my heels and heaving back as hard I could.

"By the blessed saints I had a butcher knife in my teeth for to scrape the tent. That lizard grew so angry at my challenge that it rushed out, leapt almost, and seized my leg and dragged me under the banks of the stream and lay on me crushing me under the water. But I used my knife to wound its belly."

He jabbed an imaginary knife into the scaly belly.

"Seven times and it perished. When I drug it onto the bank later on, it had a great weight. I slit open its belly with that same butcher knife and there within it was a full hundredweight of stones like to the size of my fist.

"And," he said, raising up his arm and pointing to the reptile inked there. "This crocodile here was purchased by my mates to memorialize the adventure."

His bench mate was staring across at the opposite riverbank with patent disinterest. The peg leg struck him lightly in the side of the arm then flexed the muscle beneath the tattoo when the man turned his head.

"Eh?" asked the peg leg.

"I seen that fokking lizard every day for two months."

This seemed to satisfy the man and he took up his oar again.

So did the others.

The helmsman looked around. They had drifted back to where the little crocodile had been pulled from the water. He shook his head, lowered the brim of his hat, making the rowers wait. Finally he said "And heave" and they continued their climb upstream.

Jack leaned on the gunwale, but now he kept his hand out of the water.

At noon the sky glazed over and black tatters of rain began to flock together in the sky. Again they pulled close-in to shore, pulled the canvas over their heads and ate the first meal, waiting till the shower passed.

Jack could not sleep in the afternoon's blazing heat as he'd done the day before. Even the crocodiles deserted the mud banks and lay beneath the waters with just their snouts and eyes above the surface. Late in the day a few huts appeared at a bend in the river, but whether their inhabitants slept or were dead was a matter of wager. Only at one did a blond-haired man in a leather kilt come out of his ajoupa to hail them. One of the other two boats, near behind, veered off to trade.

The forest's shadow lay nearly full across the river's murky water by the time their beam bit into the muddy beach of Bassin Bleau. Jack was glad to bid the river farewell.

63 THE INDENTURED SERVANT

A young mestizo just a year or three older than Jack met their two boats and helped haul them up to shore. The boatmen knew him well and joked with him about his girls and bastard babes. His smile had teeth only in its corners.

Jack did not relish helping his erstwhile comrades unload their cargo.

He asked, trying to sound as if he had an urgent message, where he could find Monsieur Van Clyf.

"Not here," the mestizo said coldly. He stared at Jack's new boots with envy

"Go up to the big house," he said nodding toward the road up the slope behind the landing. "See Nicolas. He is the factor down here for the plantation."

Jack marched past the envious youth with what he hoped was disdain and called a 'bonsoir' to the boatmen. Just above the river bank was a small clearing crowded with barrels, most stacked two high, many that oozed drops of molasses between their staves, like pitch from a tree. Past this clearing the wheel rutted path climbed gently through the twilit cypress, palms and ferns. Fireflies began to wink and float all around him. In a hundred paces night fell onto the jungle like a black cloak. The flies were his only light. Jack wished he had asked for a torch at the landing, but the path was broad and clear and soon he broke into a field of sugar cane.

The road became straight. A few hundred yards ahead he saw open fires.

The palm thatch of a large house glinted above them.

The compound was larger than it seemed at a distance, more like a village. It housed those who worked the cane fields down by the river. The hard dirt square before the main house had two large bonfires burning on each side of it, each in front of a double row of pine plank and thatch shanties. There were many people. He heard women laughing; two small children ran past him quick as cats; three men sang a French rondo. Smaller cooking fires in front of each shanty door were dying out and a score of people already sat on the dirt around the big bonfires. Some tossed tobacco leaves in the flames to drive away the mosquitoes. Others walked about, their shadows crossing like shuttles on the ground or leaping up the walls of the big house.

Jack was eyed curiously by some, but mostly he was ignored. He muttered "Bonsoir" to anyone whose eye he caught and crossed through to the big house.

It was very broad, two stories with an open porch across the second floor. The bottom was dark but there was lamplight above. A red haired man sat at the bottom of the stairs up to the porch puffing life into his clay pipe. White clouds enveloped his face.

"Bonsoir," said Jack.

"Bonsoir," the man said, taking the stem from his mouth and studying the bowl. He drew on the pipe once more before asking "What is your business here?"

Jack explained he had a letter for Van Clyf and wished to ask Monsieur Nicolas for lodging and transport in the morning.

"I'll get him for you." The man coughed in his throat, then bellowed "Nicolas !"

Nicolas was a hearty, barrel-chested man with a long gray braid down his back and a scar across the side of his face that let only one side of his mouth raise in a smile. He came out on the porch above them and questioned Jack about the letter. Jack feigned ignorance, say he only knew that he could keep the boots and receive a piece of eight with the reply.

Nicolas told him he could ride in the wagon that would take the supplies that had come on his boat on to the main plantation the next morning. The man with the pipe was told to lodge him with the servants.

Jack was given over to one of the indentured servants, a lank-haired Englishman of some thirty years.

He was given a meal of smoked beef and a cup of wine and seated near one of the the bonfires. Jack, who had sat the day in a boat, felt refreshed when he had finished and ready to be convivial. But most of the plantation had already retreated to their pallets in the shanties, worn down by a day in the hot cane fields.

The indentured Englishman left off talking with his friends and led him to a cluster of ajoupas immediately behind the rows of shanties, and then into one of the huts. It had two pine pallets each with a blanket folded on it. A wooden chest sat next to the pallet where there was also a bundle of reeds serving as a pillow. The Englishman pointed wordlessly to the other bed for Jack. Then he kneeled next to his own and reached beneath it, dragging out a heavy crock.

He lifted the lid and sniffed, then turned to Jack and smiled.

"Palm wine," he said. "I make the best on the plantation. You'll share a gourd with me."

Jack nodded. "A little wine makes the best pillow."

The man lifted a clay tile off the crock and pulled off a swatch of gauze and set them on his pellet. From the trunk he took two cassavas carved into ladles, dipped one into the crock for Jack and filled one for himself..

"A free man's life," he said raising his own gourd.

Jack took a sip of the tangy, bitter wine. It was as good as palm wine could be. He had never cared much for it.

"Your contract is done?" Jack asked. He had heard the quaver of anticipation unmistakably in the man's words. But the Englishman did not smile or even look up; he drank deeply from his dipper.

"Aye, done six years ago and now just ending."

Then he smiled and refilled his dipper. "Come have another. My name is John, boy, what's yours?"

"Jack" Jack said. Jack squatted on the dirt next to the crock taking more of the heady stuff after his host nodded approval. "It is good."

"I drink myself into a stupor every night or I can't sleep for thinking of it. In twenty-six days I'll be free of my contract and Lord knows what I'll do. I could go to Cayona and sail on account for the Campechy coast, or get me to Port Royal and become a rich distiller, or clerk for some merchant and buy my own share of a cargo --- I can cipher as good as any man. Or could before I came to Hispaniola."

He stopped speaking. The man's teeth creaked.

"You were sold, your contract sold again?"

"Sold and resold. You know these masters, they are mad boars, dog-fucking, devil-hearted beasts. They beat you, and beat you again if you stop to wipe your brow. A negro slave is treated like a man, but an Englishman, or French or Welsh, no, no, any indentured Christian is a mule or oxen or are made to work the same, striped with a cane, kicked like a cur if he falls. If you're indentured to them for three years, then that is the term of your life to those masters. You chop cane and haul it on your back whether you cough blood or are near to raving with fever!"

The Englishman was wild-eyed now. Spittle flecked his lips. He plunked his gourd into the crock, raised it to his lips and poured the wine down his throat.

"And when the end of your contract is near it becomes worse." He stared into Jack's eyes, or seemed to in the gloom of the hut. Then the man's teeth appeared. A grim smile pursed his face.

"I had seen it happen to my fellows, but I thought I was too strong, too quick. Ha! In the half year before my indenturement expired I lived in hell on earth. I was punched about the head each morning, kicked in the groin at noon and lashed with the cane 'til I could rise to

my feet and stumble into the fields on the toe of the over-
seer's boot. I would have died had I not begged them to
sell my contract. My master sold me, sold another added
three years of my life. And often I prayed to God I had
perished instead.

"My new master --- "

"Van Clyf?" Jack asked, trying not to let him rush head-
long into his nightmares. He had seen men strangling
their own friends in the rage of drunken remembrance.

"No. No, Van Clyf is not so bad. Nicolas, the whore-
son bastard, is not so bad. No devil like Bettesa. You
have heard of Bettesa?"

Jack shook his head. He knew little of plantation life.

64 BETTESA'S HAUNTING

"Only a monster like my first master would have sold me
to Bettesa. He must have thought it a joke."

He took a breath and made a sound that married a
low growl, a chuckle, and a pang from his gut.

"Someday," he said leaning forward, whispering like a
mutineer. "Someday I'll murder him for that little joke."

The Englishman rubbed his eyes with the back of his
hand and dipped into the crock again. He motioned to
Jack to do the same.

"Never heard of Bettesa. He was as cruel as L'Ollonais
or any other pirate in Cayona. He killed a hundred servants with his own hands and lashes of the cane.

"I had a friend on that plantation, Jean de Bueil. As the last year on his contract came round Bettesa and his factor beat him terribly. We vowed to escape together, but I held off for cowardice. Jean ran off one night. He was free for five days before they took him.

"As soon as they brought him before Bettesa, that animal, he smiled and commanded Jean to be tied to a tree a little way off from the houses.

"Bettesa took off his own shirt while this was being done and took up the cane himself. He lashed Jean, merciful God, he lashed him, till the blood and bits of skin and flesh ran off his back in a stream. He lashed him so hard the blood spattered up into the limbs, and leaves of the tree dripped blood. The bones of his back showed through the gore.

And after he'd worn out his arm, Bettesa, he --- " The Englishman gagged or sobbed, Jack couldn't tell --- "He anointed the wounds with a bowl of salt and lemon juice mingled with pepper.

"His screams." The Englishman's head waggled from side to side and tears ran down his jaw. "His screams."

He took another dip of palm wine. So did Jack and drank it down.

"He left Jean tied there. He left him tied like that a full day. I do not think he felt the flies and wasps that fed on his gory back. From his groans and screams we all thought him mad with pain.

"After that day was done, Bettesa came back to him at the tree and took up the cane again and lashed him just as hard and cruelly as he had before, so that many of us, forced to watch his punishment, retched in horror.

"And it was a wonder to us all that in the midst of this torture, Jean drew his face up from the bark of the tree and over his bloody shoulder shouted as clearly as I speak to you, 'I --- '"

The Englishman choked on his tears and began again.

"'I beseech Almighty God to make you feel as many torments before your death as you have caused me to feel before mine!' And saying it he gave up the ghost."

The man leaned back and gave a tremendous sigh. He managed a smile of pride at his friend's bravery. "It was a wonder."

"A wonder, indeed," said Jack. He drank again.

"But the miracle, the miracle was Bettesa's own end," the man said leaning suddenly forward. The whites of his eyes seemed to shine in the hut's darkness.

"Three days after Jean's death, to the hour, as Bettesa walked on the path close by that tree, he let out a mighty scream of horror and fell backwards as if struck dead. That scream was like none heard even from Jean de Bueil. There was a moment of pure silence on the whole plantation. Only the buzz of the flies that still swarmed among the bloody roots of that tree.

"But then Bettesa stood. He struck himself in the face with his right hand, again and again, then the left hand, and alternately he struck his face crying and groaning. Then howling with frustrated rage he tore the shirt from his chest and dug his nails into the skin of his own belly and clawed stripes up across his ribs, and then again and again, and again, again, again. Blood streamed down his legs," the Englishman declared with wild glee.

"Then he began to strike his head with one hand and claw his left cheek.

"Finally the factor, a big mulatto, came running from the fields and seeing him insane jumps on Bettesa's back and grabs his arms. Bettesa thrust back his head and broke the mulatto's nose and pulled loose his arms and kicked him so hard in his stones the man could not rise from the ground.

"Bettesa howled when he saw the factor's cane and tore its strap off the man's wrist. He belabored his own legs and head, dancing as bright blood streamed from his scalp over his scratched and wealed face. He tossed the stick away. I can see it now, flying up into the tree.

"He tried to strangle himself and at the same time kick at his own leg and landed flat on his back. He rose howling and now, oh God, he was clawing his face from eyes to collar bone, both hands over and over, wandering about running with blood, over and over till he had the most hideous deep gouges, torn, bleeding ruts where his cheek bones, jawbone, even his gritted teeth gleamed through at us. There was this terrible whine trapped in his throat behind his clenched teeth. It broke into a new howl, this bloody monster splashing in his own gore on the noonday path howled at everyone hiding in the shadows, raising his gory arms and then brought his claws to his throat digging, digging as if for gold. Then I saw him myself reach into the wounds of his neck with the fingers of his hands, grip, and tear out his own throat!

"Blood burst out in a font beneath Bettesa's chin and his head jerked around to look at the tree where he'd murdered poor Jean. Then he fell into the gory muck around him, surrendering his ghost to the same Spirit of Darkness who had tormented his body."

Jack took a gulp of palm wine. The Englishman was breathing in gasps.

"A fitting end," Jack managed.

"I wanted him to gouge out his own eyes, but he didn't." The man seemed calm again.

Jack ladled up some more palm wine and drank. So did the Englishman.

They sat in silence for a short time.

"That was a stern tale," said Jack.

"There are many more I could tell if I weren't so sleepy." The man leaned back and rested his head on his reed pillow. He pulled the blanket across his shoulders and groaned contentedly. "Put the crock away if you will."

Jack dipped another drink, replaced the gauze, tile, crock and gourds, then retreated to his own pallet where he had fitful dreams.

65 INTO THE HILLS

The supplies were not brought up from the river until nearly mid-morning.

Jack passed the time smoking his pipe and watching the cooper and his apprentice measure and saw staves. The first floor of the big house was given over to his shop and behind the building, a little ways off, was the unfired smithy where the cooper made his hoops.

When the wagon came up from the river pulled by an ox, Jack cursed.

Old Kit's life was ebbing each hour. He could have walked to the plantation faster. But, he thought, wiggling his toes, perhaps not in his new boots.

Jack sat with a laconic old African on the wagon bench. The silvery-haired slave did little more than switch at the plodding ox and nod his head in and out of sleep. The path did not at first climb up into the hills but skirted the edge of the flood plain, following the cane fields. Just as on the river, there was no breeze to stir the damp heat rising from the fields.

They passed three men in white shirts harvesting, bending and slashing at the tall cane with machetes while white egrets flapped and swirled in the air behind them. Every few moments one of the bright birds lit on the green carnage of cut stalks and plucked out a snail, wheeling back up above the harvesters chopping slowly in the heat.

When the road finally turned and climbed high enough for a breeze the wind had already died under the noon sun. Jack put his face to his knees and slept. It was deep in the afternoon when they finally reached the main compound of Van Clyf's plantation.

The plantation house was big, the largest building he had seen since Cayona. It was two adobe stories set on a low hill above a dozen outbuildings, with a new palm thatch roof that overhung a veranda running all the way around the second story. The same design as the factor's, but larger and all given over to the master's household.

Jack declared to an old mulatto house servant that he had a letter to be delivered by hand for the master. This seemed so extraordinary to the old man that Jack was escorted immediately up to the veranda on the far side of the house. At a shaded table a short, ruddy faced man with silvered mustaches sat inking ciphers into a ledger. He studied Jack wordlessly after taking the letter he had proclaimed as an urgent message from Master Kit, then broke the blue wax seal and read the contents very slowly.

As he finished he looked up and said, "I marvel that one so old still wants to live."

"But," he said with a wry chuckle, "I doubt old Kit is anxious to meet his Maker. What do you seek for him in the mountains? Indian herbs and roots?"

"A butterfly, sir." Jack extracted from his pouch a crude drawing of the mythic insect, tinted red, brown and spotted black. It explained the bell jar if anyone should ask. "The dust of its wings is said to be very potent."

The Dutchman pulled at one end of his mustaches, then stuck it into his teeth and chewed at it, considering. "It's not one I've seen, but the peaks he's sent you to are remote even for the buccaneers.

"Well," he said looking up. "I'll do the best I can for the old fellow. Lord knows he's done enough by me. We'll fix you up a bed in the house tonight and in the morning I'll give a chart to guide you, and some provisions, and a donkey. You'll sup with me and my wife, and tell me what's passed with Kit --- and Cayona --- these past two years."

Jack left the plantation at dawn, tugging a braying but docile donkey. After leaving Van Clyf's tobacco fields he climbed a rising path used by buccaneers who came to the plantation to trade their skins and beef for powder, shot, coins and tobacco. After the path crested a low ridge it divided like a hydra and disappeared in a broad grassy valley studded with tall royal palms.

Jack crossed the valley at a long angle heading due east. At mid morning he passed the remains of an old bonfire. It was the only sign of man he saw. The higher the sun rose the more he sweated, but he did not halt in the shade. He thought of Old Kit slowly sinking into his bed, disappearing beneath the coverlet as if into death. His fortune would sink into nothing with the old man. He would never unhook Rebecca's bodice.

Jack tugged at the donkey's rope and stepped along faster.

The sun was an hour past zenith by the time he had climbed out of the valley and descended pine wooded slopes into the next one. The veins of sun between the trees' shadows burned on his arms. Reluctantly he left the shade to cross a long, narrow meadow that shimmered lime green in the sun's white light. Only scattered butterflies moved in the air.

66 BOUCANIERS

Jack trudged down around a low bluff -- muskets banged through the dead air. Six, seven, eight, nine shots, their hard reports from far up the hill. Human howls, savage and excited, clawed through the empty air and a low thunder began to rise.

Jack pulled the shying donkey closer under the little bluff, tossed and tied his kerchief over its eyes. He locked his arm around its neck and hugged himself against the shaking animal. Six more shots cracked, closer, and then a dozen huge wild cattle pounded past into the meadow, shaking the dirt beneath his feet. And then another score of the beasts and scores, the rumbling stampede of gray hide, horn, bellowing filled the meadow. One charged past in a blur and its horn hooked Jack's sleeve. He shouted in terror. Suddenly the beast stopped, turned to face its invisible tormentors like some doomed king while the flood of cattle raced by in bovine panic.

The giant bull's wagon-wide shoulders and rippling, heaving flanks shook, slick with sweat, venous blue and glistening, the muscles swollen against the guys of its tendons. Its hind legs shone scarlet, bleeding from a botched hamstringing. The entire animal seemed to throb against the burning green grass and the blurred stampede until the bull seemed to Jack to lose anchor where it stood, drifting like an afterimage of the sun that rode on a glowing chartreuse bay. The beast seemed to stare directly at him. The head dipped toward Jack. A snort blasted from its enormous, bony head and its two bowed horns hummed sympathetically out to their tips.

Screaming a blasphemy against God and kine, a buccaneer sailed off the bluff above Jack's head like a sailor leaping between ships. He hit the slope running hard at the bull, a long Flemish blade gleamed in a hand held over his head like a rope walker.

The bull's head rose up at the man's scream and its chance was lost.

The buccaneer seemed to stumble at the bull's feet, caught himself and ducked under its left horn, spun along its flank and stopped in an instant at its rear, dropping back a step, the bloody blade upraised.

The bull's bellow was crushed to a grunt as it tumbled, sinews slit, tendons shorn properly this time.

Sighting Jack, the man did a surprised double glance. Then with a laugh he dashed into the rushing cattle and disappeared.

Another buccaneer leapt over Jack's head and into the stampede; muskets fired in volley and cattle tumbled. A youth Jack's age ran past and danced about the tossing head of the hamstrung bull, jumping aside as an eddy of the stampede stumbled over and past their companion. Then quickly the boy stepped in and cut its throat and ran off after the others.

Most of the cattle had passed. In the distance the herd stampeded into a neck of grass emptying into lower fields. Cattle unable to veer into the herd went crashing in blind terror into the trees of the forest.

The meadow, silent and windswept just moments before, was filled with two dozen men and boys prancing and strutting among huge, dark boulders that had been a score of wild cattle. The hamstrung kine and those not shot dead bellowed and snorted, twisting their heads and goring the black earth. Some struggled to rise on their forelegs, but their hinds and flanks twitched and dragged uselessly and they fell back with ogres' grunts.

The buccaneers made short work of the beeves. They stepped up behind a bull, grabbed a horn and made a swift precise slash in the great throat. Jack saw the hunters leap back, and the mammoth necks spout crimson onto the grass, the head swing up once, snort blood and fall dead.

The boys, valets of the buccaneers as they were called, cut the throats of the already dead animals to let them drain. Clouds of ravens now whirled above, cawing excitedly over the carrion. Jack could barely hear the buccaneers shouts to one another as they counted their slaughter.

He tugged his donkey across the meadow to where some of the buccaneers had sat themselves down in the grass beside a ceiba tree. They cursed and threw stones at their valets who now had the task of gutting the kine while the hunters lounged in the shade.

The buccaneers greeted Jack cordially, though anyone of them would have kicked his butt out of the way if he had stepped into their path in Cayona. Even though Jack was just the age of their older valets, when he told them his business was hunting herbs and medicines for a doctor in Cayona, the circle of brown, sinewy hunters squinted and peered at him with respect. Immediately a red headed Scotsman took off his leather cap and asked Jack to examine an ulcerous sore on his scalp. Another complained of a burning in his lungs. Jack begged ignorance of the medicines' uses and, besides, he had not yet begun his gatherings. Nonetheless, the buccaneers invited him to stay for the evening's feast. Though it was not near evening and his mission tugged hard at him, Jack was curious to watch these famous Brothers at their work. And to deny their hospitality would be rude and suspicious. He tied the donkey to a shrub and sat with them.

They watched the valets working in pairs, going from carcass to carcass slitting open the cattle's bellies and pulling out slithering great heaps of viscera. A dozen hunting mastiffs worried the cattle's legs and fought over the entrails until each had an animal opened for it. Ravens hopped among the offal plucking sweetbread tidbits or were perched on the unopened carcasses pecking the eyes.

It was some time before all the dead cattle scattered down the long meadow were gutted. The dogs gorged on the liver and tripe and soon slept in the shade next to the buccaneers, their tongues licking lazily over their bloody muzzles to dislodge the flies. The ten valets were themselves dressed in gore and covered with flies. Eight of them went to the edge of the jungle and began gathering wood. The last two valets, older looking, perhaps of longer standing in their apprenticeship, began to skin one of the closer bulls. First the inside of its leg was cut and then slit around the shank. Lifting with their left hands and stroking and flicking with their keen knives, the skin peeled back from the sinews and gleaming red muscles.

One by one the buccaneers heaved themselves up from the shaded grass and in pairs began skinning other carcasses.

THOMAS ERIKSON

In a short while nearly a third of the animals lay naked and red in the sun. Most of the buccaneers helped the valets feed three bonfires that now burned, spaced about forty paces apart.

As the valets brought their armloads of dead wood, half was tossed in the fire and half in a pile near to it. The buccaneers had cut small posts from young trees and were using axes to pound four in a square around each fire. Soon an entire hurdle was built, the fire allowed to die down, and green limbs laid over the frame to form the rack.

One bull was butchered near each fire. One of its haunches, then its ribs were lifted onto a rack to be dried and smoked in its own drippings.

All but three of the hunters went to rest in the shade again while their companions continued to watch the fires. The valets filled the wood racks and pushed the meat together with sticks to make room for more joints and slabs. It would take two or three days to smoke dry all the meat, Jack could see that.

The once empty and shimmering meadow was flattened and marred by many thousand hoof and footsteps. Carcasses and heaps of entrails buzzed and squawked with flies and ravens. Gray, fatty smoke drifted slowly into the trees.

When the racks were filled the valets marched off to wash themselves.

Jack left his pack with the buccaneers and ran to join them. He followed the troop down the isthmus of meadow where the herd had escaped and they turned off into the trees. There was not much talk. The young valets were tired and surly, and cursed as they brushed biting flies away from their eyes and slapped them off their noses.

A few yards into the trees a narrow stream ran fast and clear over dark stones. Downstream the boys could hear the splash of a waterfall.

They found two. Each was the height of a man, and splashed consecutively into pools the depth and length of a good longboat. Crusted with blood and grime, the valets whooped with joy as they jumped into the water. Jack jumped in last.

He was left out of the pummeling and splashing that ensued. While the valets chopped the water and spouted on one another, Jack sunk to the bottom and hugged himself to a large rock. He opened his eyes in the cold water. Amputated legs and feet jigged slowly in the clear water. Turning his head upstream he saw the little waterfall break into the pool, a frothing curtain of white and silver.

67 SNAKES, SCORPIONS, AND WHITE ANTS

The sun was low and brassy when the valets and he returned to camp.

Flies whirred and buzzed spinning over the entire meadow. A few of the ravens perched in the ceiba trees, gorged with entrails and sleeping. Occasionally one would glide down to peck at the carcasses.

Most of the dozen buccaneers stood or leaned against the trunks of small trees bordering the meadow. A side of beef roasted over a cooking fire and a small boar had been shot and was spitted over another blaze. Two men basted the meat with a thick sauce of pimento and pepper. The others puffed on pipes of shag and argued over the day's hunt.

Each claimed to have been the keenest shot, and they broke into factions as to the finest make of musket, whether it was a Brachie from the gunsmiths of Dieppe or those the favorites of the French, the famous Gelin's from Nantes. Jack had seen buccaneers maimed and killed over these disputes in Cayona taverns, but here it was just good natured banter.

He gave his donkey water in a bowl from his pack, then moved and tied it closer to the men so that neither wild animals nor the dogs would attack it. He dug out his own pipe and pouch and diffidently approached the gaggle of buccaneers relaxing beneath the ceibas.

The one who had leapt over Jack's head and cut down the bull, a Walloon with black mustaches that dropped to his chest, took abuse for botching his first attack. He was protesting that he brought down four other cattle that same way, not wasting powder and shot on a single one, more than any of them, but such sloppiness found no excuse from his comrades.

The Walloon was no Vincent de Rosiers, ha! they said. Two mates who had hunted with the famous buccaneer recounted DeRosier's amazing exploits chasing down cattle with the speed of a lion, slashing apart hock tendons left and right in the middle of a stampede, twenty cattle in a day without a shot.

Meanwhile the valets each set up their master's cotton tents and took their machetes into the woods to chop thatch for rough ajoupas they built over the tents. Lastly, they laid down banana leaves inside the tents and tossed pigskin sleeping bags on top of the leaves.

Jack had been leaning against a tree. Now he went and pulled his blanket roll out of his pack and propped it against a tree to lie against.

The buccaneers had paid him no mind till then, but now the one with the festering scalp turned an eye on him.

"That all you've got to wrap yourself, mate?" He pointed with the end of his pipe at Jack's blanket. Jack sat up.

"Aye, that's what they gave me at the plantation."

The buccaneer and three others that had turned toward him gave dismayed shakes of their heads and laughed.

"I can see Cayona folks not knowing, but you'd think Pierre'd set 'em straight."

"That's right, boy," said a stringy haired man with a 'T' branded between his eyes. "You'll get a snake slither over you or roll over and get stung by some scorpion, you'll see what we mean. We don't want no screechin' setting the dogs abarking."

"That ain't the worst," said the first, stabbing the air again with his pipe. "You get an army of white ants march through camp, they'll be all over a man head to foot before he's awake. Wrapped in a bag you got a chance.

"Not even the dogs can give you warning," another said, warming to the subject. "It's a fright to see 'em under a full moon, silent as death, coming down across a meadow, moving over the grass like a stream of dew in the night."

His head gave a jerk. "Chills me worse than ghosts."

The sun set and within a few breaths the night was black. The buccaneers, valets and Jack dug yams out of the coals and hacked dripping, succulent hunks from beef and boar. More than a score of them encircled the large campfire. Tobacco leaves were tossed on the fire so the smoke would keep the swarming mosquitoes at bay. A jug of brandy passed continuously around the circle. Tales of ants and crocodiles, lemurs and Arab gold, turtles, sea battles and Spanish tortures also made the round.

68 WILD HORSES
Jack left the buccaneers' encampment just after dawn, pulling the donkey into the jungle surrounding the long

meadow. The new sun's candle-yellow rays pierced the gloom everywhere. A bell bird trilled overhead.

The voices of the buccaneers and their valets as they built up their fires were quickly lost.

He found the way easy through this high jungle. The trees were not so close nor as thickly woven with lianas as the lower valleys. The ferns in consequence were much larger, giant sprays as broad as ajoupas. But it was no problem to push between them, or through the archipelagos of white and lilac orchids scattered over the green seas through which he and the donkey waded. Here and there in his path a patch of bare earth was warmed by a shaft of light, causing scores of tiny land crabs to emerge from their holes and wave their claws in the air as if angrily shielding the sun from their eyes.

One hour's walk, slowly climbing, brought him to the crest of a ridge. He unfolded the map the old man had given him. Jack reckoned he was some miles west northwest of the Mountain of the Zemes. But where he stood now the palms and stands of mahogany were too tall and dense to provide any horizon. Tugging the donkey, he climbed higher, following the ridge's crest for another hour. Finally a scarp of limestone broke the forest's curtain and he stepped out on the mossy stone to take his bearings.

Before him spread a dark green, undulating sea of forested hills and jungle. Far to the north a band of lapis lazuli, the true sea, divided the jungle from the cerulean sky. Directly west loomed a brown massif: by his map it was unmistakably the Mountain of the Zemes. It seemed like the bristling back of a wild boar arching out of the brush. Its saddle-peaked companion rose over its southern slopes to the lee. Jack felt a thrilling flush that left a tiny ripple of fear in its wake.

He smothered the thoughts and coalescing images of Indian godlings and ghosts, almost easily done under a blazing sky. Jack consulted his compass and map. He had come a short ways too far to the south. He would need to tack transversely down the slope into the valley that separated him from the flanks of the Zemes' mountain.

He tested the knots on the donkey's packs. "Gee," he shouted and gave the animal a swat on the rump. They began their descent.

Jack ate his noon meal by a deep stream that ran like a vein through the valley. It gurgled and chortled loudly, but was hidden beneath the ferns that crowded its bank and arched oar-long fronds across it. A pair of toucans settled on a branch a few feet above his head. They cocked their heads to study him for a few moments, then with their huge tricolor beaks began plucking at the purple berries that hung around them. The birds tossed each berry in the air and caught it again in their beaks. After swallowing the fruit the birds began spitting the stones at Jack. He laughed and tossed the pits back. The toucans flew across the stream to a higher branch. They preened themselves for a bit while he watched, then tucked their beaks part way beneath their black wings, stuck up their tail feathers and prepared to sleep.

Jack, wishing he could do the same, rose to his feet and set off along the stream searching for a place to ford.

The sun was low and amber when he and the donkey at last mounted the flanks of the Arawak's mountain. There was no demarcation in the jungle between the valley and the massif, but Jack felt a difference in the inclination in the slope, in the movement of the breeze. He made a small fire and a quick meal of bread and boucan. He banked the fire as dusk came and clambered up into the crotch of a tree as day was extinguished. Despite a boar's grease salve that the buccaneers had given him, he spent a night tormented by mosquitoes and dreams of snakes slithering across him.

The next morning's climb was steep. Jack could have tacked back and forth, but he worried more and more about Old Kit sinking deeper in his bed, life evaporating, while he climbed slowly through these mountains.

Now he cursed himself for lingering an afternoon with the buccaneers. The journey was taking longer than he expected, longer than the old man had guessed. Kit could be dead. Jack had dreamed it in the tree the night before. He had been looking for the old man in his room, had pulled the sheet up from the bed and there was Kit shriveled to the size of a monkey.

Though steep, it did become easier to climb as the jungle thinned, pines and ceiba again replaced the palms and ferns and lianas, and small bushes broke the mats of needles and leaves.

By noon the slope eased a little. Jack could look up the mountain's flank to where the seams of forest and patches of grass petered out to the barren brown hump of the peak. He knew it was not far to the Cave of the Zemes.

An hour later he came out into a broad dell. The high sun glowed in each long leaf of the meadow's grasses, the wind tossed its reflections across the steep-rising slope.

It shimmered like a sea of dragonflies, it seemed to Jack, under the midday gusts. He began climbing directly up the slope of the meadow, jerking the donkey's harness.

Two forested ridges converged at the head of the meadow and in its cul-de-sac dozens of Hispaniola's small, tan and dapple wild horses champed at grass scattered with vermilion flowers. He climbed toward them at a steady pace until he was almost at the edge of the small herd. In the shadows of the wood above them he saw a unicorn.

Even the unicorn far above heard his gasp and cocked its head. The horn was just a sun-caught branch in silhouette.

The closest horse, a little stallion, seemed to await his approach. He walked quietly up to it. As he reached out to pet its muzzle, the animals bolted all at once, like a flock of birds. Pale horses dashed wild-eyed past him; it was all he could do to hold the donkey in check. Nostrils snorted blasts of sour grass on his cheeks; flanks brushed at his as the horses turned at his feet in terror; and suddenly they were gone, the last three galloping past on the far side of the meadow.

His breath came back to him. He turned to look after them. Already they were far below, strings and pairs of them prancing, butts bobbing on the bright, wavering green slope like whitecaps shipped up by the sea-born wind breaking against the mountain. He shook his head. Even with the kerchief tied over his head he was getting too much sun, that was sure.

Unicorns and whitecaps.

Jack turned back up the slope and halted. Horse shit. Dozens of fresh biscuits and pies already heavy in the warm air, already speckled iridescent with flies. He watched his step, picking his way through the droppings and into the break of trees where he had seen his unicorn.

Passing through the wind-gnarled branches of the little copse he saw his goal.

69 A PLUME OF BATS

Across from him, separated by a broad, shallow dell, was a limestone bluff, just as the Arawak had described it to Old Kit. The crumbling stone of its west face was shaped like a giant axe head with a deep notch at the top spattered with white flowers. Somewhere in thick woods on the bluff's north face was the entrance to the Arawak's cave, cave of zemes, ghosts, and godlings.

Jack stroked the donkey's neck, a calming gesture not so much for it as himself. Then he tugged at the bridle. The animal bared its teeth and brayed, a sound that echoed faintly back from the hill.

It was late in the day. He made camp at the edge of the trees and gathered dead wood for a fire. He ate biscuits and gave the donkey water from a folded leaf. He started a small fire and leaned against a tree to study the clouds for an omen. He waited for sunset.

More than a score of small brown bats were swooping and fluttering in the low, gold sunlight, licking midges and mosquitoes from the air, before Jack realized they weren't birds. He jumped to his feet and ran a dozen steps into the clearing and looked back up the bluff.

Like a leaking barrel seam, a spray of bats spewed in a fan above the upper trees, then turned over on itself and drifted like a band of smoke across the brow of the bluff and down over Jack's camp and beyond.

Fixing the spray of bats like a dead-reckoning navigator, Jack clambered up into the shadowed woods.

By the time he reached where he thought the cave should be there was no trail of bats in the darkening sky. Just a few flickered past in the coppery light. He ranged back and forth over that quarter of the hill, searching behind bushes and ferns grown to rocky outcrops and depressions in the hillside. He did not want to be near the cave when night fell; he did not even want to go in during daylight.

The sun had almost set. The last red golds and deep shadows were softening swiftly to a vermilion and lavender that would be gone in a blink to black night. He turned to make his way down hill and caught a breath of something watery, cool, and with a slight reek of dung.

A soft, steady breeze blew out of a clump of glossy-leaved bushes and ferns. Jack went forward and pushed the greenery aside, uncovering a smooth-rimmed black hole broader than his shoulders.

Something whipped past his head, another shot past his face into the hole, a third struck his shoulder with a squeak, the air flickered black shadows, then exploded with squeaking. He stumbled back swinging his arms, took a tumble, and rolled away.

He scooted farther from the cave mouth on his butt. The bush before him shivered with the swift shadow stream of returning bats. Jack stood up and quickly as he could scraped with his knife a big blaze on the nearest tree. Then he followed the smell of smoke in the darkness down to his camp.

Jack did not sleep well. The donkey was restless; he wondered if wild dogs or worse were nearby. He did not want to dream.

70 THE CAVE OF THE ZEMES

He woke from a final brief nap before dawn, rekindled the banked fire and watched the first flush of sun evaporate the constellations. He deliberately avoided watching for the bats on their morning excursion. He took a long time eating his breakfast, then gave the donkey its water and made sure of the knot that secured its hobble to a strong sapling.

Finally he opened his pack and drew out the small mahogany box with the ring in its top. It held the bell jar and its nest for the magic stones.

He took out the pair of tongs that Kit had given him for picking up the stones and stuck them in his belt. In a roll of canvas he carried two long-burning torches. He unwrapped the torches, hooked a finger in the box's ring and stood up. His stomach felt full of eels. He looked up the bluff. The sun was hidden from him, but its rays should be shining across the cave mouth now. That thought made him feel a little better. He sighed and started for the Arawak cave.

The clear, bright morning made the lightless hole of the cave's mouth seem all the more a refuge of night creatures, bats . . . Jack turned his thoughts and himself away from it, to look over the rolling humps of green, the horizon dark-edged by the sea. Far Tortuga was invisible, Rebecca, Louis, Jesús . . . Old Kit near dying. Like a drowning Midas Kit's hands reached above the water for Jack to grasp and turn his fortunes to gold.

Jack shoved one torch deeper in his belt, used his tin-
derbox to light the other, waited for it to stop sputtering,
then with the mahogany box held in his other hand and
using his elbows he slid into the cave feet first.

It did not help that the first thing he saw in the torch's
light was a skeleton stretched out before him. The eels in
his stomach began to wriggle.

He was in a huge limestone hall, the biggest thing he
had ever been within, so deep his flambeau's light barely
touched the farthest walls that rose at a dozen different angles to a jaggedly peaked ceiling higher than the
tallest mast. Belly of the beast. The entire ceiling was
festooned with a brown, shaggy mat of fur that gleamed
here and there with tiny garnet eyes. The cave stunk of
their shit. Some of the bats dropped free and swooped
past his torch and then realighted on the ceiling. When
he saw the bats would not panic and swarm past him in
a mad, maddening frenzy, he let out a breath he had not
known he was holding.

The skeleton at his feet was not an Indian's. The remnants of boots, belt, dagger, and yellowish hairs clinging
to the skull told him as much. He doubted it was a good
omen for his own task.

Jack could see nothing else in the cave but the lone
skeleton and the high, shaggy tapestries of bats. A thin,
acrid mist of piss settled through the air. The thought of
leaving right then flickered through him. He went forward immediately to put the urge behind him.

Twenty paces into the cavern the light of his torch caught out a patch of dull white to his left. Cautiously he went toward it. There, in a low, natural doorway were more skeletons, these a broken tangle of ribs, skulls, shins, and finger bones, apparently kicked to each side to make way. Perhaps by the man at the entrance, Jack thought.

With his flambeau held straight out before him like a sword, he squatted down and advanced through the door.

The cave room was filled to the walls with human bones. No bigger than a tavern's common room, its floor was heaped, the walls lined with reclining dead --- at least three score, with skulls of every size, a whole village that had come here to die, to die at peace with their gods.

A spasm of horror shook through him and left the torch shaking at the end of his arm. The eels writhed in his stomach, his knees seemed to change to sand. The dead surrounded him on all sides in a silence broken only by the occasional squeaks from the outer cave. Clamping his teeth so they would not chatter, Jack raised the torch and waved it in a slow arc.

Except in the middle of the stone floor, where they had been kicked aside, the skeletons lay where death had found them. The path of scattered bones led to the wall on his right, to a natural stone shelf. The narrow shelf was rubbled with broken clay, carved wood and dirty feathers. There was not a single golden glint.

He approached slowly, careful not to step on even a finger bone.

Here, too, the skeletons had been knocked aside into unspeakable piles. All except one. Jack paid it no mind.

Setting the mahogany box on the edge of the stone shelf, he tried not to think of what lay behind his back staring with empty eyes. He raised his red torch above shattered gods. No moon stone, no gold that he could see.

He did see, in the wavering light, strange heads the size of his fist with strange faces of monkey, men, and devil, crude as those the boys drew on a wet beach, but with round ring eyes that pooled the blackness in a dead stare.

Jack did not want to poke about in these Indian holies. Besides, he could see they had been combed by other desecrators before him. Then he saw a speck of sky blue deep in a crook at the back of the ledge. Leaning over, it looked to him like a dirty ball of turquoise, but he knew it was an Arawak moon stone.

"Ah, now," he said and the sound of his voice was very strange.

The stone was thickly covered, almost mossy, with the magic mildew that he had seen only as specks on Kit's own stone in Cayona.

Jack shoved the end of his torch in a crevice. He quickly undid the latches on the box, upended the lid and placed the glass bell in it. Then he took the tongs and gingerly picked out the stone and set it on the wet velvet in the bowl carved into the box's base. He unwound a thin wire from the rim of the bowl, tied it to a small knob on the base and stretched over the moonstone, then tied the other end to a second knob. There were knobs at eight compass points to secure the wires that would hold the moonstone in a fine net. But before he secured the other three wires he had to look for more stones. The longer he could help Kit live, the better for his own fortunes.

Jack picked up the torch again and searched along the shelf, even pushing bits of the broken gods off promising lumps. Then, after glancing quickly over his shoulder at the skeletons, he used his knife to stir the rubble.

Nothing more could be found among the shards of the gods. Jack was shivering in the damp cold. He was ready to quit the cave. His courage, tested so long in this haunted chamber, was ebbing. He had the treasure he had come for, didn't he? He turned to finish securing the stone he had found, but his eye was caught by a gleam of blue from the floor.

He stepped over a shin bone and bent down with his torch.

Wedged in a crack was another small, azure-fuzzed stone. Jack tried to pluck it out with the tongs but the claws were too wide. He tried his knife but only succeeded in rolling it deeper into the crack. Bending with his cheek close to the floor he reached in with the tips and fingernails of his thumb and middle finger. Barely pinching it he lifted the holy pearl slowly out of the wet crack.

Jack stood up, stepped over to the rubbled ledge and placed the slippery, blue-fungussed stone with its twin in the velvet nest. He smiled: Two! Perhaps he would not give that new one to Old Kit. He would not only be wealthy for his efforts, but immortal, exalted . . . he felt lightheaded, warm, too warm for the cold cave. Jack turned and sat against the low shelf. His arms hung at his sides. The torch, set low, cast the shadows of skeletons on the rough walls. Everything was taking on different significances . . .

He stared out over a diary of the dead, where everyone's face was frozen in the last expression: hard bone eye sockets: all fifty-three skeletons but one seemed to be fading, receding, all but the last Arawak: whole and reclining at the far end of the shelf of broken gods. It glowed. The bones leaned against a stalagmite, the skull laid back against its peak.

Its forehead sprouted a conical thorn. The last Arawak's bones glowed the hue of a horizon on a clear March morning at sea. The cave's walls, dark in the weak torchlight, faded into dark night. The tips of Jack's finger and thumb glowed like the Arawak skeleton.

"Fool!" he screamed at himself, though it was only a whisper.

He shuffled over to the soft blue skeleton. Resting in the skull beneath its open teeth was another magic stone.

And beneath its raw white hand resting on the cave floor an opal dove's egg horded and cast brilliants . . .he saw Kit pick his stone from beneath the bell jar with silver tongs and kiss it briefly like a miser's diamond. Kit's philosopher's stone, he said he was inured like Mithridates . . . a gilded finger bone pointed towards him. It had lifted its forefinger. A voice rose from the Arawak's hollow chest and mouth boomed, and echoed in the cave to its deepest cracks. "There is yet a spark," it called, not to Jack, but behind it as if over its white, frozen shoulder, to someone in a recess without depth.

The Arawak's skeleton chuckled with delight, then hiccoughed. Jack shuddered and seemed to be falling. The torch leaped from his grasp and sailed across the star-filled sky and was extinguished in the sea and he fell still deeper into an impenetrable blackness. . . He lay on his bed of thatch beneath the Tree smoking his pipe. Crabs roasted in the coals. There was no moon here in the cave of the bones. He lay on his back, the cold stone behind his shoulders, beneath his head, then it wasn't. He floated above Van Duyn's wall, tossing on a limb and staring into Rebecca's room. She was in a translucent shift; she lit two candles beside a mirror, then selected from a priest's pyx, wet with her tongue, and applied to her cheek a tiny black paper rose; and bending back, back to look, her nipple silhouetted, she turned, he turned and tumbled with a cry toward the spiked wall . . . fell between the spikes that were the maggoty ribs of a bull, its flesh eaten away by dogs, crows, sun, ants and flies. Wild mastiffs barked at his appearance and drew back in fright from their midnight worrying of the carcass. Some howled at the full moon, full moon through the meat crusted ribs, the dogs growled and crept forward. Jack pulled back deeper into the carcass and screamed, he could not scream. Dark, lumbering shadows dashed up, circling, snapping at his hands, the rib ends, worried the bull's thigh, snapped at his boots. The dogs devolved into hideous crocodiles . . . hideous crocodiles into . . .

Hatuey woke with a start. He was in his own hammock in his father's ajoupa. He was alone. A dream, a black dream. Late morning sun came through the door. Outside he could see his mother's back, her shoulders moving as she ground something in a bowl. It was hot, quiet. Except for his mother's grinding the only sounds were children calling and the distant, soft soughing of the surf.

He had had a fever dream. He would get up. His legs would not move, but it did not surprise him. He looked down along his long, bare copper legs. Did he want them to move? Did his dream? His hands and arms lay still beside his naked hips. I am an Indian, Jack thought.

"Aho!" Hatuey exclaimed in fright. The dream was speaking in his head, though his eyes were open. Silently, Jack cried out too, tried to twist out of the Arawak boy's body, to escape the dream.

Hatuey sat up. Jack was carried with him, thought as his dream thought, knew the dream's words, saw what his dream saw. His mother came quickly through the door and took hold of his shoulders.

"You're shaking," she said and made him squat down on the mat. He leaned his head against her bare breast as she stroked his hair.

"You've been sweating, but the fever is gone." Now she helped Hatuey stand. "Climb back in your hammock. You are weak."

Hatuey shook his head and pointed out the door. "I'll sit by you."

He sat down clumsily next to the stone bowl where his mother was mashing a yam for him to eat. He was in the shade of the thatch awning, but he stretched his legs out into the sun. His head felt empty, yet too full, like clear water, as if his dream still tried to fill it. He heard his mother digging through baskets in the hut. She was muttering to herself in words it seemed he had never heard.

He put his hand to his forehead, then cupped it above his eyes, peering past the palm trunks, the beach, to the canoes out in the cove. In the farthest of the three boats he could make out his uncle pulling in his nets in his slow, lazy way. Around Hatuey the women squatted and worked in front of their own ajoupas. Two women sat talking together as each made a personal zeme for a child, carefully incising features on the godlings they held in their palms. They would probably bake them in the nearby coals of the fire old Anacoana had banked around her new jars. From a basket she was shaking sandy dust over the fire to slowly smother and cool it. Beneath a coconut palm a man carved designs in a low stool. And across from him a woman fit a big iguana into its pipkin to cook all day by the fire. Children ran and jumped, laughing as they snatched at a shoal of orange butterflies that drifted through the village eluding each tiny grasp.

He heard the deeper laugh of his father and saw him emerge with two other men from the giant ferns along the stream that trickled down to the cove. They had their thin, sharp hunting spears, but no agouti or opossum.

Still, one man did have a large breadfruit under his arm. They greeted another man and his wife who each carried a pineapple plucked nearby. Everyone in the village walked naked to the breeze, except for the hunters whose penis shields, tied with thongs around their waists, protected them as they dashed after animals in the forest.

Hatuey was bewildered to be thinking of the breeze on everyone's skin. Fever. The thought of them all covered in fur like monkeys ran through his head. He shivered as Jack struggled to open his eyes, to breath his own breath.

As his mother touched his shoulder they heard a terrible shout of sorrow. Hatuey clambered to his feet. A woman's scream, then a frightened child's, and another. His father was running to the ajoupas behind their own. Hatuey's mother already ran that way.

He stumbled into the chaotic, shouting, screaming, and crying of half the village. Women pushed past him with tears on their faces, carrying babes and pulling toddlers away. He pushed past them and the younger boys into the ring of men. Jack cried out. Hatuey's fever-weak knees shook.

To steady himself he grasped his thighs with his hands. Hands! He jerked his hands away, grabbed his own shoulders. The horrible man slumped against the ajoupa had no hands. Hatuey first saw only the bloody wound in the middle of his face where the nose had been, two ragged holes clotted with blood that blew crimson bubbles as he gasped for breath. No hands.

He waved two black and scabbed stumps unbelievingly before his own eyes and wrenched the heart of everyone with his cry. And there on his chest . . .

The Spaniards had cut them off, he said in an odd, choking voice.

And burnt his arms in the fire to stop the blood. They had come to his village to make them slaves, the same beings who had come the year before as peaceful traders, and come again every full moon.

"It is Atopo," someone said behind Hatuey. Atopo was from the village less than a morning's walk over the mountain.

The village warriors had fought them same as if they were Carib raiders, Atopo gasped out, but there was no hope. And to show the other villages there was no hope in war, that they all must submit; they took a dozen men, a dozen women . . .

Atopo raised his mutilated arms to them. All of Hatuey's people groaned and cried out in their sorrow for their brothers and sisters. Atopo carefully brought the stump to the gory hand that lay hanging from a cord around his neck.

"Flee," he said in the strange language Jack could understand.

In his dream he was pulled by his Arawak mother back to the ajoupa.

His father was there, too, shouting words, but it was as if it all happened in silence. It was taking his mother and father so long to fill a basket with what they needed. His father disappeared. A young man he took to be his older brother came in and handed Hatuey one of father's spears. A little sister and brother huddled at the back of the ajoupa.

A frightening noise struck the air, then two others, breaking the shell around his head. His father ran in and pulled his mother by the arm. They all ran, the whole village ran away from the stream, ran for the mangroves.

Hatuey looked back and the loud bang hit his ears. Dream monsters like monkeys with spears ran among his people. One raised a bright stick and clubbed down a woman as she passed him, spewing blood over Hatuey's arm.

He veered for the thick ferns of the hill, his legs were so tired, fever tired, they would catch him, he ran so slow, dream slow --- the spear shoved into his back and he cried out . . . He woke with a scream and then screamed again as the bones stuck him in the back, cracked and clattered as he rolled onto his hands and knees. Before him in the blackness of the cave was a wisp, a twist of blue smoke, an azure skeleton reclining against a rock next to the shelf scattered with the shards of its gods. Jack froze stiff, dare not move, shivered with fear. The skeleton glowed with the same hue as the magic stones . . . Suddenly the skeleton's bones flared, burning, hurting, bright blue, lighting the cave like the azure corona around the zenith sun. Jack sat back and shielded the glowing bones from his eyes.

If the bones moved, or worse, spoke, he would shit his pants; he could feel his bowels tensing for the move, expecting death. The light was cold, dimmed suddenly and he looked to see there between its sparse and rotted teeth a golden stone, a spherical nugget, a nugget that faded to silver as the light in the bones also dimmed; the stone was cerulean, then azure, and now the only faint light in the cave, glowing there in the Arawak's mouth.

The Arawak spoke but Jack did not hear it. He stared at the magical Philosopher's Stone and knew here was his treasuring. Crawling forward he fell into an abyss . . . he had stumbled from the cave without remembering how. It is still night. The bull's carcass and the wild dogs have left the meadow and the pied horses have returned. He reaches out to pet the muzzle of the closest and it rears up with an awful slowness, muscles rippling like thick honey, nostrils flaring, his mane moonflowing, then leaps forward, gone like an arrow, shedding all flesh, and the field follows, skeleton horses in the blue moonstone light, bucking and galloping, the last ridden by the dwarf Francisco, armored in rusty cuirass, spurs hooked in the white ribs, saluting Jack with his raised dagger. He cannot find the donkey. Is it bone, too? Suddenly terrified, he raises his eyes to the star-thick sky. Slowly, very slowly, slow as honey he raises his own hand before his face . . .

Hatuey sat beside his sleeping son. He absently waved at the flies that tried to settle on the boy's eyes and lips. The lips murmured, sometimes cried out in the fever that burned the child, fever that spotted his face, limbs, across his chest where his little frog zeme lay, rising and falling with each breath, unable to protect the boy's spirit from evil.

But Hatuey's own spirit drifted, thinking of a conch he had eaten as a boy. And a little violet crab. Breaking the claw, Jack pulled the meat out with his teeth and lapped it on to his tongue. He had loved conch when he was a boy. It was many years since he had even seen the sea. Once, before the boy was born, he had sat at the fire weaving cotton yarn into a net while his wife cried. The medicine man ministered to his zeme and broke the spell.

Poor Higuanama. He looked up to his wife in her hammock. Her eyes were open, quiet. She smiled faintly to reassure him. He could not smile back, only nod. She burned, too, and the spots just this sunrise appeared on her cheeks and between her breasts. But she and his son would not have to fight the evil spirits long, spirits sent by the Spaniards, nor flee the dogs sent to flush and ravage them. They would flee this little conuco where they had hoped for refuge, flee the world, all of them.

Their zemes would guide them to the island beyond the sun where the spirits of all ancestors dwell.

A faint sound of work came to him. The women's mortars pounding, mashing the cassava roots. Higuanama had had to abandon her bowl, but by sunset there would be plenty of the poison juice for all. Then they could carry themselves, the jars of poison, and their zemes up to the holy cave.

Jack quaked and tried to awake. Hatuey shuddered, his mind tumbled in panic, then settled. A spirit had entered him, not his own zeme or any he knew, and then the spirit fled in fear, not willing to join him. There were many strange zemes and attendant spirits about this wretched camp, zemes of his clans of the north coast, zemes of the Cibao and Xaragua, even one carried by a wanderer from distant Higuey. But the holy cave would welcome all, the old priests knew. They had spoken with the zemes of the cave.

He shooed a green fly from his son's eye. Then Hatuey rose, went to the doorway and set on his wife's low, wide stool. He picked the pestle out of the bowl and studied it. Then he began mashing the root. Woman's work, but on this last day of the world it mattered little. He stuck his finger in the bowl and dug out a dollop of pale paste. Then he and Jack opened their mouth. Jack reached out to stop him and his hand touched the stone pillar of the cave, touched the lips of a zeme, was Hatuey's hand touching the lips of his son. Hatuey took the bowl that was passed him and, raising his son's head, poured a little juice in his mouth. The boy raised his head a little himself and sipped twice more in his thirst. Hatuey raised the bowl and drank half the thin, bitter juice, then passed it to his wife.

The blazing torchlight from the altar showed the tracks of her dried tears.

She drank it all and looked at him and Jack saw his own face reflected on the surface of her eyes. Hatuey and she grasped hands, and Hatuey turned his eyes toward the altar. The priests in their scarlet, blue, and green-feathered headdresses chanted first to the altar and then to the people sitting pushed close together over the whole floor of the cave of zemes. The altar was crowded with clay, wood, even stone zemes, tall zemes of clans, of families, the small zemes of every soul within the cave, little frogs, great owls, and bats, birds, snakes, every spirit gathered for the journey. The little bowls among the zemes were heaped with the golden rings, pendants, and bracelets of all who sat in the cave, covering the priests' magic stones, a final offering for a peaceful journey. Hatuey's eyes sought the zeme of his clan. He squeezed his wife's hand. The zeme spoke . . . Jack whispered so softly his lips did not move. Jack whispered so that his ears might hear.

He was inside a nacreous egg, was a pearl himself, guarded from the vicissitudes of the silver sky . . . His mouth bit wet stone, licked his own blood and he woke.

Nightmares, nightmares he thought, just nightmares like a drunk's madness. Just drunken nightmares. Jack rose up on his hands and knees. He could see faintly, there was a weak light behind him. He turned his head over his shoulder. The bones of the Arawak priest shone very faintly, covered with the thin, aqua-glowing moss. Shone, but were silent. It was the only light; his torch was out, lost.

Jack pulled his other torch from his belt, fished out his tinder box and lit the torch with a twist of paper. The flame waxed, the skeleton's blue light waned, disappeared, and the bones seemed the same stained ivory as all the others. Nightmares, haunted nightmares, meant to test my mettle, he thought; he had to think, kept thinking.

He stood. All his limbs, his neck, his back and chest ached. But there was no fear, no eels.

Somehow, by dreaming he was one of those whose bones lay in the terrible jumble of this cave, somehow some initiation had been passed; or maybe all fear had been drained from him and he must be filled up with it again.

He secured the wires to hold down the second blue coated stone, replaced the glass bell over his ugly, price-less gems, fastened the box over it, and then slowly picked his way out of the Cave of Zemes into the main hall of the cave, never looking back.

Only a few dozen bats hung from the vaults of the cave. The rest had fled.

At the cave mouth he paused by the buccaneer's bones. He kicked the plunderer's skull off his neck to avenge the sacrileges. Then Jack crawled out the hole, pushed through the leaves of the bush, and stepped into the world.

Behind him, in the cave, the azure skeleton's right arm reached up and the bone forefinger wiped the tiny peak of stalagmite from its forehead like a drop of dew.

"A close alarm," said its voice to the presence behind it in the dark.

Jack heard, but did not hear, the words' echoes whispering past him, carried out of the cave on the wings of the dusk's last bats. He shivered.

The sun was below the western mountains. The empty ceilings of the cave had told him that. High above, immensely high, white clouds drifted in the clear air. The wind carried the scents of pines, grasses, earth, ferns; bell birds chimed in the soft shadows of the trees. Jack rubbed out the torch in the dirt and started down the hill.

At his camp wild dogs had killed and torn apart his donkey and, worse, all his baggage. Parts of each were strewn all down the slope into the tall grass. The flies were thick on the donkey's carcass.

There were no dogs he could see, but he knew they could be back to feed.

He built a fire and ate some scraps of biscuit he found in the grass.

Worst was the shredded water skin. It would be tomorrow past noon before he had more than the morning's dew. It seemed a bad omen. Despite the medicinal treasure he had found in the cave, the old man might be dead even now.

Dead and buried and his golden treasures shared out to all but Jack. But, at the least, he had the magic stones. He had them and their secret, worth a pretty penny.

Jack climbed into the tree with his little treasure box and slept without a dream.

71 AT KIT'S DEATH BED

The pirogue's keel bit into Cayona's beach and Jack leapt onto the sand. He ran as hard as he could with the mahogany box clutched to his chest. As soon as he got to the Aeolus someone could ride him up to Kit's house. Few were on the streets in the torrid midday.

"Hey, is Old Kit alive?" He shouted at familiar faces in the shaded doorways. All he got were shrugs and a shouted "Not for long." But it was a hope, Kit on his death bed or not, that he might have arrived in time.

In front of the Aeolus a planter in town from the Ringot, an old client of Kit's, was just arriving. When Jack breathlessly told him he had a potent medicine for Old Kit that one of the doctors wanted at once, the planter pulled Jack up onto the wagon seat and geed his horses up the hill, snapping their reins and cursing them, rattling and bouncing along the ruts. Jack curled over on the bell jar's little box as they careened around the bends.

The Aft Gascon, apparently back in the dying old man's graces, opened Kit's door.

"The doctors are with him," he said, his long face solemn, speaking slowly.

"It's the end at last."

Jack pushed past him and ran up the stairs, down the hall and burst into Kit's bedroom. The clutch of doctors gathered at the foot of the bed turned, startled, frowning, started to protest. But the old housekeeper, sitting beside Kit's bed with her splinted leg propped on a stool, silenced them with a squeal of joy and a shouted hosanna.

"I have the herb," Jack said between pants as he approached the bed with his box. "The herb that has sustained him all these years."

He sat the box on the bed table.

Old Kit's open eyes were blank, the face so much a corpse's that Smeeks, seeing Jack's look, spoke up.

"He lives," the chirurgeon said solemnly. "At the moment."

As if to prove it, the old man spoke, but as if with his last breath, words catching on a dry, tightening throat.

"Carry me aboard the ship, I must sail with the tide."

Smeeks turned away shaking his head.

Quickly Jack undid the latches on the box, lifted off the case, then the bell, and twisted free the little wires securing this treasure. He drew the tongs from his belt and plucked the largest Arawak stone from the bowl. Smeeks and the other doctors crowded behind him as he bent over the old man.

"Master Kit," Jack said. But now there was not a flicker or twitch in the stretched and sunken face.

He hurriedly dabbed Kit's dry, cracked lips with blue slimed stone.

There was no motion, no tongue eased out to lick the blue flecks.

"I'm afraid he's lost," said Doctor Piron.

"Jack, let's pry open his mouth and drop it . . ."

Kit's tongue slowly protruded and ran over his lips. They all stared in silence at the otherwise dead face. The gray tongue licked out again and retreated. For long moments nothing happened. Then Kit blinked once; and again. The dry orbs began to glisten. Then his head moved a little to one side, a little back, then back again. His face turned and the eyes seemed to find the doctors' faces, to search among them as his head moved slowly until his gaze fell on Jack and halted. Very, very slowly the corners of his mouth turned up and his right eyelid dropped.

"Hurrah!" Jack shouted and threw his arms in the air, almost losing the magic blue stone from the tongs. The doctors were exclaiming in delighted amazement. The housekeeper wept into her apron.

Old Kit's head rolled back and he let out a sigh of contentment.

Smeeks slapped Jack on the shoulder. "You've done yourself proud, my boy. That must be a very potent herb. We'll give a little, bit by bit, so as not to strain his old heart."

Jack put the stone and tongs beside the other magic stone and replaced the glass bell.

"You look a bit ragged Jack," said Smeeks. "My advice to you is to wash up and go treat yourself and your friends to a little sport and celebration."

Smeeks reached into his coat pocket and pulled out a heavy leather purse. He held it out to Jack.

"It was my fee. Take it and spend it. I imagine you'll have quite a glorious fee soon enough." He winked at Jack.

Jack took the money without a word. Old Kit was breathing softly but steadily, and a pinch of color was in his cheek.

Smeeks also glanced over at Kit, laughed and smacked Jack on the shoulder a second time.

"I'll wager you could buy the whole fleet in Cayona bay if you've a mind to."

72 THE BRISTOLMAN'S REVENGE

The Aeolus was roaring, bellowing out of its double doors. The window shutters, flung open, spilled out trumpeting, guffaws and curses. Bypassing the crowded doorway a few men and wenches clambered in through them as word of free drinks ran down the street like a refreshing stream.

"I found a magic bean," Jack answered all his credulous new boon companions.

Black haired Maude, the finest beach whore in Cayona, came up behind and ruffled his hair and winked when he tossed a doubloon between her sweat-gleaming breasts. He guzzled from a bottle of sac with his head cocked back. A drunken drummer now beat like a crier outside the Aeolus' doors, and was jostled down on his butt by a surge of fish pirates, armory clerks and a slew of beach doxies. Jesús came in the door and hailed Jack. Someone tripped on the drum and a fight started, hidden from view by the swilling forest of tattered sailors and velvet suited cutthroats with their parrots, whores, and monkeys perched on their shoulders.

Jack drank deeply again and tottered backwards hard against someone.

He turned with a smile and so did the one-eyed Bristolman off the Prosperous.

Jack's smile froze in a grimace. The old sea-artist's pale eye stared and his smile grew wider and opened. He didn't quit smiling until he had the hook in. He leaned forward and gaffed Jack's shoulder with his stubby arm, then pulled down, crimping his wrinkled elbow and setting it deeper near the bone in one motion.

Jack howled into the man's grin, screamed out of his twisting viscera, pain scream hardening to fear to rage and then loosening back to fear. But the hoary grin fell, the yellowed eye blinked. The pirate went for his knife too late. Jack grabbed his broad wrist with both his hands and lifted his knee hard into the dirty codger's stones, raising him up with a grunt. But his fat, sweaty wrist twisted like a python in Jack's grip, the hook dug, indigo flashed cold shattered knives, red broke, flashed beneath his eye, knocked his head back, the old man lunged and butted him again, pounding Jack's lips against his teeth, a spin of arms, shouts surrounded him, the wrist slipped loose, the gaff wriggled and dug fiery, the knife sliced down his palm, he grabbed and turned the jabbing point into his hip, then to the side. Jack butted down, too, smashing the Bristolman's nose and the old man stumbled back, easing for a moment on the hook and Jack lurched with him and bit the bleeding nose like a dog.

The circle of shouting, screaming men and women roared louder, then was gone in the red flash of pain that struck like a spear from his shoulder through to his heel, he groaned, kneed up to catch the Bristolman's thigh as his knee went up for Jack's own groin. Still biting down hard he twisted and jerked his head till he tore off the end of the pirate's nose. A maddened shout went up around his ears and then sank, the hook mauled deeper, tugging. Growling. Yellow pegs of teeth grazed Jack's nose and he butted down, banged down his forehead at them, the pain lanced fire from his shoulder to his soles like lightening, he smashed with his head again as the old man jerked back his arm, freed the knife. Jack shoved forward against his bloody chest, pushed, pushed, grabbing blindly for the knife, expecting to feel it plunge into his liver, shoved, they fell, Jack landing atop, the Bristolman's shout like bellows in his face, Jack's free hand sliding desperately down the blood-slicked arm for the knife hand, quick, as the man jabbed for his kidneys, Jack held it away. His left arm, almost dead with pain and trapped between them found the pirate's culls and squeezed them like a lifeline.

The Bristolman kicked his heels against the planks, howled and shouted, and tried to roll him off, but Jack spread his legs and rode on top, squeezing for his life. The pirate bit deep into Jack's cheek; Jack pulled back and thumped the side of his head against the bloody end of the nose and was bit again. The old man's patch rode up into his gray hair, the withered socket filled with fresh blood. Jack's left arm was not there anymore, was gone, useless, burning in an invisible flame, he fell to its side, off the Bristolman's blood slicked barrel chest, the old man had Jack's ear in his teeth; he couldn't pull away; red, black, black fire, gold flame of gold, the hook was out! It bit again beside his neck, it pulled and he was rolled with it, the pirate's wrist wriggled free. The horrid face above Jack dripped blood into his eyes, their faces held close by the pirate's hook. The Bristolman leaned and raised the bloody knife high, red knife, Jack jabbed up with his right thumb gouging into the puffy, bloody good eye as the knife stabbed down into the meat of his arm. Both croaked out shouts of pain. The pirate leaned on his knife, pressed his mangled face against Jack's grimacing lips, put his shoulder to it, the point pushed through Jack's arm into his breast, pressing into a rib, splitting it slowly. Blood was all he could see, smell, even feel except for the point of the knife that pressed searching for the final font, to tap the flood of blood to burst and wash over him --- Jack pushed up against the knife and rolled hard on the candent steel hook, a bursting sun, the gory bulk above him shifted, slipped and tumbled, rolled, dragging Jack with the knife turned in the muscle of his chest. Jack's head lay on the pirate's chest. Both took one breath without moving. The knife jerked out of him. He tried to reach up to fend it off, but now his right arm would not move, the left seemed to lay in some cold mountain stream far away. The pirate, gasping and wheezing, rose on one elbow and Jack slid down his crimson slick paunch into his lap. The old pirate sat up and jerked Jack by the neck with the hook so that his head lay on the man's knees looking up. He could not move, staring at the face of his death. A gray, empty socket and blinking blood caked eye, the mangled, gory knob at its center, the gap-toothed, gasping grin that dripped dark blood. The teeth came together, the knife rose above him --- a black trumpet poked the Bristolman's ear. The blunderbuss boomed and Jack was jerked hard by the hook in his neck. The top half of the pirate's head was gone in the gray cloud of smoke, broken off like a melon, only a swatch of scalp fallen to where the back of his throat had been.

The corpse still sat, spurting great gouts of black blood, held up by the arm still hooked in Jack's neck. Jack could hear the bedlam of curses and cheering, but he could not move, not even his eyes, did not have any desire to move. Above him the Aft Gascon stood with a smoking blunderbuss and his pistol out, pointed at the crowd. Beside him stood the Aeolus' taverner and the cook also with ready blunderbusses arrayed in the same direction. He made no sense out of the words, the sounds, but he knew they must be facing down the Bristolman's mates, that his own partisans were turning with the Gascon . . . the hook was out, a rag wiped his eyes clean, he was being lifted.

"Ah, Jack," the Gascon was saying. "When Master Kit bid me fetch you or he'd have me hanged, I didn't think to find you putting my neck in the noose like this."

He was being carried.

They were walking through the kitchen, then were in the hot, bright sun. Louis was holding his legs, silent and grim. Somewhere others gabbled and chuckled about what a famous brawl it had been.

Someone wiped the blood from his eyes again and they sat him in Kit's palanquin, propped him against a corner, shut the door.

Louis looked in with a grim smile. "You'll be fine, Jack. Old Kit will have the chirurgeons doting on you worse than baby Jesus himself."

The palanquin was lifted and he almost fell over in the seat, then managed to lift his right hand to the gilt painted window edge and grip it weakly.

The Gascon and the other bearer sat out at a trot. Louis and Jesús ran along beside.

"That's right," said the Gascon. "He'll have Smeeks and Piron sleeping at the foot of your bed. You got Master Kit sitting up and set to dance a jig.

"He'd crown you prince of the West Indies if he could." The Gascon gave a merry laugh. He knew he would have fine prize himself for Jack's rescue. "We've got to take care o' you, your Highness."

Jack could not speak. He had no desires of any kind. He stared at his crimson hand. The bloody fingers

seemed a great distance away, numbly clutching the gilded wood in the hot sunlight.

His lips parted with the notion of a smile. Blood
and gold. Like every tale told in Cayona. Jack Higgins'
tale now.

The sun blazed on his gory hand and on the blood-
smeared gilt, pierced his eyes, the only pain he could
feel. He could not close his eyes, did not want to turn his
head from the sun's glare consuming his hand, a light so
bright the crimson was black, the gold white. White so
bright it was black.

Far, far away, nearly drowned in the darkness, he heard a
voice say "Kiss it, Jack."

But he was drifting out on the darkness, the empty
darkness, silent again, empty even of his own . . .

"Kiss me, Jack," he thought he heard, far away,
Rebecca whisper to him.

Something softly touched his lips. He tried to kiss
her.

A bitterness came to the tip of his tongue, bitterness
that glimmered and ran like a small stream to the back of
his throat where it pooled, and he inhaled and swallowed
it at once, the glimmering stream flashing and coursing
up behind his eyes, cascading into his heart, the bitterness now sweet, a tumbling, golden rush through his
body and all the air around him . . .

He opened his eyes. Rebecca's sea-blue eyes gleamed above him. She gasped. Jack heard cheers and shouts far away.

"Kiss me," he told her.

Finis